Free

Also by the same author:

The Death of Me
Central Publishing Ltd. 2002

Meet the Hormones
Upfront Publishing Ltd. 2003

Free

PAUL VINCENT

UPFRONT PUBLISHING
LEICESTERSHIRE

FREE
Copyright © Paul Vincent 2003

ISBN 1-84426-255-3

First published 2003 by
UPFRONT PUBLISHING LTD
Leicestershire

Printed by Lightning Source

Chapter One

The first letter written to me by the stalker was typed on a word processor and sent in a nondescript envelope, so I mistook it for junk mail and didn't read it.

It's not as though opening mail usually pays dividends. In my experience, good news comes by phone and bad news comes by letter. We all learnt years ago which envelopes are bills and which are junk mail; I don't open either, but at least I know which is which. On the rare occasions that a piece of junk mail or a junk email is addressed in such a way that I do open it, I get cross with myself at having been taken in. I vow not to be caught out again and open even fewer letters and emails in future. I have no idea whether this is a further retreat into myself or a heroic stand by a defiant consumer.

So I can only presume the stalker's letter resided happily in the pile of letters, flyers and half-read magazines that sits in the corner of my kitchen.

Before that, it would have spent a week on my doormat, because it turns out it was sent to my address in England while I was on holiday in Northern Spain.

I had gone down there with Gabrielle. It was our first trip away and it wasn't going particularly well. I felt that what little momentum we had was already petering out. It was four months since our first kiss, as good a milestone as any, and five weeks since she'd finally agreed to come away with me.

Despite this, her first and only sign of commitment, she was emotionally more elusive than ever.

I had gone to considerable lengths to find a Citroen 2CV with a sunroof so that we could drive down through France in it as a laugh.

When I explained this, Gabrielle replied, 'I can see why you'd think that was fun. But it's fine.' She spotted a look on my face and added, 'I like it that I can say what I feel. That you don't take everything personally.'

'That I don't take relationships personally,' I mused.

Such an exchange may sound negative, but our strength was that we could always say exactly what we thought; always the truth, effortlessly shared. It was how we had gone about conversation from day one.

I first met Gabrielle at a pavement café on a Friday morning. A dark haired woman with blonde eyebrows was standing in front of me, looking about for somewhere to sit. There were plenty of empty tables but she sat down at mine.

'They're in the shade,' she explained.

'Ah,' I replied.

I had been reading some paperwork. I moved it off the table to make some space.

'You seem sad,' she said.

'Do I?' I said. 'Well I suppose that's the effect I was going for.' I was pleased with my reply.

'You're on your own,' she said.

'Obviously,' I replied.

'I mean, you're not waiting for anyone.'

'How would you conclude that?' I asked.

'Body language. People who are waiting for someone to arrive have a more open body. They might look at everyone who comes into view. People who are on their own are more self-conscious and curled in on themselves or the book they're reading.'

'Or they bring paperwork with them to try and look busy,' I replied.

'Precisely.'

Gabrielle was entirely correct. I did make myself go out and drink in cafés, I did take props with me because I was self-conscious. Without them I might never get out at all.

She was demonstrably younger than I was, and I couldn't understand why she was interested in me. A few dates later I asked her.

'I'm fed up with dating little boys with optimistic condoms in their wallets wearing a round patch in the leather.'

No worries there, then. I was old enough to have an optimistic Viagra in my wallet wearing a little diamond shape.

Gabrielle had longish hair which was usually pinned up with two of those chopstick things women use. The chopsticks were dazzling white against the deep black of her hair. She looked taller than she was, because she always held herself square and upright. She wore simple, well cut clothes ranging from Jigsaw to Armani. She had two favourite bags, both of which had broad leather shoulder straps; decent leather, well crafted and solid. Her overall look was of a person who was comfortable with herself, who was complete and had a lot to offer. She was a godsend, but a godsend that had come at the wrong time.

I was on the verge of moving to Biscay in Northern Spain. I thought life would be different there. When you travel you never feel self-conscious sitting alone; when you are abroad it would be strange *not* to go out and sit at a café table and admire the view, no matter how long you'd been there.

In Biscay I would be free.

And I would have plenty to do. I had sold up my overpriced box of a house in Cambridge and had bought a house in the Basque countryside that I was planning to do up. Even after all that then happened, buying that house was a choice I would still defend; it is a good part of the world in which to live.

They say that it rains so much in Bilbao that they made the Guggenheim silver to reflect back into the town what little sunshine they get. This is unfair. The Basque Country may get wet but it also gets a lot of sunshine, so as a result the countryside is an extraordinarily rich green. The landscape is riven with a dramatic kind of hill that has almost sheer sides and flat tops.

With a flourish that is more mid-European than Hispanic, their farm houses look exactly like Swiss chalets. In Spanish they are called *caserio* and in Basque they are called *baserri*. Typically the ground floor is a kind of stable where you keep your cow and a couple of sheep at night, while upstairs there is a living quarter which is kept warm by the livestock below. There is a kitchen affair on the ground floor behind the stable, and the whole thing is set in about five hectares of orchard land and vegetable plot.

Idyllic.

Or it would be, if the building I had chosen hadn't needed quite so much work doing. On the plus side, it had several walls still more or less intact, a fine original timbered roof, and its very own spring of crystal clear water. On the minus side, the spring rose up in what should have been the middle of the kitchen, and the original timbered roof had somehow fallen away in one piece and been dragged clear by a previous owner.

So I had a lot on my hands, but it represented a new and exciting phase of my life. It was not, incidentally, the result of some sort of mid-life crisis. My father came from Bilbao and my mother, being from Eire, didn't make me feel especially British even though I had lived there most of my life. It was more a matter of getting back to my roots.

My decision *was* the product of some good timing though. My employers, the English firm Banbury PLC, had recently taken over an engineering company near Bilbao. It was in the same field as Banbury but was non-profit making. It was non-profit making not for altruistic reasons but because it was badly run, and Banbury were looking to put some key workers in place to turn it around.

The English are poor at languages so they were tickled pink to discover they already had an employee who spoke Spanish and even had a working knowledge of Basque. They made me a truly great offer to relocate; a good pay rise and rent free accommodation. If I had been attached, the latter would have been a decent sized house, but in the event it was a small single bedroom flat in the heart of Bilbao. I didn't bother to tell them I wanted to move there anyway and instead took to haggling about the exact terms. I couldn't believe my luck.

I took Gabrielle out to see the *baserri*. On the last stretch of road before it came into view I stopped the car and blindfolded her with a scarf she'd been wearing, before driving on. I parked and led her by her fingertips to the edge of the hill. I slipped her blindfold away.

'Now look,' I said.

The hills ahead of us had crevices and folds within their sides. The greens that covered them were so impenetrably deep they needed a crucial amount of light to be seen at all. Yet the colours were so rich that in full sunlight they dazzled. The sun may slip behind the thinnest of clouds but the drop in light levels that resulted would make the darker creases flicker and disappear, then reappear at random; quickly enough to make you doubt your vision. When clouds stream across the face of the sun, the effect is awe-inspiring; the entire countryside rippling, speckling and dazzling.

'The Spanish call it *La Desaparicion*,' I said. 'The Disappearing.'

I had been longing to share this with Gabrielle. This was my gift to her, and on that day the effect could not have been more perfect.

She watched it for a while, then turned to the house with its neglected builder's sand and gathering weeds.

'Don't ever blindfold me again,' she said.

I walked with her into the shell of the building and marked out invisible lines where the rooms would go. I didn't know

5

what else I could do or say, except doggedly explain my dreams.

I told myself off. So she didn't fall over herself praising the view. The poor woman was not to know the invisible hoops that she was supposed to be jumping through in this relationship.

'So you've got a job starting soon in Bilbao,' she said.

'Yeah. I've exchanged contracts on my place in Cambridge. I move in five weeks. I can get the keys and show you the flat I've been given. If that interests you.' I had no idea what interested her.

'And if you'd been married, they'd have given you a house,' she said.

'Correct.'

She looked in her handbag for something that obviously wasn't there. A nervous habit. She zipped the bag back up and exhaled. She chewed on her lower lip and looked left and right as if eyeing up her escape.

'You really shouldn't wear those shorts,' she said.

'They're Paul Smiths,' I said.

'Well he can wear them then. You haven't got the legs.'

I felt the car keys in my pocket.

'I'll marry you,' she said.

Just like that.

We drove down to the nearest village and found a bar.

She said, 'Look, what's the worst that can happen? We come out here for a couple of years, it doesn't work out and I have to go home again. I think we've clicked. I don't know about you, but I don't click that often with people. This job of yours coming up obviously means we've got to take a chance when no doubt we'd normally be cautious. If it wasn't for the job, we'd date for a while and see how it went. Well, that's life. Sometimes you've just got to go for it.'

'What can I say?' I replied. 'That is wonderful. We need to celebrate. This calls for white wine made to a Champagne method, and a night of unbridled passion.'

'Or we can use the bridle if you'd prefer,' she said.

We got through four bottles of Cava and were in no state to drive back to Bilbao so we found a hotel.

I always think of that as the first day I fell in love with Gabrielle. I also think of it, rightly or wrongly, as the day the first letter came.

Had I read it I would have seen that on the top left of the envelope it had a number one printed.

Inside it said,

Dear Sal
I will send just 8 letters to you. By the 8th letter, you will either love me or I will have killed you.
You know me.

It was unsigned.

The truly awful thing was that the stalker's letters were the very least of my problems. They were barely a footnote to the crises that lay ahead.

Chapter Two

Gabrielle was my first waking thought and my last thought at night. Not least because she moved into my house.

My home in Cambridge was situated at the exact point where city infilling met modern building regulations. It was built on some reclaimed railway land and it was minuscule. It had heat-retaining glass; it had insulating blocks under the floors, in the walls and above the ceilings. It was stiflingly hot. I had the daily choice therefore of either dying in a pool of my own sweat or throwing the windows wide open; in which case I would be woken every morning by the dawn chorus of the birds coughing, and the 5.15 through-train whistling its way to King's Cross.

I had always bought decent sized furniture though. I figured that I would soon move to a bigger house and would regret compromising on wardrobes, beds and kitchen tables. So I spent five years paying an outsized mortgage while edging round outsized furniture.

The bedroom was particularly irritating because the wardrobe wouldn't open more than three inches before the doors got stuck against the bed.

Fortunately, Gabrielle didn't take up too much space when she moved in. She only brought two cases with her. Not much to show for a lifetime, or perhaps she wasn't planning to stay long.

'I'll pick up the rest sometime,' she said.

And she only wanted the simplest possible wedding.

'I don't want guests, you know?' she said.

I was very happy with that. I have so few friends it would have been an embarrassment any other way. Table upon table of people from her life and, er, my mother and perhaps Ian and Sally who I knew from university.

In order to get married in the tight timetable available, we were offered a Tuesday in four weeks time at the registrar's office on the hill.

We met at a pub, the Mitre, at the foot of the hill. Ian and Sally were there already.

'Gabrielle phoned us up,' said Sally.

Then other friends arrived. Gabrielle had been cold-calling her way through my address book. Colleagues, ex-colleagues, a cousin I didn't even like; all jostling to smile.

I then discovered Gabrielle had contacted the local music college and hired four students: a trumpeter, a trombonist, a viola player and a guitarist. They ambled into the bar wearing assorted Oxfam dinner jackets and bought each other pints.

Gabrielle joined us in a massive meringue wedding dress. It was, literally, a joke.

I hope.

I had already noticed that Gabrielle had a penchant for raiding the dressing-up box of life. She had gone for the flounciest, whitest, puffiest apparition of a dress, with a train that went on for a week. It must have cost her thousands, unless she'd stolen it from Princess Diana's memorial museum.

She was helpless with laughter from the fun of it all. She was more than a bit drunk.

She kept calling out, 'Look at me, I'm a bride! Look at me, I'm a bride!'

She combined this with eyes that rolled up and a slow sway to the side.

She downed three vodkas and flirted with everyone, especially me.

At the appointed hour we marched, literally marched, the half mile up Castle Hill with our band at full volume. Tourists photographed us, bank clerks on their lunch breaks looked up from their cardboard mugs of Starbucks coffee.

It was perfect.

We had a reception of sorts at my place. Cava and paella. Gabrielle told the vegetarians to 'Pick bits out' and give them to her.

As she walked around, every man in the room followed her with their eyes. If at any moment that day I didn't know where she was, I just had to follow the sound of males simpering.

Sally and her cronies clustered around her wanting to know details.

'Salvador was so surprised when you said yes to marriage,' said Sally attempting to ad-lib her way to some gossip. 'He felt you were cooling.'

'It was our first holiday together,' explained Gabrielle. 'I was bound to be nervous. But I hid my nerves well enough, under a thick smear of stroppiness and ill will. I was in love. It comes out in funny ways.'

The women purred and turned their heads to look at the bridegroom.

It was perfect.

And it was perfect having her live with me.

The mundane became exotic. The bangles left in the soap dish. The blister packet of contraceptive pills half out of the cardboard packaging. Her insistence on me not talking for half an hour every morning as she drank several coffees at the kitchen table, while doing the crossword with a felt tip. Her recipe where she attacked red peppers with a blow torch until they blistered and sweetened. The warmth of her bare skin against me on the sofa. The way she reeked of sex after we'd fucked, then pull her trousers quickly on as if to trap in the smell. The way we'd be in a bar and she'd slip her fingers down into her trousers then waft them near my nose while ordering vodka from the barman.

She was a total delight.

I sometimes wondered what on earth I was offering her. Here was this wonderful woman with a triple S rating: Sexy, Solvent and Sane. It was plain what I was getting from her, but hard to tell what she was getting from me.

I had a week between finishing my English job and moving. I spent it at home packing.

Gabrielle helped a little in the evenings, but largely by rationalising. For example, she got my entire pants and socks drawer and poured it into a bin sack.

'I swear you've had some of that underwear since you were at school.'

She was probably correct but it was an emotional wrench to see it go.

'I'll buy you some new stuff,' she said. 'Sloggis. Anything less is just pants.'

I wondered what was I going to wear in the meantime.

I was quite keen to do my own packing after that.

The last Tuesday before we went, I was busy at home and the doorbell went.

I wandered down the stairs wondering if our next house would have a doorbell. Our house. Our. The best word ever.

There was a man standing there. A little older than me perhaps. He looked, what exactly? Like an off-duty policeman. Greying, solid; a man used to being polite to people whom he despised and who despised him in return. He looked soiled in the way one gets from travelling too much or has been unhappy for too long.

'Hello,' he said.

'Hi.'

I waited for him to explain why he was on my doorstep, but he seemed loathe to begin.

'This is going to seem strange,' he said.

'Okay.'

'Does Gina Lawrence live here?'

'No,' I said.

I tried to remember the names of the people who had bought my house and would be moving in the following week. I had mostly had dealings with the man, but there was a woman as well and I couldn't place her name. She might have been a Gina.

'Gina Tremain?'

'What?' I asked.

'She might be called Gina Tremain.'

'No,' I said.

'Does a woman live here at all?'

'I really don't think that is any of your business,' I said. 'May I ask what this is all about?'

'The person I am looking for is about five eight. Medium to long hair. Probably blonde but she could be brunette.'

'I really don't know what you're talking about,' I said.

'Downy arms,' he said. 'There's a slightly raised sort of mole thing at the base of her neck. Look, can I come in?'

'I'm in the middle of stuff,' I said.

'She's my wife,' he said.

'Pardon me?'

'Gina is my wife. We're married. She, I mean, we lived together. She's my wife.'

'Er, okay,' I said.

'One Friday morning she literally went to work and she never came back. She's my wife. She's taken a hell of a lot of tracking down, but I have reason to believe she now lives with you.'

'I think you've got the wrong person,' I said. 'But, you know, good luck with the search or whatever.'

I went to close the door, but he became agitated. He put a hand against the wood.

'I am going to have to close the door now,' I said.

'Your name is Salvador Gongola, right?' he said. It always sounds so foreign when English people say it. Like most Basques, I have a very silly surname that is impossible to pronounce in a way that sounds English.

'I'm closing the door now,' I said.

'I won't give up, you know. You see, I have the right to expect that she at least explains herself. She's taken a lot of tracking down. She needs to talk through things with me. She simply walked out, don't you see? She owes me at least the chance to talk.'

Chapter Three

It might have been because we were moving away to a
foreign country, slipping out of one life and into another;
but whatever the reason, I found it easy to consign the concept
of weird men on doorsteps to the dustbin, along with the
drawer of recipes I'd snipped out from the Sunday papers that
I'd never got round to using; a mysterious round battery in an
envelope marked *Do not throw away*, and the guarantee for a
food processor I couldn't recall owning.

That evening, when Gabrielle returned I could have asked
her if she'd ever been called Gina Tremain or whether she had
been married before, but I chose not to.

She was beautiful, she felt I trusted her. She saw me as
someone with whom she had fun, with whom she was safe
and above suspicion. I had had enough relationships to know
that one doesn't move away from that position voluntarily.

It made me want to enquire about her in a general sense
though; to get a better feel of her. I decided to ask about her
job.

She had previously muttered that she was something to do
with the police. I tried to recall what she said. She didn't say
she was *in* the police; her formula of words was more like she
worked *for* the police.

'So what exactly are you doing about your job, exactly?' I
asked. Too many exactlys.

'Exactly,' she replied. 'Exactly what I've been wondering. I thought I'd just walk out.'

'What do you do exactly?' I asked, 'If that's not too er…'

'Personal? I think it's fine for a husband to ask what a wife does for a living.'

We were still at a stage where it was fun to say words like husband or wife. Husband. I could wrap my lips around the word and issue it into the air like a smoke ring.

I chopped salad on a wooden board and Gabrielle got a beer from the fridge and sat opposite me.

'I work for a unit that collates information for the police,' she said.

'What?'

'It's a bit like Intelligence but it blatantly doesn't deserve such a grandiose title. It's dull. You see, nowadays there is so much information about: from road traffic cameras, to the thousand witness statements that might be gathered in a house to house inquiry, to the twenty people who ring in on their mobiles every time they see a crash or a crime. And it all needs collating and storing in case it's needed. It's a glorified clerical job, really.'

She went on to explain why she hated it so much and would be glad to leave. I suspected her grievances had been marshalled and polished over a considerable period, but were interesting nonetheless.

Gabrielle was peripherally involved in the unit that liased with MI5; they shared intelligence about the IRA. She remembered vividly the day they were due to have a joint meeting with six women from Military Intelligence.

Gabrielle sat with her five male colleagues and they all waited for business to begin.

There was some small talk and after about ten minutes a silence descended.

Eventually Gabrielle spoke up.

'What are we waiting for?'

Her team leader replied, 'I'm waiting for their boss to turn up.' It hadn't occurred to him that they wouldn't be led by a man. When he discovered his mistake, it didn't even occur to him to look shame faced.

Gabrielle said that was the first day she realised she didn't like her job. She'd heard that most of MI5 was run and staffed by women; it was famous throughout what she called their 'industry', but she hadn't realised until that day just how male dominated her own unit was.

'But you know,' she said. 'One doesn't leave a job over something like that. But when you want to leave, you start *dwelling* on reasons like that.'

On a later occasion Gabrielle had got to her desk to find a basket full of clothes sitting on top. A note said, 'Washed and ironed by Thursday, please.'

'What did you do?' I asked.

'I took the laundry basket out to the car park and set fire to it. That went down well.'

Gabrielle was in her stride. I began to wonder how I got the idea she didn't want to talk about her past. There was no stopping her now.

'And then there was the wanking incident,' she said.

'The wanking incident?'

It turned out Gabrielle had been seconded to a unit in North London. She'd gone to the mess bar with a friend and colleague called Amy.

'Is everyone here up to something?' asked Gabrielle. 'There's a bit of an atmosphere.'

She recognised a PC she liked, but he looked sheepish about what was happening.

Eventually he said, 'The lads were going to have a wanking competition.'

'Were?' asked Gabrielle. 'Don't stop on my account.

'Well,' said the PC warming to his theme. 'The lads from SO19 are in and they challenged our lads…'

'Who are SO19?' asked Amy.

'The armed police,' said Gabrielle, 'I had a try out for them once. There is only one known example of a non-male being accepted for the squad, Sarah Nuttall.'

'And who knows what sex Sarah is,' laughed Amy.

'So I didn't take it too personally when I was turned down,' said Gabrielle. 'So how does the wanking competition work?'

'Eight of our lads stand in a row and face eight of them and they all drop their trousers.'

'A head to head,' suggested Gabrielle realising there was a rich vein of puns to be mined.

'Mmm, and the two men on the end start,' said the PC. 'When one person comes, his team mate can then start…'

'Yeah I get it,' said Gabrielle. 'So when's it coming off?'

The lads from SO19 stormed in. Storming into places is what they did. They were wearing black top-to-toe combats. They always tucked their trousers into their boots, presumably to stop snakes climbing into their boots: a big hazard in Golders Green.

Gabrielle recognised someone she half knew called Steve Salmon and bounded over to chat.

'You're not going to spoil our fun are you?' moaned Salmon. He liked Gabrielle.

'I thought I'd join in,' she said.

'In a wanking competition?'

'I can see I'm up against stiff competition,' she replied.

'Well how do we know when you've come?'

'You'll know. My face twists and I clutch the furniture a lot. Oh and I gush. I'm a woman who gushes.'

'We wouldn't know which team to put you, you've got connections with both sides,' said Salmon.

'You could toss for it,' said Gabrielle. 'And Amy could be on the other team to even it up. Do you come easily Amy?'

'Bit of a goer, me,' said Amy, trying to be as feisty as Gabrielle but turning pink with the effort.

'Hop it,' said Salmon.

But Gabrielle hadn't hopped it. She'd gone on to get drunk that evening, and made a bit of a nuisance of herself. But somehow when the story came out, *her* name had kept cropping up rather than the names of the sixteen men present. She never discovered whether the others had been reprimanded, but she was the only one from her particular Met unit and her boss had taken the line that she had brought her section into disrepute.

Gabrielle was quite convinced that had she been a man she'd have had a superficial telling off and been handled in a boys-will-be-boys manner. But this man seemed genuinely cross with her.

'And I was suspended,' she said to me.

'And none of the men were?' I asked.

'My mistake was that I had a row with my boss about it. He doesn't like me and it gave him a reason to suspend me. I just couldn't fit in. Day after day I walked the walk, I talked the talk, I dressed the dress and got drunk in the mess. But I just had this nagging sense that I was never going to belong.'

'So,' I said. 'You kind of work for Police Intelligence.'

'Kinda,' she replied.

'How amazing. How wonderful. You don't look like a copper.'

'Thank God for that,' she said.

I was mildly surprised to learn what she did for a living, but then I'd have been equally surprised if she'd told me she was a plumber or an actuary.

She went on to tell me that she could see that a lot of the problems were a symptom of her wanting to leave. If she'd really wanted her career, she'd have not hung around the wanking competition for example, or she'd have grovelled more when told off.

'What fun,' I said.

'How so?'

'You're obviously fun. But I knew that already. It's fun that we have months ahead where we can ask each other simple stuff about our childhoods and what our favourite drinks are, or films or what our first record was that we bought.'

'CD,' she said. 'In my case it was a CD, old man.'

So if I had to analyse the time that we both spent in Cambridge I would say there was no real evidence that Gabby was mad or particularly weird. Any strange tales that did exist, such as the story about the wanking competition, were largely provided by herself. And they very much felt like anecdotes; atypical or extreme highlights that she offered up from the past.

The only incident of which I had direct experience, and which might remotely be described as weird, came one evening after work.

I wandered home to find Gabby in the garden with my Black and Decker Workmate, electric saw and two large planks of wood.

I got closer. The planks of wood turned out to be the wardrobe doors from our bedroom. She was sawing through them.

'Er, can I help you?' I asked.

'Yes, hold the other end of the door, would you?' she replied.

'I mean, what exactly are you doing?'

'I am exactly cutting the length of the wardrobe doors. Then we can open the wardrobe without it being caught on the bed.'

This turned out to be correct. She shortened the doors and reattached them to the hinges. From that day on she could lie in bed and open the wardrobe with her toe. She would select what to wear while still wrapped in duvet.

Was this mad? Not really. It was fun. Should she have asked me first? Probably.

We walked into the house holding a door each. At the threshold, Gabrielle knelt slightly to pick up some letters. She passed them to me.

'You should open your post more,' she said.

'If it makes you happy,' I said.

After we'd got the doors upstairs I sifted through the mail.

There were two envelopes that were obviously bills; so I opened the third, which had a number two on the top left of the envelope.

It said,

Dear Sal
As I arrived without warning, so I will leave without warning.

I turned it over in my hand.

'What do you make of this?' I asked Gabby.

She looked for no more than a second, then shrugged.

I scrunched it up, binned it, and forgot it.

Chapter Four

We got to our new house in Spain late on a Friday morning. It turned out it was rent free for a reason. It was a plague-era slum.

Gabrielle walked silently from room to room, taking in the lost plaster, mildewed walls and rotting woodwork. In fairness, it did have the advantage of being big and sunny.

Gabrielle said absolutely nothing to me. She couldn't; she'd left by the front door.

I stood looking out of the window. It was at least a great view. The house overlooked the port town of Portugalete. The hill we were on was so steep that although we were only about 400 yards from the edge of town, we were a couple of hundred feet above it. I could see a Velux swing open in a house below and a mop appear. It ran lazily up and down the glass to clean it.

Beyond the flats and houses of Portugalete I had a great view of the river as it snaked towards Bilbao. Tugs and freighters moved silently on the baize green water, past a similar number of rowing boats: eights and coxless fours.

Gabby returned.

'Are you all right?' she asked.

'Yeah, why?'

'What have you been doing?' she asked.

'Gazing out the window, I guess.'

'For an hour?'

I looked at my watch and shrugged.

'Help me get all the paint and stuff out the car will you?' she asked. 'We've got a busy week ahead.' Gabrielle turned out to be a 'virtue out of necessity' kind of a gal. Her plan was to knock off any loose plaster and highlight the resultant recesses with bright colours. The rest of the room would be whitewashed and the plaster edge between the two would be picked out in crimson, orange, or leaf green.

She dressed in a kind of 1940's land girl uniform. A headscarf, a white blouse knotted at her waist.

'Look at me, I'm a decorator!'

I had bought her a jokey Spanish phrase book to help her learn the language. All weekend she had a paint roller in one hand and 'Useless Spanish' in the other.

'*Beberé el aceite de oliva ahora!*' she read. 'Now, I will drink the olive oil!'

She dipped the roller in the emulsion.

'*Arrepentido acerca del incidente con la salsa,*' she said. 'I am sorry about the incident with the sauce.'

It transpired she could learn a language almost instantly, even when drunk.

She was a very thorough decorator. The front door was south facing and caught a lot of sunshine so she was determined to repair it carefully then give it several coats of gloss. To do this, she took it off its hinges and put it on trestles for a few days. She even went to the trouble of boarding up the front doorway. Gabrielle took total control of the whole house, and got itchy if I helped at all.

I decided to busy myself with the garden. The hill that the house was set against was so steep that the outhouse attached to one side actually backed onto what was the first floor internally. I kept all my tools in there, and built some solid shelving all the way up the far wall, but I hated going in because there always seemed to be a rustling going on somewhere beyond where I could see. You'd think that self respecting mice would stand stock still when a human opened the door and stood in front of them, but this lot were brazen.

I made a bit of a rockery on that side of the garden, but put most of the plot over to grass which banked up dramatically and appeared to need constant cutting. I would stand at the top of the bank and pull a hover mower up and down it by a rope attached to its handle.

As well as the decorating and gardening in those first weeks, we went for a number of walks to get to know the area. The first of these was on a Sunday morning; we took ourselves down to the river.

Portugalete is probably most famous for its huge transporter bridge which is described by the local tourist office, rather optimistically, as 'Bilbao's Eiffel Tower.' More the Eiffel Tower's evil country cousin. It has two eighty metre high towers of steel lattice that support, at its top, a bridge that spans a whopping 164 metres from one bank of the Nervion river to the other. Suspended far beneath the bridge, by long cables, is a large cable car affair or gondola, that carries the cars and people from one bank to the other.

The bridge is very narrow, very long and very very high. A couple of stabilising cables stretch horizontally and disappear beneath some houses either side which, perversely, have the effect of making it all feel less secure, as though the whole edifice is held in place by a couple of No. 8 screws and a frayed red Rawlplug. As the trolley system then moves along its rails at the top, the entire construction sways like a drunk at closing time.

Mystifyingly, you have to pay good money to go to the top. Most rational people would pay good money to not have to, but everyone takes the lift up there just once in their lives, to walk over the river, admire the view, and say goodbye to their lunch.

We took the cable car over to Areeta and had coffee in its shadow.

Areeta has a population of a little under 5000, and a churchgoing population of a little under 5000. After church on a Sunday they like to promenade: twenty-year-olds and fifty-year-olds alike, arm in arm, saying hello to anyone they know; which is everyone. They often wear olive-coloured suits: the men wearing their jackets over their shoulders and have ironed handkerchiefs poking out of their breast pockets. Their wives push a buggy or hold a dog lead; their green jackets are more tightly fitted, perhaps revealing the top of a white blouse with white ruffles. It's like stepping back in time.

Areeta is being rebuilt and the council are putting in extra walkways by the river, but in the meantime there is only about twenty yards of pathway available, so the entire populace have to walk up and down in ever more congested circuits for the hour before they join their mothers-in-law for lunch.

We joined the throng. We walked arm in arm and felt the sea air stroke our faces.

'Oh God, I'm now going to have to wear green and dye my hair,' said Gabby.

'Why?'

'I'm the only woman here over twenty-five who doesn't have dyed hair.'

I studied all the women around me. Sure enough, their hair was shades of rust, or bottle blonde, or a profusion of vibrant highlights. Not a strand of natural hair colour amongst them.

We walked along some more and apropos nothing Gabrielle turned to me and said, 'I love you,' in that way you do when life in general is exciting and it needs expressing.

I was going to reply but I was thunderstruck by the sight of a man about ten yards away. He was standing by the huge statue that pays homage to the gods of the sea.

It was the man who had been on my doorstep; the one who said he was looking for 'Gina.' There was no mistaking him, he was looking right at us.

The crowd obscured my view for a second or more, then he was gone.

'You okay?' asked Gabby.

'Yeah. Yeah, fine,' I said.

Chapter Five

My new job was agreeable enough, and I soon settled into the routine of it. The factory was situated near the airport. To get to it I could either take the motorway down past Bilbao or go across the transporter bridge and use smaller roads. With the instinct of a tourist I chose the latter.

The company was on two sites, Bilbao and Pamplona which is to the south east. I was in charge of the maintenance of both; pest control, security, car parking, and infrastructure.

It was a pleasant enough site, a couple of warehouses, a couple of factories, an office block, a large car park, as well as some lawn and ornamental lakes to help distract from the intermittent drone of jets taking off.

I took the view that I needed to meticulously dress the part. I had bought a couple of new suits in England and some over-priced ties. I spent what felt like an hour in the mornings ironing white shirts before putting them, scorching hot and starchy against my skin.

No one at work appeared to notice in the slightest, but it made me feel very managerial which was probably half the point.

My assistant was a woman called Olaia. She was the sort of person my mother would describe as 'working to a level of her own satisfaction.' But it wasn't just that she was lazy; she had a major criminal record.

This was not surprising as, one way or another, just over half our Basque speaking staff had a criminal record of some sort. The local Basque youth see it as a badge of honour that they must try and get arrested for doing their bit for their liberation army, ETA. Daubing graffiti on a bank, a bit of light stone throwing at the police, planting a bomb in the sand for a tourist to sunbathe on; these were all considered reasonable acts as far as the youth of Biscay were concerned.

Banbury UK threw a wobbly when they found out all this, but to sack every employee with a record would leave us with a severe staff shortage and too few Basque speakers. So Olaia, along with all her colleagues have been 'pardoned' by Banbury; an action that must have irritated all concerned.

Looking at Olaia, the phrase 'proud looking' springs to mind. She's a typical Basque; taller and with a fairer skin than most Hispanics; a long straight nose and a handsome, almost male chin. And an attitude. Even her tits looked aggressive.

It has always been the tradition around here that upon the death of the parents, it is the eldest child who inherits everything without any division of property. So throughout history, women were as likely to be in charge as men. The rest of Spain was traditionally among the most chauvinist societies in Europe, so this was a factor that set the Basques apart. One law doesn't make us wholly feminist, of course: any culture whose favourite sports include wood chopping, ox-lifting and turnip throwing, must surely have a certain macho slant to it, but it is no surprise for example that ETA is the only terrorist organisation in the world known to be run by a woman. In Ireland, by contrast, the 'loyalist' paramilitaries won't even allow women in their ranks. The German authorities recently announced that in a hostage situation they would shoot women terrorists before the men, because they are less likely to negotiate and more likely to shoot. If, as I often daydream, Olaia was in ETA, I can imagine she would go out in a flurry of bullets taking forty victims with her, and using her dying breath to mutter that a 41st had somehow got away.

Olaia hated me. As far as she was concerned, the factory had been working perfectly well until we all turned up, and all we had added by coming from England was another layer of meddling. I would take issue with her on this if it wasn't for the fact that I'm scared of her, and that she was probably correct.

Our firm makes and maintains turbines for the wind farm out near Pamplona. It is the biggest wind farm in Europe, and Banbury was hoping to position itself as the world leader in renewable energy. We were currently laying the first electrical superconductors outside of America (the first serve an area of Detroit that rejoices in the name of Frisbee) and as a result we should be able to move three times the normal amount of electricity with near perfect efficiency. Exciting times. Well, in my opinion at least.

Olaia was prone to sulking. On one occasion I had politely enquired where she had been the day before. She hadn't showed for work.

'I told you,' she said, 'I was off for personal reasons.'

'You were seen sunbathing on the beach in Areeta.'

'I didn't say I was off work for altruistic reasons or family reasons,' she replied. She liked to irritate me with her very precise use of English – better than most Brits could manage – and then deliberately misuse the language as if she *didn't* have a grip on it. She might say something like, 'I have said before, I cannot possibly work during my menstrual cycle.' Then she'd let me catch her smiling at her own joke.

In common with a lot of Basques she also had a near perfect English accent; not a hint of throat or Hispanic lisp. Oddly, this made her excellent use of English all the more disconcerting.

Our mornings at work would usually follow a set pattern. We had just the two desks in our office: for Olaia and myself. Various Spanish workers would walk in and out, talk to Olaia and ignore me. They used Basque as their preferred language because they knew I'm wasn't strong in it. They occasionally looked at me as they spoke, nodded to each other and apparently made decisions without consulting me.

I felt all the more excluded by the fact that the locals seemed to like *other* British people, and had done for centuries. The British had brought the Basques steelworks, railways and even football. They had asked our architects to design their palaces and their Metro. We had a shared history of not getting on with the Madrid government. The Basques love British pop songs and British tourists. It was just me who was singled out to be left alone at my desk.

I was only in my second week there when I received some mystery post. The system was that I read all the post that was written in English or Spanish, and Olaia read anything in Basque.

My In Tray that day contained a piece of typed paper that was written in English.

It said,

Dear Sal
I think you should read this.

It was stapled to a photocopied leaflet about birds. The latter was in Spanish.

I took it over to Olaia.

'What do you make of this?' I asked.

'It is a leaflet about birds,' she said.

'Yes but why would someone send it to me?'

Olaia barely looked at it and shrugged. She flicked her right hand left and right: a piece of Spanish body language I didn't understand, or possibly a gesture of no significance. Either way, I had a feeling that Olaia knew more than she admitted. But then I *always* felt that.

I asked if she knew where the envelope had gone.

'What envelope?' asked Olaia.

'This letter must have come in an envelope. It might give me a clue where it came from,' I said.

'I take most letters out of the envelopes as a service to you and then I put them in your in-tray. But if I think the letter is private, I do not do that.'

'Where do you put the envelopes?' I asked.

'In the bin.'

I peered at the bin but decided it wasn't worth working my way through its contents. It was only a silly piece of mail.

Whatever my frustrations at work, I always had the joy of going home to Gabrielle. In those days I could think of her for only a moment and my spirits would rise. She was by far and away the most exciting person I had ever met, and she was sharing my life.

Occasionally I had trouble knowing what to say to her, as though she were some sort of exotic creature who wasn't quite one of us. I found the trick in such moments was to get her talking about herself. I remember once we had a picnic at the top of the cliffs which are about a quarter of a mile behind our house. She must have talked for a solid hour without drawing breath; all about her experiences working alongside SO19, the firearms squad in London. She conjured up images of men in black uniforms sheltering in the shadows with their Heckler and Koch submachine guns and their night vision goggles, waiting to storm into houses. She joked that they loved it so much that even if the negotiations were going well, they used to try and storm in before their shift ended, rather than pass the fun onto the next crew.

'Have you ever wondered why it is always *dawn raids*, not *midnight raids*? Well that's why,' she said.

The conversation was so detailed that I felt quite the expert by the end. I knew that there had been no successful hostage-taking in Europe since the early seventies; that night vision goggles work less well when you put the lights on in the house; that SO19 had at least four ways of getting through any given door; that they had funny grenades that bounced into a room and exploded several times while shooting erratically from wall to wall. Gabby told me all these details with such relish, it was clear that this was a bit of the police work she sorely missed.

Gabrielle fell silent and looked a little bored. She stood and dusted herself off, then walked to the edge of the cliff.

She jumped off.

She was wearing a summer dress and a straw hat. She slipped off her sandals, put her right hand on the top of her hat, tucked the skirt between her legs and without saying a word, stepped forward.

My first thought was that she would die; it was a hell of a drop. There must surely be rocks below. At the very least she'd break her legs.

She shot down for several seconds. The fall itself was undramatic, and within an instant she had pierced the water and disappeared from view. There was barely a splash, but such a profusion of bubbles within the water where she'd dropped that the colour of it changed to a lighter green. Then the bubbles became fewer and fewer until I was no longer precisely sure where she had jumped in.

I waited. What else could I do? After what was surely a full minute I felt sick with anxiety. How the hell could I get down there? Was it possible she had surfaced round the corner where I couldn't see? I leant forward but there was nowhere she could be hiding.

Then I could see her. She was treading water a long way out. She was shouting something I couldn't hear. She still had her hat on – how the hell had she managed that? Her hair was plastered in black bars down her face. She was laughing so loud I could hear her from the cliffs.

'How did you know it was safe?' I asked her later.

'I didn't,' she replied.

I suspected she might have seen boys jumping in from the same spot previously. Either way, we both spent the day giggling about it. It was delightful.

In those weeks I too got a chance to delight. My impromptu jokes sparkled like new.

'I made this recipe out of my head,' I'd say while cooking. 'Brawn.'

Or in traffic:

'Patience comes to those who wait.'

Or on a Sunday morning:

'I'm a complete animal in bed. A sloth.'

Despite my jokes, she seemed to love me.

What impressed me most was the way she threw herself into her new life. There was no lip-chewing about leaving England; just plans and excitement for the future.

'I'm going to get a bar job,' she said one day. 'It would be a good way of getting to know people. What the hell, I could even make some money.'

'Then we won't see so much of each other,' I protested.

'I'll see if I can get day shifts. Anyway, it's only an idea.'

Sex was a slight puzzle. She said she was 'gusher' but she'd never 'gushed' with me. She didn't look at me across the sheets and know for the first time what it was to truly be woman. But it was early days yet and Gabby had a direct attitude to sex that made it easy enough. 'Tie me up, tie me down; I can forgive everything except indifference or leaving me with a hair in my mouth I can't remove.'

She frequently asked me what I liked sexually.

'What do you like? What do you *really* like?' she'd say.

But I had no real answer. I liked to please her. I didn't think it right to tell her what pleased me. She saw my lack of answer as a wall between us, but it couldn't be helped.

When she got a job, that was a slight wall between us, too. She worked in Bilbao old town, in a *tapas* bar, or a *'pintxos'* as they are known around here. It was situated amongst the tattoo parlours and sex shops that litter that part of town.

Behind the bar there were a number of posters of criminals. Beneath their grimacing faces was the word PRESOAK: to the untrained eye, an exhortation for them to be thoroughly washed, but in fact 'presoak' is the Basque word for prisoners. It was the Madrid Government's policy that ETA prisoners weren't allowed to reside in jails within the Basque Country and weren't allowed to converse in their native language. The posters were presumably put up because the Madrid Government was well known for cruising backstreet bars looking for tips on how to formulate their policies.

To an English person the whole phenomenon in that bar was mystifying. Here were groups of partygoers who loved endless nights of bar hopping and dancing, but who were nonetheless keen on discussing for hours the need to reshape the territory according to boarders that existed, briefly, a thousand years previously. Even in a good year barely eighteen per cent of voters supported them, so *they had no chance whatever* of getting what they wanted. Nonetheless, I've seen piles of twenty-year-olds spend a vibrant evening re-living how Franco used mustard gas on thousands of them in 1937, before piling into cars to storm off to an all night beach party thirty miles away.

That then was the bar where Gabrielle found her first job. She did four day shifts and two night shifts a week, which was a fair deal considering the locals were largely nocturnal and needed most bar staff at night.

I sneaked down to see her one evening and was amazed to find she was the centre of attention; there was a crowd of locals in front of her end of the bar, and a little to her right a man, who was probably the owner, watching her antics fondly over his half moons while he dried some glasses.

A Basque said something Gabby plainly didn't understand.

She paused, placed one finger in the air to request silence, then pointed around the crowd one by one.

She said slowly, *'Sospecho todos. Sospecho nadie!'* ('I suspect everyone. I suspect no one.')

She had reason to believe she had worked out who had mocked her, so she brandished a knife in his direction.

She proclaimed, *'El nunca procreara otra vez!'* ('He will never procreate again.')

There was a roar of approval as she used her phrases; phrases from the book I'd given her. She hadn't noticed me at the back of the bar. I shrank a bit as I watched her.

She then did a trick I'd never seen. She held a sharp looking meat cleaver in one hand and an egg in the other, then threw the egg high in the air. She caught the egg sideways on, on the edge of the blade. It cut half way into the eggshell. The egg white slowly ran down the blade and away, leaving her with the yolk which she put in a glass. There was no shortage of people wanting fresh advocaat after that.

When she wasn't performing party tricks, she was doing non-specific flirting. She would place her thumbs in the waistband of her skirt and run them forwards and backwards in a subliminal 'I'm going to pull my skirt down' manner. When listening to what men said she would idly tease her lips with a finger. When talking to women, she would make conspiratorial jokes and wink. She was a natural at being the kind of barmaid who drummed up business.

I felt I ought to back off, so I left the bar. I had a horrible feeling Gabrielle saw me leave, though.

Another aspect of that bar that made me think, was that they had porn on the TV. The Spanish have a lot of very graphic porn that blasts out free on their mainstream terrestrial channels, interspliced with adverts from companies who plainly don't mind being associated with it. 'No flicking in the advert break.' I could watch it for hours when Gabby was out, but never if she was around. But there it was, on the wide-screen in the bar, going largely unnoticed. Even after seeing that, I still didn't watch it in front of her.

In a funny sort of way, the experience in her bar was a challenge for me to make some progress with the natives.

I didn't have such a broad point of contact as Gabby, I only really had Olaia as company, and it always feels a betrayal to seek female friendship when you're married, even when, as in my case, there was no sexual element to it. However, she was my only real option, so in my free moments in the office I took to reading my father's diary.

That is not as odd as it sounds.

My father had been a child in Andalusia when the Spanish famines had hit; famines that appeared to have passed the British consciousness by altogether. It was so bad that there were literally no cats or dogs in the streets possibly because they could not even find rats to eat, or they themselves been eaten. The exodus from the country towns was so severe that they were later used to film the Spaghetti Westerns with Clint Eastwood in. I'd say that the townsfolk left and the tumbleweed moved in, but I think that even the tumbleweed got eaten. Certainly, according to the diary, they resorted to boiling weeds and grass to feed themselves. The world's response to this? The UN, almost as its inaugural act, slapped a trade embargo on us because they didn't like Franco. The only country that helped us out was Argentina, where General Peron arranged for a huge sum of money to be sent.

My father kept his diary throughout this period and I genuinely enjoy reading it. The binding on the book is stitched by hand, and the paper is of such a poor quality that it has what appears to be knots of straw in it. The pencil he used to write it is still tied to its spine with browned and brittle string; down its side is printed 'Staedtler GmbH Nuremberg.' My father told me he was proud of this pencil, that as he held it he would imagine the world beyond Franco's Spain; the glamour of Paris and Rome. For the first twenty years of his life it was his sole foreign possession.

I would sit at my desk in front of Olaia and ostentatiously reading the diary, asking her occasionally about details that came up or what specific words meant.

Did she remember the influx of thousands of country folk trying to find work in Bilbao? Did she remember the shanty towns they then lived in?

Olaia regarded my questions with suspicion; of course, she didn't remember events that occurred in the 1950s, she was too young. But I had no other way of making conversation. Occasionally she'd answer, but mostly she sat at her desk ignoring me.

I would sit for hours thinking, 'Look my way. Just look my way.' or 'Tell me about your life. Tell me the gossip. Let me in on the loop. Anything.'

I had already exhausted the obvious tactics of asking about how the factory was run. There was so much that puzzled me. The car park appeared to have twice as many vehicles as we had staff, the security guards never seemed to be where they should be, and most bizarrely I kept finding short scaffolding pipes in and around the grounds that no one seemed to claim. I raised these issues with Olaia but all she could manage was a shrug or a 'no idea.'

She did offer a few tips occasionally. When a certain inspector came it meant Health and Safety and we had to run around unlocking all the fire exits, but when another inspector called it meant Security and Local Anti-terrorist Measures so we had to quickly run around all the fire exits making sure they were properly locked.

'Well which should we do in the meantime?' I asked. 'Lock them or unlock them?'

She shrugged.

One morning I found another anonymous letter in my In Tray.

It said,

Take this seriously.

There was another leaflet enclosed. It was in English this time. It was eight pages long and on the subject of different types of sea birds.

I was just asking Olaia what she thought, when the phone on my desk rang.

It startled me.

'Hello?'

'Hi, it's me, Gabrielle.'

'Hiya.'

She said, 'Sit down.'

'Already done.'

'I know this wasn't our plan,' she began.

'We had a plan?' I asked.

'But I appear to be pregnant.'

Chapter Six

It sounds naive, but at no stage had I asked Gabby about contraception. When you are teenagers you might decide to have sex and then you'd discuss it. But for some reason, when you meet a fully formed woman you assume she knows what she's doing and if she has any requests like 'please wear a condom' you assume she'll voice them. And there was the fact that I had seen her pills lying around. I had never actually witnessed one leave the packet and touch her lips, but that wasn't the point.

Then there was the matter of periods. In my (limited) experience, women who have sex during their periods don't understand those who don't and vice versa. Men don't pry or argue, they just accept the particular woman's position on the subject. So I think I assumed that Gabby had shortish periods, because looking back there wasn't much evidence of them, and it was rare for her not to be interested in sex.

So the first question was when did she get pregnant.

'It must have been quite early on,' she said. 'Sorry.'

'No need to apologise,' I said. 'I'm interested, that's all.'

I threw my arms around her.

'It's terrific,' I said. But I'd left it too long to sound convinced.

We talked in general terms about parenthood and the future, but after a short while she unexpectedly said, 'Actually, I don't want to discuss it.'

'Oh,' I said.

'It's been a bit of a shock,' she said.

'Okay.'

'Tell me,' she said. 'Why didn't you say hello when you came to see me at work the other day?'

'What?'

'You came down to see me at the bar and then you walked out without saying hello.'

'I'm not sure what you mean,' I said.

Gabrielle rubbed her hands over her face several times.

'Did you come down to the bar where I work the other night. Yes or no?' she asked.

'No,' I said.

'I could have introduced you to some people. There's lots of people down there you might like.'

Deep down I wanted to ask her whether she was pregnant when she decided to marry me. But asking two questions like that in the same vein would sound negative. I knew enough about relationships to know that in the long run it pays to be supportive. Relentlessly positive. 'I fancy having an affair.' 'Okay, sweetheart.' That sort of thing.

It was a few days after that, that yet another letter came. I think it was at that stage that I started to feel panic. I fully appreciate that it would have long since been apparent to a third party that I had a major problem on my hands, but they would have had the advantage of a condensed view of events. The letters, the visit by the ex-husband or whatever he was, the trouble at work; it was all spaced out over a reasonable period. A period that involved major changes and turmoil; I had huge amounts on my plate and from my perspective I had a truly great woman in my life and a brand new future. It was day after day of virtual heaven. Buzzing around the hills on Vespas that Gabrielle hired. Picnicking on the nearby beach. The scent of a room after Gabby had been there. Laughing over tequila, learning about each other's lives, stroking her flawless back as she lay against the sheets. What more could I have asked for?

The letter had a number four on the top left of the envelope. It said,

Mostly red with splashes of yellow on the left. Mostly turquoise, a grey turquoise, on the right. Orange, the colour of Jaffas in front. The best. My favourite, I think, as I look around.

I had absolutely no idea what it could mean. I looked at the envelope again. It was posted in Spain. It had been written on a word processor. I felt panic rise up from my stomach, up through my diaphragm to my chest. I drew in breath over and over again, almost to stop myself crying. But I didn't want to cry. I just wanted it all to go away. I think with the first few letters I found it a bit too surreal to feel it was a true threat; as though this was happening to someone else. This was one letter too many. I felt sick with fear.

I tried to concentrate. I spent an hour looking at that letter. But I had no idea what I was looking for. It was on plain white paper. There was nothing special about it; quite a cheap paper I would have thought, but I was no expert. I held it up to the light; there was no watermark.

The black lettering on it had bled very slightly on most of the letters, particularly on the letter O. An inkjet printer rather than a laser printer, I would have thought.

I thought about the sentence structure. Did it ring any bells? Did I know anyone who spoke like that? Of course not. It was deliberately written in bursts of varying lengths. It could be anyone. There was no telltale sentence structure. No words that were unusual or that I associated with anyone in particular.

It could have been anyone.

I think what I found most disturbing in the weeks and months was that the pressures on us were so varied and inconsistent. I felt that a stalker, for example, would have a clear game plan, would employ just one tactic to terrorise and toy with me; perhaps silent phone calls or following Gabby down the street. But as the story unfolded it was bewildering and relentless in its variation.

Chapter Seven

At work I was still enjoying reading my father's diary.

He spent a lot of time detailing his life in the shanty towns outside Bilbao.

His mother and father would spend their days trying to get work in the city; at the docks or waiting on tables. The shanty town had been created by people stealing bits and pieces from building sites or scavenging in the countryside. A piece of corrugated iron would do for a roof, but was freezing in winter and oven hot in summer. So the kids would be sent out to look for rocks to weigh it down and give it some thickness and protection from the sun. But if the home was left unattended, people would come and steal your rocks or your entire roof. My father and his sister had to spend their days keeping guard.

The problems were compounded by Franco who refused to let the shanty towns have water or electricity. Bizkaia had been anti-Franco during the civil war, and it was a running sore for him that people now flocked to be there.

I made my usual attempts to talk about this with Olaia, but she was having none of it. She maintained a stony silence for the first three hours of the day. Then unexpectedly exploded.

It turned out she was upset with her boyfriend. She hadn't previously shared with me that she even had a boyfriend, but evidently she was in such a temper that even I was worth talking to.

'I came home last night, from working hard all day.' She said this with no apparent irony. 'And he had been down to the old town. He had a new tattoo on his back which he says I must admire. It was a… (she stopped for the word) lizard. The black ink was still coming out of the skin in black dots.'

'Oozing in beads,' I said idly, and bizarrely rather than look annoyed that I'd put her English down, she looked pleased that I had made it sound more literary.

'He said do you like it?' She continued, 'I did not like it. But I thought I had to say something. I said I liked the red eye of the lizard; it was a good touch. He looked at his back in the mirror and he said, "No that's just a spot," because he is so stupid. I knew it was a spot and he said, "you should have another tattoo, Olaia."'

'You have a tattoo?' I asked. But evidently this new spirit of sharing didn't extend as far as me asking questions.

She said, 'He then suggested I got my lips tattooed.'

'Your lips?'

'On the top lip he wanted me to have "I love" and on the bottom lip, his name, "Anartz".'

'Classy,' I said.

'I said, "What about work? I can't go to work with that on my lips."'

'A fair point,' I ventured.

'He said I could put lipstick on and when I came home every evening he could kiss the lipstick off.'

'What did you say?' I asked.

'I told him I do it when he had my name tattooed in the head of his penis.'

I laughed.

'The trouble is,' she said. 'He is so idiotic, he would do it. He said I should do it to give us something in common. We then had an argument, so now the only thing we have in common is that we hate each other.'

This revolutionised my view of Olaia. I originally thought she was… well I don't know really, but nothing like that. I was happy out of all proportion that she had chosen to speak to me.

I pondered what I would say in return, but didn't want to screw up this first bit of communication. In the event, however, I was robbed of the chance because I made the mistake of looking toward the window.

The man who claimed to be Gabrielle's husband, was looking at me through the glass.

I was terrified.

I sat entirely still.

Then I reasoned with myself that I needed to go on the offensive. He should be made to feel the one who was in the wrong.

I ran out of the office, down the corridor and out into the sunshine. It would take me another ten or fifteen seconds to get round the building to my own office window, but I ran as fast as I could in case he hadn't moved quickly enough.

He hadn't moved at all.

'Now will you talk to me?' he said.

'You're not even allowed on this property, mate,' I said. 'This is private property.'

'You need to talk to me. I need to talk to you,' he said.

'Get off this property,' I said.

'This is not a matter of opinion,' he said. 'We need to talk.'

Eventually I said, 'Fine, okay, let's hear what you have to say.'

'Shall we go somewhere?' he asked.

'No,' I said.

Bizarrely, at that moment I saw two security guards sauntering along with shotguns under their arms. I am in charge of employing the security guards, and they are not supposed to be armed in any way shape or form. At that moment, however, it was definitely the least of my problems.

'The woman you are living with now calls herself Gabrielle,' began the stranger.

'Okay,' I said. 'First of all, what is your name?'

'Alex Lawrence.'

'Okay,' I said. 'I'm going to need a pen and paper. I'm going to get a pen and paper.'

This led to the rather stupid situation where I needed to walk back to my desk. I thought it would be a sign of weakness to run, but it would take too long if I sauntered. So I loped in what I hoped was a nonchalant manner until I was round the corner of the building, then I ran like hell back to my office. Once in my office, I wandered around slowly, in case he was watching me through the window.

I sneaked a look at him. He was still standing just where I'd left him. Unnaturally straight, I thought. Only mad people stand that straight and that still.

I ran back round, then sauntered into view.

We stood facing each other again.

He reached into his pocket and I hated myself for flinching.

He retrieved a photo and held it out.

'This is her,' he said. 'Yes?'

The photo was definitely Gabrielle, but with short blonde hair. It was one of those boozy, girls-on-the-razz type photos. She was in a bar wearing a yellow boob tube. My eye was drawn to her nipples. She looked very drunk; heavy eyelids and one of those smiles that was either happiness, or the prelude to throwing up. I wondered if she looked happier there than she'd ever looked with me.

A photo in itself meant little. Gabrielle and Alex could have been colleagues or acquaintances. After all, I was convinced this man might well be a cop, so it could have been that he had worked with Gabrielle and perhaps had a crush. On the other hand, how did he have the time to come all the way to Bilbao if he had a full time job? He would have to be seriously mad or seriously motivated to... to do what exactly? Talk to her? Irritate me?

'Why do you want to talk to me?' I asked.

'We were married on May 12th 1995,' he said. 'At the Camberwell Registry office, South London.'

He fished out a piece paper and unfolded it. It was a photocopy of a marriage certificate.

'Why won't you even look at it?' he asked.

I took it and looked at it for a carefully calculated amount of time. Long enough to show I had seen the names on it and was now in a position to dismiss the evidence; short enough to show I was not prepared to engage on this man's terms. The name on the certificate was Regina Gabrielle Tremain.

'Okay, so you might have been married,' I said.

'We are married,' he said.

'If you claim you are married, why are you stalking me at my work?' I asked. 'Why have you come all the way out to Bilbao? Why don't you simply take it up with Gabrielle?'

'I have a right to fight for my wife,' he said. 'Fight for the chance to make our marriage work. And in answer to your other question, I've moved here. I work here.'

'If she has chosen to leave you in such a dramatic manner, then there's little you can do,' I said.

I was annoyed that I'd apparently conceded his central point that they were married. I was too afraid to contemplate the concept that he'd moved here permanently.

He started talking at length. He walked in little circles as he did so; sometimes he seemed to be almost talking to himself. He had the air of an aggressive man, but also of someone who was deeply sad and confused. He had obviously been through a lot mentally and was probably telling the truth. In his mind, at least.

I didn't listen, or rather I half listened.

He was saying how he'd had no particular sign that Gabrielle wanted to move on. They had seemed happy enough. They'd had a holiday planned; a villa in a town south of Venice. He spent a long time wondering out loud about why the marriage might have failed.

'Perhaps I was too stay-at-home for her,' he said. 'I was happy, you see? Perhaps I'd settled too much. She's very energetic and fun. She once said to me I was too passive, that she kept coming up with all the fun stuff for us to do. It was never me.'

'But I *like* watching sport,' he continued. 'And we can't go out endlessly, it's just too expensive.'

I became very aware of my surroundings, in that way you get when you are going to faint. Colours changed. Noises were either too loud, or I couldn't hear at all. I was aware of the office blocks and the foundry. The warehouses. The green landscaping at the front. The ornamental lakes. Three ornamental lakes. Count them, one, two three. This man was obviously married to Gabrielle once. Or he was a hell of a fantasist.

A plane took off from the nearby airport. Surely that airport is too close to the factory to be safe.

I heard myself saying, 'I've listened enough.'

I was walking away.

He was saying something but I couldn't catch what it was.

I said over my shoulder, 'You've had your say. Thank you.'

I was safely round the side of the building now.

I kept walking. I half imagined he would run after me.

I made it to the door. I was soon down the corridor and in my office.

I stood in my office by the external wall, so that I couldn't be seen through the window.

Of all things, my scalp felt itchy. I scratched at myself.

I realised with a jolt that Olaia was still at her desk. She was looking at me puzzled. She started talking about her idiotic boyfriend again.

Chapter Eight

Now there is something about human nature that means we would rather believe the word of a complete stranger than someone we live with, even when that someone has never apparently lied, works hard every day to make us happy, and has made life almost perfect.

I recognised this phenomenon, so I wanted to tread carefully when challenging Gabrielle about her past.

If I waited until we were settled into a meal, say, then it might look calculating to then bring up the topic. I opted to spontaneously bring it up when I next saw her, but affect a kind of nonchalance.

She wandered into the house looking sunny.

'Hiya,' I said.

'Hello gorgeous,' she replied.

She made herself a gin and tonic and opened a packet of Rich Tea fingers. She started chatting about something that had happened that day and dunked a biscuit into her gin before eating it. It's a trick I'd seen her do several times before I then tried it myself. It's surprisingly nice, providing the drink isn't too strong.

'That can go towards my five portions of fruit and veg a day,' she said.

'What?' I asked.

'The junipers.'

She'd made that joke twice before.

'Oh, I had a funny experience today,' I said. It didn't sound even remotely nonchalant.

'Mmm huh?

'Yeah, a man came to see me at work who... well he claimed he was married to you.'

I watched her face. Not a flicker. No change in colour. No shadow crossed it. On the other hand, she was slow to answer and a little too matter of fact about what should have been strange news.

'Who?' she asked.

Did she have lots of ex-husbands?

'He said he was called Alex Lawrence.'

'Yeah,' she said. 'Yes I know.'

'You know?' I asked.

'Well I didn't know he had come to see you. But I know who is. He used to imply to people that we were married.'

'And he is…'

'We used to live together,' she said.

I let that hang dramatically in the air. Largely because I didn't know what to say.

'It was…' she began, then stopped.

'It was just a bit of a shock for me, that's all,' I said. I was annoyed that I was virtually apologising. On the other hand I was demonstrating that I wasn't out to get her; whatever she did was fine. She was trusted. Which she wasn't.

She did the deep breath, just-about-to-tell-all thing.

'I can see how you might think I should have mentioned this before,' she said.

'You don't know that I thought that,' I said. It sounded aggressive.

'It isn't always true that people talk about previous relationships. Previous marriages, yes, but not necessarily relationships,' she said.

'So you weren't married,' I said.

'Sometimes in life,' she said. 'One makes a mistake. Sometimes in life, something goes so horribly wrong that my every instinct was just to forget the whole incident and move on. I moved in with Alex and everything was perfect. It seemed perfect. And we did have a good couple of years and we shouldn't forget that.'

She'd said 'we' a lot.

'I was younger, so when you're younger, we don't know so much about ourselves or how we should do relationships, so I don't necessarily blame him, or me. But it got more and more frustrating, and he got more and more pent up. He saw everything I did as an attempt to push him away. He would get jealous and obsessive about us. I realised one day that it wasn't teething problems, it wasn't problems we would work out, it was simply a complete nightmare that was never going to improve. It was the little things, it was the big things. He was a tightwad, he was petty, he was unbelievably tight with money.'

'You've said that twice,' I laughed.

'The stress it deserves,' she said. 'Even though he was the one doing all the spending; and he was violent, and ruthlessly dominating. I know he was unhappy. But that doesn't excuse it.'

'What sort of things did he actually do?' I asked. 'I'm not disagreeing, I'm just interested.'

'All sorts. He would start one project, and spend weeks on it, then drop it, then we had to do something else. Then he'd get frustrated we didn't have enough freedom so we'd change this or that, plan to go abroad or something, but he never actually wanted to go away. We were forever changing things, discussing things, but it was never right, he was never happy. Then he got passed over for promotion. Then he would obsess if I went out at all. If I went out with friends, he would make up some reason why I couldn't go, or he would accidentally pop by, wherever we were. He was just checking up on me. God forbid if I wasn't exactly where I said I'd be, because we'd moved on to some other bar or something.'

I was struck that when she'd described her job to me she'd stuck to specific anecdotes, but when describing her marriage she was mostly going for generalities. I couldn't work out what that meant, possibly that it was more painful and she didn't want to consider the details, or possibly that she had taken a view on what happened that couldn't be adequately supported by specific facts.

'What did he do for a living?' I asked.

'He used to work for a civil engineers,' she said. 'They sort of put the infrastructure into buildings. Now he's more of a bureaucrat. But he drank more and more. That was probably the single biggest problem in fact. He was deeply unhappy, and stressed, I could see that, but it didn't excuse how he treated me, and at the end of the day I do have my own life and my own health to consider. It's not wrong to consider my own happiness ultimately.'

'No,' I agreed. 'So what did you do?'

'So one day I moved out. I simply didn't come home. I made a lame excuse that morning to go in late to work, and I waited until Alex had left and I packed two suitcases and I took them into work with me. I had no idea what I was going to do. I stayed with a colleague. She was most reluctant to put me up. I realised how few friends I had at that time. I think partly because I had put so much time and mental effort into my relationship. We weren't married but I had been deeply in love and I think that's the point. It makes walking away a bigger, more difficult decision. I want you to know I really tried, but sometimes in life you just have to walk away. I promised myself I would never look back, and that the rest of my life started then and there.'

'Fair enough,' I said.

'But I am not my past,' she said.

'What?'

'I am not my past,' she said. 'Although...' She fixed me with a look that meant what she was just about to say was very important. 'The man is mad. And very very scary. It is a big worry that he has found us. I mean, what kind of a person comes all the way out to Bilbao "just to talk" with us? We should take precautions.'

Gabrielle got herself another gin, and had a think.

'Perhaps he's just come out the once,' she said. 'And when he's said what he wants to say, he'll go.'

'Yeah, maybe,' I said. 'But this is not the first time he's done this.'

'What?'

'He came to see me when we were in England.'

Gabrielle looked fierce.

'He's made contact with you before?' she asked.

'Yes.'

'Well why on earth didn't you tell me?'

'I don't know,' I said. 'I thought he was mad.'

'Someone came to you and claimed he was married to me and you didn't bother to mention it?'

I was silent. It took me too long to come up with an answer.

'I didn't realise it was you,' I said. 'He said he was looking for a blonde woman, and I thought he must have meant the woman who was moving into my house.'

'But you didn't sell your house to a woman. It was a man.'

'But he might have had a girlfriend,' I protested. 'I was confused.' I pulled a comical face to denote my addled brain.

'You're just lying to me,' said Gabrielle.

'I'm lying to you? How the fuck was I supposed to know that you were in the habit of changing your man every time you dyed your hair a different colour.'

I didn't see her hand shoot towards me. She had a glass in it, but I'm sure she didn't mean to hit me with the glass per se. Then she was thumping and slapping me over and over again. I was trying to hold her wrists and I more or less had things under control when she started kicking me instead. Then her head was sort of shaking quickly left and right as if confused. The next thing I knew she'd run out of the room.

I was surprised to see blood on the table and work surfaces. Vibrant lines of red, as though someone had flicked a paintbrush. I then noticed smears around the kitchen where it must have got on my hand and I must have touched everywhere. I went off to the hallway to find a mirror. I had a gash on my cheek about two inches long which ran exactly on the vertical from the corner of my mouth upwards.

Large drips of blood kept rising out of the wound and joining the mess on my neck, or dripping off my jaw and onto my clothes. My shirt was particularly bloodied. It was a work shirt that wasn't particularly new, so I made the decision to throw it away; although later on I couldn't recall for certain whether I actually got round to doing it.

There was the noise of Gabrielle stropping about on the landing. Thumping on the floorboards and slammed doors, a pause, then more thumping of floorboards for extra effect.

I found some kitchen roll and wet it under the kitchen tap. I managed to clean most of the peripheral blood away. I then got a bigger handful of kitchen roll, held it hard against the wound, and went to lie on the sofa. For my sins, I get a bit faint when blood appears.

I thought through the situation a bit. It was possible Gabrielle was telling the truth about not being married to Alex. For example, he had only showed me a photocopy of a marriage certificate, not the certificate itself. He could easily have faked it by making a copy of any old marriage certificate, Tippexing out the names and changing them, then photocopying that photocopy. Okay so I was probably deluding myself, but the fact remained it was possible.

I gazed at the ceiling for a long time, then my eyes started to meander around the room taking in every detail one by one, the way you do when you're ill.

It is a room that has a couple of large windows but they look onto the garden that banks up behind. In other words it's not overlooked by anyone.

Lying there, I suddenly realised what the stalker's letter had meant.

Mostly red with splashes of yellow on the left. Mostly turquoise, a grey turquoise, on the right. Orange, the colour of Jaffas in front. The best. My favourite, I think, as I look around.

I got the letter and ran upstairs holding the kitchen roll against my face.

'Read this,' I said to Gabby. 'What does it remind you of?'

She read the letter carefully. She didn't reply for a long while. She turned it over to see if there was anything on the back.

'The decorating I did downstairs. All the coloured patches where the plaster had gone,' she said.

'So, whoever wrote this letter has been looking in at our windows,' I said.

'Yes,' she replied.

She read it again carefully.

'No,' she said. 'The red patch isn't visible from the window. Whoever wrote this letter has been in that room. Who wrote this?'

'I have no idea. But I think I'm going to have to go to the police.'

'You got sent a letter like this and you didn't bother to tell me?' she asked. 'What the hell is wrong with you?'

'I have no idea.'

Chapter Nine

A true story. In 1971 there was a study that showed that eighty-seven percent of all acute mental illness in Malaga was due to shock. Actual acute shock. It turned out that most of the patients were young men working in the catering industry: waiters, hotel staff and the like.

For centuries, rural Spanish workers had been used to a life measured in hours. Work was something to be done at some indeterminate point over the next day or week. The animals had to be fed and fences kept intact and that was largely it. Suddenly better paid work was available that involved waiting on tables in busy restaurants and hotels. Every minute counted, and you knew your boss could easily replace you. As a result, the Spanish hospitals became overcrowded with young patients suffering from breathlessness and insomnia, panic attacks and night terrors. Construction companies were called in because they had to build extra hospital wards to accommodate them.

So I don't believe that the Spanish are mischievous, but I do believe they frequently take life at a pace that we can't comprehend. From what I'd heard, this was particularly true of the police. I went down there hoping for the best, but preparing for the worst by taking a thick book to read.

A further problem is the sheer complexity of their system. The Spanish have several police forces, and it's a brave person who declares they understand who does what.

The Guardia Civil are the ones who used to wear the comedy tricorn hats and green tunics. They variously drive around in four-by-fours, ride horses or, and I'm not making this up, in rural areas they get about on donkeys. I have no idea what the Guardia Civil do. Nothing probably.

There's the Policia Municipal who hang around towns in blue uniforms and chauffeur's caps. Their speciality is to shrug imperceptibly when asked a question, while eyeing up the woman over your shoulder. Their other function is to blow their whistles at tourists who want to cross the road.

There's another lot called the Grupo (full title Grupo Something Something No Doubt Very Important) who are a bit like the SAS. They storm into your house throwing hand grenades, on the off-chance you're a terrorist.

There's the Cuerpo Superior who, I think, look into murders and stuff.

But I was convinced I was looking for another sort of police: the Policia Nacional, who wear brown uniforms and sort out the problems of a city. The trouble is that the Basque Country is semi-autonomous and now has its own police system independent of Spain proper. For the purposes of catching ETA this must be a little like putting Gerry Adams in charge of Irish counter-terrorism, but who knows. In either event, I thought they were my best bet and presented myself at a police station to enquire after them.

It was one of those high-ceilinged buildings that looked as though it had survived centuries of different regimes and revolutions. I sat waiting in an echoing hallway.

A cleaner appeared at the top of the stairs with a bucket. She emptied it out, then chased the murky water down the steps with a mop. The stairs were fully carpeted, but no one appeared to think this strange, even though the carpet already smelled like a dog with an advanced case of distemper.

I was surprised to be called through. I had only been waiting about three minutes. A very pleasant-looking man ushered me into his office. He asked me to sit, and I explained everything.

'What do the letters say?' he asked.

I explained.

'They are about the colours in your room?'

I took a chance he meant this as a joke and laughed.

He looked puzzled.

I fished in my briefcase. I showed him my threatening letters.

He showed me his.

He pulled on the drawer of his filing cabinet. It was jam packed with correspondence.

'These are my death threats,' he said with a flourish. 'Do I look dead to you?'

'I think I know who sent mine,' I said hopefully.

'People get death threats in the Basque Country. It happens all the time. We can't possibly chase up every letter. Especially when there is no specific threat. This is just a letter about colours. But I will get someone to write it down. It will all be done properly.'

He looked at me afresh.

'You are English?' he asked.

'I am Basque,' I said.

'Your father is from?'

'The Basque Country.'

'Your mother?' asked the policeman.

'Is from Ireland.'

He then said something odd.

'Are you from the English Intelligence?'

'What?' I said.

'Are you with the English Intelligence, or the English Police?'

'Er, no.'

Back at work I asked Olaia about this. She didn't break from her typing.

'You should have said yes,' she said.

'Why?'

'There is a lot of British Intelligence in the area. He would have shown more interest. The police are told to co-operate by their bosses. Are you sure you are not British Intelligence?'

'Is this some joke I am not getting?' I asked.

'No. It is like this. Your Tony Blair was keen to have an ally in the Madrid Government. He offered the British Intelligence to come here and help against the struggle for independence. After all the English and Americans have done to us, the Madrid Government suck up to them. There's no predicting what they will do.'

'You're saying the British are here, acting against ETA?' I clarified.

'Yes,' said Olaia. 'Because ETA and your IRA have strong links. That is their excuse for coming, anyway. They pose as married couples on honeymoon or they set up a bar or a small business. The Basque Country is... what word do you use? Village-like. We all know what goes on. What about your wife?'

'What about her?' I asked.

'She is in the police, you said.'

'So you do listen to what I say.'

'Of course!' she said. 'What an odd thing to say.'

'Oh.'

'But you should have said to the police you worked for the British.'

'Why?' I asked.

'They would have helped you. And also you have a father from the Basque Country and a mother from Ireland.'

'So?'

'So they probably now think you are working with ETA. We also get a lot of IRA Irish here,' she said.

'Do you think I work for ETA?' I asked.

This was the first time I ever saw Olaia laugh.

'No,' she said.

I laughed too.

'But I wouldn't know,' she said in a more serious tone.

'Why?'

'ETA is an organisation of many thousands of people. Each little, er…'

'Cell.'

'Each little cell acts on its own. Not even the head of ETA would know who everyone is. So if someone is arrested they do not have much to say. It makes ETA invincible, I think.'

A glint caught my eye from outside.

I thought at first it was the sunshine catching the water in one of the artificial ponds, but I was astonished to see a gun barrel protruding from a first floor window. There was possibly a second one beyond it.

'Olaia, quick, follow me.'

We ran out of the building and round the block. Well *I* ran; Olaia wandered along behind in a resentful manner.

In my hurry I couldn't really remember at which window I'd seen the guns. They'd disappeared now. I was soon in the right building and taking the stairs three at a time. I shouted to Olaia that I would check the rooms to the right of the stairwell and she should look in the rooms to the left.

I opened several doors only to reveal bored office workers who occasionally looked up from their desks.

There was nothing to see.

I eventually found Olaia in a staff room. She was sitting having a cigarette with two guards. The two guards I'd seen with guns on the previous occasion.

'So?' I asked.

She shrugged.

Chapter Ten

The picture I'm trying to paint is that there were a number of strange events all jostling for attention. My instinct was that some of the problems amounted to nothing; they were just the quirks of life. Some of the other problems were no doubt more important.

The mix was already rich and confusing, but there is no situation on God's earth that can't be further darkened and confused by the presence of my mother.

My mother came to stay.

My mother can be on an entirely different continent and still wind me up; so four weeks (four weeks!) under the same roof would be a living hell. In England she lived in a small modern flat which could easily be locked up and left for months on end. I always feared, therefore, that if she stayed she might get too comfortable and never leave.

My mother is called Jancie; part anagram, part monster. She's always seemed unduly old: somewhere between the age where you sigh in a satisfied manner when sitting down, and the age where you are congratulated on getting to the chair in the first place. 'Nearly there, love. Well done!'

To look at she's a mild old lady. To know, she is a selfish, mad, attention-seeking vindictive old bag who inexplicably smells of potatoes.

I tried to prepare Gabby psychologically with various descriptions of her antics.

'Everyone thinks their parents are mad,' she replied.

'She has spent most of the last twenty years in the kitchen talking to the oven mitt on her hand,' I said.

'So?'

'So she thinks she can hear it talking back.'

'Your dad's dead. She gets lonely,' said Gabby.

'He was the brains of the outfit.'

'Oh you're always negative about people,' she said. 'She sounded fine on the phone.'

I met her at the airport. Her eyesight is very poor so she had various staff buzzing around her. She's had cataract operations but the only positive result as far as she was concerned was that it gave her something juicy to moan about. She can, at best, make out vague shapes. Her first words to me at the airport were, 'Sal! When did you put on so much weight?'

'About the time you lost your social skills, Mum.'

How could she conclude I was fat? By smell?

I consoled myself that if my mother was still capable of being rude then she was also still capable of looking after herself for a few years yet.

I brought her home and Gabby was very charming. My mother had the temerity to be charming in return. She made light conversation, praised my new wife and what she'd done around the home, then joined with Gabby to make a few jokes at my expense.

'She's lovely, your mother,' Gabby said a few days down the line.

'Wait until you see inside her handbag,' I said.

'What?'

'She's got the rings from each of her five dead sisters in there. And a small bottle of little black gallstones which, as far as I am aware, are not hers.'

'Sal, there is nothing wrong with your mother,' she said.

Mercifully, the very next day I caught my mother putting her coat on.

'Where are you going?' I asked.

'I'm driving to Ipswich. I've got a friend who's going into hospital there next week. I've got to visit her, so I'm going tomorrow to see how long it takes. Note the chevrons.'

'Mum,' I said, 'You're not in England, you're in Spain.'

My mother became raw. 'Don't you think I don't know that?' she hissed.

We were at an impasse. I could have mentioned her eyesight or the fact she doesn't drive, but it didn't seem relevant.

I said, 'Well don't forget to take a pen and paper with you, in case you see any trucks being driven well. Note down the numbers to ring.'

I felt obscurely cheated and, worse, Gabby hadn't been around to witness what she was like.

My mother then launched into an attack on Gabrielle, and what she called 'her spending habits.'

'It's none of your business,' I said.

'None of my business that woman is bleeding you dry?'

'She's not bleeding me dry,' I protested.

'She is forever coming back into the house with more stuff she's bought,' said my mother.

'We've just moved house; it's an expensive time. You have to buy stuff when you move.'

'You don't have to buy clothes,' she said,

I thought of the lingerie Gabby kept buying for my amusement; the new clothes from Corte Anglaise that made every man and woman follow her with their eyes as she walked through the streets of Bilbao.

'She has a job,' I said. 'In fact she's been working harder than ever.'

'She spends more than she could possibly be earning at a bar job,' said my mother. 'I've seen it.'

'She works hard,' I said.

Indeed, in the ensuing weeks Gabby took more shifts at the bar, but I presumed that was to avoid being stuck with my mother. Although I had a lingering feeling that Gabrielle became jealous of the time I spent with Jancie.

One night Gabby woke me up.

'What's that noise?' she asked.

'No idea,' I said. 'What noise?'

There were a number of noises to choose from. After our initial newly-weds joy at our house, we had discovered it was noisy at night.

Whenever there was half-decent weather, the hairpin road up to our house was put to good use by skateboarders. A group of lads with mopeds pulled the boarders behind them up the hill and the 'neeeeeeee' strain of their motors echoed round the countryside, through our open windows, and exactly hit the resonant frequency of my eardrums. It takes them seven and half minutes to pull the skateboarders up the hill (I have timed it) and it's followed by the tinny rumble as the skateboarders shoot back down (this takes four and a half minutes.) The mopeds then return to the bottom and the whole process starts again, and again, all the way through to four in the morning. The noise doesn't then stop as such; it is merely upstaged by the sound of festivities when the rest of the Spanish start spilling into the streets shouting and laughing, slamming their car doors, and generally making their way home. Before I lived here, I thought the dark rings under the eyes of Hispanics were genetic, now I know it's because they never sleep.

Even when the Spanish aren't making a din, we have what I can only assume are mice in the attic space above our room. It can be a scampering or a rustling, and sometimes, bizarrely, a thumping. It's a very old house so who knows what it's all about. There is a loft hatch in the spare room and I did once tentatively poke my head up there. There was nothing to see; I could only presume that the mice got in from the outhouse at the back which shares a bit of the wall.

But the noise that night wasn't the whine of mopeds or the rustling of mice: it was more a shuffling and creaking. Quiet footsteps somewhere beyond our bedroom door. We strained to hear in the darkness. It started again. Movement, followed by a pause, then a sigh.

'That is my mother,' I said.

'No there's someone out there,' said Gabby.

'It is my mother. She spends the nights pacing up and down the corridor.'

'Are you sure?' she asked.

'Positive. You're a good sleeper and don't usually hear it.'

'Well why does it keep stopping?'

'She is pausing outside our bedroom door to listen.'

'Why?'

'To see if she's woken us up yet. She wants us to know she can't sleep.'

We both gazed at the ceiling in silence.

My mother walked around (eight seconds), stopped (three seconds), sighed (one to four seconds according to effect required), then walked on again.

I woke up sometime later and Gabby was no longer in bed. I had no idea where she'd gone. My mother was making up for the fact that she never sleeps by snoring loud enough to shake the walls.

No doubt I would receive a phone call from her at work later, giving me a blow by blow account of her disturbed night. I would then ask in an apparently polite tone whether it mattered that a retired woman felt a bit tired during the day, and she would reply that I 'obviously didn't understand.' She's quite right of course. I genuinely don't understand why, if a night's sleep is so important to an old person, they would be so hell bent on having afternoon naps. Or why old folk moan that the music that youth play is 'too loud' and spend the rest of the time moaning that they can't hear anything because it's not loud enough.

I set off to work and drove down to the river and waited in my car to use the transporter bridge. I queued for five minutes, which is about average, and at the other side drove off through Areeta to find the motorway.

I was still puzzling where Gabby might have been that morning when my phone rang.

I did the 'retrieve the phone from pocket while driving' shimmy, and discovered it was my mother who was in a complete state.

As far as I could work out, the following had happened:

Not long after I'd left the house, my mother had stopped snoring and had surfaced for the day. There was a knock on the front door which she answered in a dressing gown.

In the morning sunshine she could make out the shadows of two men. One short, one medium height. There was possibly a third.

The taller one talked steadily, while the other hung behind. Jancie's Spanish is reasonable but she needs people to speak slowly, partly because of her poor hearing and partly because first thing in the morning she gets a little confused.

The men were now pushing into the house. They separated and moved into other rooms. Jancie's eyes are so poor that she needs to be close to someone to be sure they are even present, so she listened hard and decided that at least one of them was in the living room. She felt her way down the corridor. She was walking into the living room when the man walked back past her holding something heavy. She followed him as fast as she could.

She was shouting now.

'Who are you? Get out of my house.'

One of the men called, in Spanish, from another room. She felt both of them walk past her quickly. She decided they were stealing all the possessions of value and loading them into a van.

Jancie walked steadily along the corridor and felt her way up the stairs. She would have rung the police but she couldn't think what the number was. I had shown her a button to push if she wanted to ring my mobile; the second 'memory' button. She picked up the receiver and pressed it.

By the time she got through to me, I was on a busy stretch of the motorway about five kilometres from the airport. The Spanish have a habit of driving at 70 miles per hour with only four inches between their bumpers, using their brakes with a faith that would make the Pope feel inadequate. At the moment the phone rang I had a car attempting to overtake me on the inside even though there were already two cars side by side with me travelling at the same speed.

When I first heard my mum on the phone, I have to admit that my first emotion was irritation, because it was likely that she'd simply mistaken the sound from the television or some such nonsense.

'Are you quite sure?' I asked.

'Yes I'm quite sure,' replied my mother in a loud whisper.

'Okay,' I said. 'Lock yourself in a room and I'll try and call the police and come straight back.'

Jancie shut her bedroom door but then realised there was no lock. The men now seemed to be upstairs. She felt her way around the room for a chair to prop against the door although it seemed to her like the sort of measure that only worked in films.

She dithered for a while, listening to them moving about the house and then she decided they were downstairs again. She'd go to the bathroom. There was a lock on the door there.

In the corridor she was sent spinning by someone rushing past. She thought the man might have already gone again, but her confidence had deserted her; she didn't want to move and couldn't think what best to do. She was by the door to our bedroom and eventually decided she could go in there and find something heavy. She stood by the bed and felt around. When she had come to stay, she had insisted we stop and buy some flowers for her to give to me. I'd promised I'd place them in a vase in my room. The flowers had long since died, but Jancie wasn't sure whether the vase had been washed and returned to my room, or left downstairs. It was somewhere to start.

Feeling around she found an aerosol. Perhaps a deodorant. My mother is a resourceful person and wondered if I had a cigarette lighter. She could light the aerosol and use it as a flame thrower. A resourceful person with a violent streak.

She ran her hand over the chest of drawers, feeling the various objects and trying to think clearly. The men hadn't actually attacked her so perhaps they should be left to do whatever they wanted. On the other hand, they were stealing her son's possessions; she'd stood up for herself all her life and wasn't going to be helpless now.

While hunting for a lighter, she came across a Polaroid camera. She could take a picture of them as evidence.

Meanwhile, I had managed to drive back as far as the queue for the transporter bridge. I counted the cars in front. Fifteen. The transporter took ten vehicles at a time across the river and it had only just left. I jumped out of my car and ran down to the first vehicle in the queue. My best bet was to persuade that driver to let me in.

The man looked passively at my frantic face through his car window. He eventually wound it down.

In my panic, my Spanish didn't come so easily. I said, '*Alguien me ha robado mi madre.*' ('Someone has stolen my mother.') I then said in Spanish 'The house of mother has been stolen.'

Astonishingly enough, the man looked blank.

'My mother has been stolen,' I said, in English, slowly and loudly this time, which goes to show how barmy I'd become.

I ran back and drove my car to the front anyway.

The man laughed. He spoke English to me. He was evidently from Yorkshire, in a hired car.

I explained my problem and he reversed up a little to let me put the nose of my car in front.

Chapter Eleven

When I finally got to the house it looked shut up, and there was no sign of my mother.

I gingerly opened the front door.

Perhaps I had been correct earlier; my mother really had been stolen.

I walked slowly forward.

'I've called the police,' I shouted out in Spanish and then in Basque.

There were papers and letters all over the floor as if there had been a fight. The television had gone, the video had gone, the stereo had been taken, along with one of the two speakers; all replaced by rectangles in the dust.

The mantelpiece looked less cluttered but temporarily I couldn't recall what might have been there before.

I called louder for my mother, feeling braver at the apparent lack of people present. Again there was no response. I decided to walk noisily through the house, banging doors and calling out as I went. I checked every room, I even checked under the beds and in wardrobes, feeling very self-conscious as I did so, which was stupid, because no one was watching.

I decided I shouldn't disturb anything. The police would need evidence when they arrived. I went back outside and leant against my car, waiting for them in the sunshine.

A short middle-aged man was visible in the distance. He walked in a businesslike manner along the road towards me. I was listening out for police sirens but there was nothing.

The man was ten yards away from me now.

'We have your mother,' he said.

'You have my mother captive, or she is safe with you?' I asked, or hopefully that's what I asked, given that my Spanish evidently breaks down under stress.

The man wasn't sure what I meant. I decided, based on nothing but his demeanour, that this man had somehow saved the day for my mother.

'I want to take you to your mother,' he said in English.

'What happened to her?'

'I found her. She was walking. She has said she had problems with men in the house.'

I followed this stranger to his home which turned out to be tucked up on the hill with us, behind the next bend.

My mother was at the kitchen table. A mug of hot chocolate sat in front of her undrunk.

'Hello mum,' I said.

'Is that you Sal?'

'How did you end up here?'

'I decided I had to leave the house,' she said. 'I walked up the street so that someone would at least see if I was attacked.'

'Well done,' I said.

We hugged.

We thanked the neighbour and walked back to our house, linking arms as we went. There was still no sign of the police.

'I tried to take their photograph,' said Jancie. 'I used your camera.'

'That's brilliant,' I said.

'Well I wouldn't be much good in an identity parade,' she said. She was very upbeat considering her morning. Although, she is rarely happier than when she's been the victim of an injustice.

'So we need to get the photograph developed,' I said.

'I don't know. I used your big Polaroid camera and then the man tried to take it off me, so I hit him with it. I think I got his shoulder but I might have got his face. I think he took the camera away.'

'Oh well, you tried.'

I figured that if I carefully walked through the house disturbing as little as possible I might be able to find any Polaroids that were taken. Even if the burglars had looked for Polaroids they might not have found all of them in the mess.

In the event it took no looking at all. I found three.

'It's likely they didn't even want them, which is odd,' I said. 'Unless they thought it was a normal camera and the negatives were still inside, which is unlikely. Most people know what a Polaroid camera is.'

I looked at the Polaroids. Two of them were blurred: a shaky shot of a wall and another of what looked like a man's arm and a bit of banister. The third was definitely the face of a man though. It was a little blurred but certainly good enough to identify someone from it.

'What on earth happened?' I asked.

'What do you mean?'

'Well the man looks burnt. Half his hair is sort of frizzed and his face looks charred. He looks right raw.'

'Yeah, he was cross,' said my mother.

It's possible to love someone and for them to drive you to distraction at one and the same time. At that moment, and when my mother went on to explain what she had done, I was totally in love with her.

It transpired that she couldn't find an aerosol to use as a flame thrower, so in desperation she had sprayed the intruder at close range with a can of oven cleaner.

I was still giggling as I tiptoed round the house looking for other clues. Not much to be found, but as I wandered back to the front, I noticed a letter on the floor by the doormat. It was addressed to me, but what scared me was the number five printed on the top left of the envelope.

Inside it said,

Dear Sal
Are you scared yet?

I stood in the doorway. I looked long and hard at the roof tops and windows in the town below. Someone, somewhere was watching us, watching our house. They knew when we were out, so that they could deliver letters. Were we visible from a hotel room perhaps? Or was there somewhere a car could park and the stalker could watch us with binoculars, and he only did it from time to time? Probably the latter.

I went back in the house and closed the door. It suddenly seemed very cold.

Chapter Twelve

I thought my biggest problem was where the hell Gabby had got to.

I was wrong.

I decided to take myself into Bilbao and talk to the local police and ask them why they hadn't turned up to investigate our burglary.

I found a parking place in central Bilbao. I had heard a number of reports that ETA Youth spends a lot of time pouring acid into parking meters. The idea was to stop the collection of money that then gets sent off to the Madrid government. I had no loose change on me that day, so I could have done with such a godsend. But needless to say there was no chance of me finding one. In fact, I've never even *seen* one. I was forced to leave my meter unfed which turned out to be an expensive mistake.

I went into the police station.

I was arrested.

All I had done was tell my story to the man at the front desk, given him my name and address, and show him the stalker's letter and the Polaroid. I waited patiently on a bench in the hallway and a couple of minutes later a policeman turned up. He looked at the photo, but brushed aside the letter, presumably because it was in English. He asked me to follow him down a corridor to a room.

The room was empty apart from five chairs and a desk. There was no window. I turned to see the door close. I sat there for a long time, then on a whim I tried it. It was locked.

I sat down and waited.

A small plain clothed man came in.

'I am from the Cuerpo Superior, the Super Corps,' he said.

I laughed involuntarily. The phrase Super Corps has a comic book element, no matter how many times it is repeated.

He passed a form and a pen across the table. It had several questions on it. Helpfully, all the questions were in two languages: Spanish and Basque.

'My Spanish isn't so good that I'd feel confident writing all my answers in it,' I said.

'You must write down who you want informed of your arrest,' he said in English. 'And there you write who your lawyer is. And there you write whether you want the British Consul informed.'

I felt the colours in the room change.

'Are you saying I am being arrested?' I asked.

'You have come to turn yourself in, yes?' he said.

'No,' I said. 'What exactly are your charges against me?'

'We will clarify your charges when the documents are prepared,' he said.

'I haven't got a solicitor. I'm English, I've only been here a while, why would I have a solicitor? Why have you arrested me?' I asked again.

'Just fill in the form,' he said.

I felt that even by filling in the form I was allowing the whole process to occur. I tried to give myself thinking time by asking what some of the questions meant.

The policeman got out his cigarettes and passed two over to my side of the table. I rarely smoke except, obviously, to annoy my mother; but passing them back felt impolite, so I put them in my top pocket. The rate things were going I was going to need them to bribe someone not to bugger me in the showers during the lengthy jail term for a crime that I not only didn't commit, but the nature of which never even got explained.

'Well, I suppose if I don't fill out the form, nobody will know I'm here,' I said, to no one in particular.

Nominating someone to tell was a difficult one. Gabrielle was the obvious choice but I suddenly felt that was a mistake. My mother was a possibility, but she was mad. I had visions of the police ringing up my mum to tell them I was in prison and her replying 'That's nice' then putting the phone down and calling up the stairs to my empty room that someone on the phone says I'm in prison. Four hours later she'd be wondering why no one had fed her.

I put her name down. At least she was likely to be in if they phoned.

'No, don't put her name,' said the policeman.

'I can't think of anyone else.'

'You can't name someone who is a... how you say? a convict.'

'What?' I asked.

'We are arresting your mother as well.'

'You are arresting my mother?'

I went blank with the enormity of it. I tried to concentrate on the specific question of naming a contact person. Gabrielle then, or someone who had more local knowledge? They had arrested my mother. Why? In shock, and more than a little desperate, I wrote down Olaia's name, her mobile number and our number at work.

'What are we being charged with?' I asked again.

'That will be explained,' he repeated. 'We are arresting you as a precaution.'

The man stood up and knocked on the door. It was opened from the outside.

'Can I keep the photo please?' I asked. 'It is my evidence.'

The man weighed it, literally, in his hand.

'It is our evidence,' he said.

I was escorted down two floors to a cell.

It occurred to me to run, to make a bolt for it. Away down the corridors and out into the afternoon; to hide out somewhere and set about proving my innocence. What was the alternative? To submit to being locked up for an undefined period by a police force who obviously thought nothing of incarcerating people at random.

I walked dutifully into the cell.

Again there was no window. There was a short white plastic stool and a plastic covered mattress on the floor with no sheet. There was a plastic basin, and in the corner a toilet that was resolutely bolted down.

At the doorway I had to give up all my remaining personal possessions; my watch, phone, keys and wallet. 'Can I have a receipt?' I asked. 'I need an itemised receipt.'

One of the two guards said, 'You'll get them.'

He gave me a plastic bottle of water, then looked me up and down, as if eyeing me up. It probably meant nothing, but I was a middle class person with no experience of the prison system; I had no idea what I should or shouldn't be panicking about. Whatever his conclusion, he then produced a packet of cigarettes and gave me two before shutting the door.

I felt that I shouldn't have signed the contacts paper. Getting that form filled was probably the minimum needed for them to demonstrate they had paid lip service to the law; that and giving me the bottle of water. Without those two elements, they might not have locked me up.

Chapter Thirteen

I was moved from the police station to a proper prison which was in the countryside. It was a very long drive in a windowless van. I had no watch but I think I was in there for at least an hour. It felt like two.

When I finally got there, the prison was modern and well appointed, which was something at least. It smelled of cigarettes and drying plaster.

There seemed to be a system where trusted prisoners were put in charge of just about everything. One of them opened the cell door and brought in a large platter of rolls, meats, cheeses and another bottle of water.

I really couldn't complain about the food.

'Can I have a wash today?' I asked.

The man looked non-committal, or perhaps he didn't understand.

I tried being nice.

'I'm afraid I haven't been in a Spanish jail before,' I began.

This made him cross.

'You are not in a Spanish jail,' he said.

I wondered how this nightmare could get worse.

'I'm not in Spain?' I asked.

'These are Basque lands under the illegal control of the Spanish and French governments,' said the man.

'Oh good grief,' I said, which I regretted. I wanted to curry favour and was now praying that this man's English would leave him unsure as to what 'good grief' could mean.

'You are right,' I said, 'I meant this is the prison of the state oppressors.' It sounded clumsy and pointless.

The man shrugged. He felt in his pocket.

'These are for you,' he said.

He gave me a packet of cigarettes.

Some time later the door opened and I was taken to an interview room. It was the same man as on the first night.

'I want you to tell me what you're doing here,' he asked.

'In prison?' I asked.

'In Bizkaia,' he replied.

'I work here,' I said. 'I moved here on a temporary contract. I work for Banbury UK.' I thought the last detail might help my case. I'm not sure how.

He consulted some papers.

He said, 'Your mother is from Ireland.'

'No, she is from England.'

'She has an Irish passport,' he said. His tone implied I was lying and he was going to push me into telling the truth. But the truth was that my mother came from England and she happened to have an Irish passport because her own mother was Irish and she was born there.

'She moved away from Ireland when she was ten,' I said.

'So your father is from Bilbao and your mother is Irish.'

'It's not like that,' I said.

'It's not like what?'

'What's your point?' I asked. He was expecting me to be adversarial and it was easy to fall into that role. I had hoped to be helpful and thoughtful, to demonstrate they'd made a mistake.

'You spend your time with known terrorists; terrorists known to have strong links with your IRA. I need to know what you're doing here.'

'Who?' I asked. 'Who is a known terrorist?'

He consulted his notes.

'Olaia Mujika,' he said.

'Oh, come off it,' I said.

He obviously had no worries about slander and felt he could merrily label people as criminals regardless of the facts. That year alone, the French and Spanish had arrested over 140 ETA suspects, so if Olaia hadn't made that cut, she was either very small fry or not involved with ETA at all. But that didn't stop him labelling her a terrorist.

The interview then changed direction.

He said, 'We have to decide what charges to bring against you and your mother. But first, I must say that assault against a policeman is a very serious offence. You cannot expect leniency.'

'I have not assaulted a policeman,' I replied.

The man from the Super Corps sifted through his file. He produced the Polaroid that I had given him.

'Do you deny that your mother took this photograph after she attempted to assault and set fire to this man,' he said.

'He's a policeman?' I asked.

The man nodded.

'Oh joy,' I said.

'You are saying, "Oh joy?"'

'That doesn't translate well. It is English irony.'

'"Irony?"'

I was left on my own in a cell for the rest of Saturday, apart from mid afternoon when I was escorted off to the shower block. The shower and toilet appeared to be one and the same, with two raised foot shaped sections for me to stand on. There was no soap or shampoo, but the water was hot. Too hot, and there was no way of adjusting it. I put my hair under it for as long as I dared. I hate having dirty hair so I hoped the scalding water could sort of melt the grease.

When I got back to the cell someone had left some paper, envelopes, stamps and a pen.

I lay on the plastic mattress for a think.

What were the possibilities?

The first possibility was state terrorism. In the UK, those of us who were Wasp middle class sorts have no experience of being arrested for the sheer hell of it. The Spanish were known to be arresting people in large numbers. They were showing a zero tolerance of ETA, its political party and anyone who helped them. The government was gambling that the majority of the public would support them, no matter how many human rights they trampled over, no matter how many houses they raided at dawn with guns and hand grenades.

So that was possibility one. But would they march into the house and steal our stuff? I thought not. It just didn't fit the facts.

Okay, possibility two.

Possibility two was ETA itself.

I was head of security at a major engineering plant. Was ETA quietly trying to drive me away? Was there something they wanted from me personally? Or did they do this to every British person who took one of their jobs?

The ETA must have links with at least some of the police forces, because the latter are set up and recruited regionally. They would probably have friends in mediocre places who could get involved.

This train of thought would mean that someone like Olaia was sending me the letters. This was possible. She would have had my home address from the moment that I was offered the job. She might even know how to get keys to my place here in Portugalete. After all, the house had been owned by the firm for some time, and her job was site maintenance.

This line of thought was possible and fitted with the facts. It didn't explain Gabrielle's ex-lover, but then neither did my option one.

Option three, therefore, was Alex.

I felt that Gabrielle had been a little cagey about what Alex did for a living. He could work for the Intelligence services and be out in Bilbao for that reason. After all, how had Gabby and Alex met in the first place? Or, conversely, when people live together they might take an interest in the other's work and think about it for a career for themselves. If he worked for Intelligence then he would have connections with local police and he could feed them disinformation.

One problem with this theory was the coincidence of both Gabby and Alex moving to the same part of Northern Spain at a similar time. It felt far-fetched. Unless he'd asked to be moved here once he'd discovered Gabby had moved. Or, alternatively, Alex hasn't moved to the Basque Country at all, and just said that because it sounded less barmy. Either way it seemed he was mad.

Option four. There was something weird about Gabrielle. She certainly had access to the house, so writing the letter about the colours in the living room wouldn't have been hard. But would she organise a burglary of the place? What on earth would she have to gain?

That was the least likely option. None of the options seemed to fit the facts entirely but it was a reasonable conclusion that Gabby wasn't the threat.

Bizarrely, I slept incredibly well. I suppose the last few days had taken it out of me. I had such deep and enjoyable dreams that when I woke I was truly surprised to discover I was in prison.

On the Sunday morning my door was unlocked and left open. I stayed on my stool for a while and could see prisoners walking past left to right pulling mattresses behind them or carrying chairs. When the stream of people had slowed to a trickle, I poked my head out and went for a wander.

With an innocence that made me smile afterwards, I went up to the doors of the cell block and tried them to see if they were unlocked too. I thought perhaps on Sundays everyone was allowed out on an honesty system.

I eventually found all the other inmates in an exercise yard, sitting or lying on mattresses and smoking. A lot of them had beer or were smoking dope. In Britain everything that is even remotely pleasurable is considered a privilege and therefore not allowed. In Spain it is considered a right; although, let's face it, being locked up for no apparent reason was already punishment enough.

Everyone in the prison looked relatively neat. I realised that with my lived-in clothes, my clotted hair and my facial scar where Gabby had hit me, I must have looked one of the roughest there; the most like a convict.

'Is anyone English here?' I asked.

A dark haired man called to me. He was possibly about fifty but a lifetime of tanning or perhaps sailing had prematurely aged his face. He said he was called Rob.

'What are you in for?' I asked.

'I was in a car accident,' replied Rob.

'So?'

'So in Spain they often arrest everyone involved in a car accident and keep them until they have it on paper who is taking responsibility, and have charged the people who should be charged.'

He sounded very nonchalant. He explained that he lived locally and had seen it all before.

'What are you here for?' he asked.

'I have no idea,' I replied.

'When did they pick you up, Friday night?'

'I took myself into the station then, yeah,' I said.

'Big mistake,' he said. 'If they want to arrest you, they choose Friday nights. They know that you won't be able to drum up a solicitor until Monday morning. If you do make a phone call it'll most likely end up on a lawyer's answerphone and even then it'll probably be ignored. Plus the police can put in for overtime. They solve a lot of cases at the weekends. In either event they're allowed to hold you for seventy-two hours for no reason.'

'But there is no case,' I protested. 'Can I not apply for bail or something?'

Rob laughed. 'You could, but the court for that is shut in August.'

'You're kidding me.'

I made a joke about summery justice, but he didn't get it.

'Where's your spot?' he asked.

'What?'

'Where have you put your mattress?' he asked.

'I haven't.'

'Oh,' replied Rob, plainly disappointed. 'The trick is that one person bags a spot in the morning shade while the other bags a spot that will be in the shade in the afternoon. You'd better sit on my mattress with me then. You'll remember next Sunday though, eh?'

'I won't be here next Sunday,' I said.

Rob had a good laugh at that, as did the people around.

'Do you smoke?' I asked. 'They keep giving me cigarettes.'

'They must fancy you,' he said.

'You're kidding.'

'Yes I'm kidding,' he said.

I didn't recognise my name. They spoke it over a tannoy so it could have been the acoustics.

I continued chatting to Rob who, despite sitting resolutely in the shade, had his head turned up and his eyes closed as if sunbathing.

Eventually a trustee came over.

'Salvador Gongola?'

'Yes?' I replied.

'You are free to go,' he said.

'What?'

'Collect your stuff, you are free to go.'

Chapter Fourteen

As I left the gates, I was shocked to discover the prison was absolutely in the middle of nowhere, in some very nondescript countryside. It looked like miles to the nearest town.

There was no one to meet me.

I turned back to the gateway, and felt rather foolish knocking on the big wooden door.

Eventually someone spoke over the intercom.

'Yes?'

'I don't have any transport,' I said.

'What?'

'I have just been released and I don't have any transport.'

'Who are you?' the man asked.

I explained and the intercom went dead.

Far off, possibly from the exercise yard, I could hear a cheer go up, I had no idea why. Then there was the silence of the countryside again.

The intercom sparked into life.

'You have transport,' it said.

The intercom went dead.

I stood for a while wondering about my next move. Rather pathetically I started walking down the road.

I was about a hundred metres away from the prison when I heard my name being called by a woman. I turned to see the figure of Olaia standing by her car, that was now by the prison gate.

She drove down to where I was standing.

'I was just getting my car round from the car park,' she said.

'Thank you for picking me up,' I said.

'You look crap,' she said.

'I didn't even have a razor. Do they often just lock people up for the fun of it? Is my mother okay?'

'She is still in prison. They say she assaulted a policeman. I get you a coffee?'

'Thank you.'

Olaia drove me to the nearest town. The buildings all looked new, blocks of flats and shops and light industry all thrown together in one place; a combination that allows workers to go home for a siesta without travelling far. Never mind that the weather in the Basque country is so similar to England that you would rarely need to sleep out the midday sun.

We settled at a pavement café.

'This is one of our new towns,' she said.

'I know,' I replied. 'My father was brought up here.'

'Really?' she said. She was being sarcastic.

Olaia looked at me through heavy eyelids and stubbed out the cigarette she'd been smoking.

At first I couldn't work out why she'd suggested we stopped at a café. She had nothing she wanted to say. But it turned out the police had woken her up with their phone call and she needed a coffee and a fag.

To fill the silence I used information from my father's diaries.

'I always imagined that my father lived in countryside like this,' I said.

Olaia looked at me neutrally.

'In the evenings when his parents came back from work or trying to find work, my father would go out to the countryside and the woods,' I said. 'In the spring he picked young nettles which they would boil.'

'They ate nettles?' asked Olaia. She was incredulous at what I was choosing to talk about, rather than interested.

'You have to boil them with the slightest bit of water and they form a sort of cotton wool mush,' I said. 'But it doesn't have much flavour so they cut up the roots of the ox-eyed daisy. Later in the year they used to get puff balls from the woods and cut them into slices and fry them.'

'Franco,' said Olaia shaking her head sadly as if she'd been there. As if either of us had been there.

'Franco kept his troops at the station in Bilbao,' I said. 'Anyone they suspected was coming in from the country to find work was returned on the train to their home town. So my family would take the train in from the next village, wearing travelling clothes and carrying badly stuffed suitcases. Then they'd be given free passes to travel all the way back to Andalusia to visit the family they'd left behind.'

I'd overdone it.

Olaia said, 'I know my own history, Senor Gongola.'

'Yeah,' I said. 'Thank you for picking me up.'

I am plainly mad.

Later, as she was driving me home, she said, 'Why did your mother set fire to a policeman?'

'It was oven cleaner. There's no telling with her. She thought she was being robbed.'

'Was she?' asked Olaia.

'I think so.'

Olaia saw me safely to the door of the house. She stood outside holding her keys, so presumably had meant to go at that point. But I must have looked helpless or something because she undid my door for me then, after a pause, came in.

She looked at the mess; some of our stuff had been put into piles, presumably by Gabrielle, but there was still an air of chaos about the place.

'Okay. I'll make a few phone calls,' she said.

'You don't have to do this,' I said.

'I am your assistant.'

'Yes but this isn't work.'

Olaia then said something that sounded rehearsed, a grievance perhaps.

'I help,' she said. 'You English think that if a person works nine-to-five that is a good worker, even if they are not a good worker. In Spain I work and help when it is needed most. But you English think this is no good.'

I must have looked a complete state; deflated, tired, still in the same clothes from Friday. She stopped telling me off.

She said, 'Sit down and I will make you an English cup of tea.'

She brought me the tea and disappeared off for a wander around the ground floor.

She said, 'Either there is a policeman who breaks into houses or they are mistaken and he is not a policeman.'

'I think they would know whether a policeman reported for work looking singed.'

I realised I had chosen the word 'singed' because I thought she wouldn't know the word. To alienate her, to put her in her place. What the hell was wrong with me?

'Or there is something we don't understand,' she continued. 'I will make phone calls, but it is hard on a Sunday. I will find out more tomorrow perhaps.'

She looked at the documents and letters that lay around the floor in piles.

'Do you not read your post?' she asked.

'No,' I laughed.

'Even with your strange letters you have been getting?' she asked.

How did she know about the letters?

'What letters?' I asked.

'The letters you got about the wild birds,' she said.

'But they were at work.'

She shrugged.

'You should still open your mail,' she said. 'Have you got a gestor?' she asked. 'I know a good gestor. He is part English like you. He advises the English who live here.'

She went off and made a phone call. She returned with a number on a piece of paper.

'This is his number,' she said. 'I think that is all I can do today.'

She said a few other things but I really wasn't listening. I thanked her and she took herself off.

A gestor is a splendidly Spanish phenomenon born of the fact that Spanish bureaucracy is impenetrable. If you want to build a house or even rent one, if you want to employ someone or sack them, if you want to be born or are planning to die some time in the future, don't forget to put aside an extra four months for the inevitable bureaucracy.

There will be a lot of forms to fill in and it will not be the least bit obvious where to get the correct ones, so you will need to queue for an hour at an information desk to find out. You will then need to travel across town to find the relevant office or offices where there will be another queue, often to discover that the clerk you really need will be missing. There will be yet another desk where you have to deliver the papers and this will almost certainly be in a different office or even in a different town. There will be yet another office where the papers are 'reviewed' and a further department to have them certified, all of which will have separate desks, and clerks for which you queue in order to get an appointment.

There are no short cuts. Crying doesn't work (I've tried it) and there are simply too many officials to make bribery cost effective. The only option is to employ a gestor.

A gestor is a gofer who runs around getting documents for you. Well, not runs, so much as saunters around looking smug. He keeps a supply of the forms you need and a list of what supplementary documents are required. Most importantly, he knows where the elusive officials take their coffee. In two cases I know of, the gestor *is* the elusive official in question: their offices are hardly ever open because they are run off their feet helping members of the public who couldn't get hold of them in the first place. Bafflingly, the Spanish find this all very amusing.

Gestor should be pronounced 'jester' because when you see his bill, you'll realise he's having a laugh.

Despite all this, Olaia was correct. I needed a gestor.

Safe in the knowledge that I had now made a decision, I set about doing nothing. I sat for such a long time in a chair that I wondered afterwards if my brain had stopped. I could not recall a single thought that I'd had.

I realised with a start that there was someone in the house. We have no pets, so any movement or noise at all is suspect.

'Gabby?' I called out.

Nothing.

I crept through the house. *I* felt guilty, as though I had no right to disturb the intruder.

The noise was upstairs. A floorboard perhaps, creaking underfoot. Or possibly I was spooking myself. Perhaps the house settles after a hot day, creaks a little, and I'd never noticed it before.

I dashed up the stairs two at a time. I ran into the doorway of each room in turn. There was no one. But I thought better of opening every cupboard and checking under the beds.

I wandered off to the bathroom.

I sat on the side of the bath as it filled. I had no plan for getting my mother out of prison. That was tomorrow's problem.

There was a definite noise from my mother's room. I went tearing back. The window was wide open and swinging. I ran to the window and looked out.

Nothing.

I tried to recall how long I had taken to get into the room. Would that have been long enough for someone to jump out of the window then get round the house and out of sight? Possibly, but only just.

I ran round to our room and onto the balcony for a better view. Well, a different view.

Still nothing.

The window might have been open all along. The hills have strange acoustics. I was jumpy; anything was possible.

The fact remains that I was convinced someone had been in the house.

Chapter Fifteen

I heard the front door open.

I ran down the stairs two at a time.

It was Gabrielle.

She hugged me.

'Thank God,' she said.

'Where've you been?' I asked.

'I've been trying to get food and wine and stuff to welcome you home.'

'You've been gone hours,' I protested.

She looked at her watch.

'An hour and a half. Two hours,' she said. 'I couldn't find a bloody shop open for love nor money on a Sunday afternoon, so I went all the way into Bilbao and blagged some stuff from work. I've got bread, cheeses, red wine. Olives. Tons of stuff. Where's our car?'

I must have looked dazed or something.

'I'm sorry,' she said, 'I should have been at home. I didn't know when you'd get here.'

'Why didn't you ring or visit me or something?' I asked.

'I tried to. I had terrible trouble getting an official to even tell me where you were. I didn't know where to start for one thing. Well, initially I didn't even know you were arrested. I mean, it's not the first thing you think of when you can't find someone. They claimed you didn't put me down as your next of kin, is that true? So they wouldn't deal with me. I had to do everything through Olaia. When I finally tracked her down.'

This did make a sort of sense.

'Why did you put Olaia down, not me?' she asked.

'I didn't,' I said. 'It wasn't like that. I don't know. After they said my mother had been arrested I thought it was safer to name someone they wouldn't take in. Do we know anything about my mother?'

'It was hurtful, that's all,' said Gabby. 'And weird.'

'I just thought that at a time like that, I needed to do the most practical thing even if it seemed weird.'

Olaia was as good as her word, and the following Monday she tried to chase up the authorities on my behalf.

I tried to get a bit of work done in case I was going to have to spend the rest of the day chasing up officialdom, defending my house from intruders, visiting my mother on death row, or whatever fun the Spanish could come up with.

Olaia and I had arranged to spend the morning in the guard hut that is situated in the car park.

As anyone who has ever worked in site management will testify, the biggest problems will always be about parking. The plant could be bombed by terrorists, cockroaches could invade the canteen in a plague of biblical proportions; but all that will concern the staff will be the visitor who put a car in their parking spot, or the gross injustice of having to park ten yards further from their office than a colleague in Accounts who they know for certain gets marginally less pay and has only been working there six months.

There was certainly something odd going on at the factory, in that there always appeared to be twice as many cars as workers in our car park, so Olaia and I had decided to take an interest.

The two gun-toting guards were with us in the guard hut, along with Juan Crusie. Juan Crusie was a runty little man who was a colleague of Olaia's. Whereas Olaia was largely in charge of security, he had the pest control and building maintenance remit; but they were able to fill in for each other if need be.

We were all out in force that day, so it was pretty cosy in the hut with Olaia determinedly phoning around to try and track down my mother.

'You may find it strange,' she said to me. 'But I have to watch what I say on the phone.'

'Why?' I asked.

'The Spanish bug them.'

'Come off it,' I said.

'Really. The Spanish bug the telephones a lot,' she said. 'They are hoping to get information about ETA. Yours is probably bugged.'

'I doubt it,' I said laughing.

'Irish mother. Basque father. Criminal record,' she said. Like a mantra.

I think she was half joking.

Certainly Juan was laughing at my expense. I couldn't quite see why.

'I thought phone tapping wasn't allowed in this country,' I said, largely to keep the conversation going.

'It's not allowed as evidence,' said Olaia.

Every time a car came into the car park, I wandered out to talk to the driver and check they worked at the factory. A bolshie-looking guard would hover behind me looking at the countryside.

In between times, I did some paperwork and the guards talked amongst themselves in Basque. They appeared to be discussing the superconductors we were laying down. The superconductors only work if they are kept cold, so they are sheathed in a tube of cooling agent which is pumped along and topped up by a couple of pumping stations along its length. My Basque isn't that strong but I was surprised at how much they seemed to know about the technical side of all this. A guard in Britain can rarely talk about anything more complex than the results from Uttoxeter and the latest size of Jordan's breasts. Perhaps it was a cultural thing; that Basque guards are more interested in the world around them than their British counterparts. It seemed strange, though.

'I've found your mother,' exclaimed Olaia. 'Well, more or less.'

'Great,' I said.

'She's in one of two prisons, both about two hundred kilometres away.'

'What?' I asked.

'It's a tactic,' said Olaia. 'They pretend they have made an error with their paperwork, and say they are not sure where they put her. Wait two days and they will tell you. It is a tactic of state oppression. Or incompetence,' she conceded.

'I'd heard,' I said. I'm not sure what I meant by that.

'Yeah?' she asked. 'You see, they think you will believe that they are inefficient and lazy. When asked, they can claim that, but it is a tactic of oppression.'

'I don't know. It's odd. My mother is just a dotty old woman. I think state oppression...'

'She is Irish!' said Olaia barely below a shout. 'This is how the Madrid Government treats us!'

The guards made no effort to hide their grins. Enjoying, I think, that Olaia was prone to losing her temper for the sheer hell of it, and they knew what was coming.

'You English,' Olaia went on. 'You have no idea what it is like. We have soldiers who crash through our doors at dawn. For years we were not even allowed to speak our language. Can you imagine it? You are not allowed to speak your own stupid English in your own stupid town? Can you imagine that at all?'

'I am very sorry,' I said. I think I was apologising on behalf of Franco.

'You get one little bit of inconvenience. Your bloody mother is arrested and sent off and you think it is the end of the world.'

'I understand and I am sorry,' I said.

Olaia stared out of the window for a while with her arms folded.

'I will help you though,' she said with a flourish.

'Thank you.' I said.

'Because the Madrid government is crazy and it is my duty to help you against them.'

'Thank you,' I said again.

'So I will take the rest of the morning off to help you,' she said.

So that was it. She fancied a few hours off. Considering she'd done more to release my own mother than I had, it seemed more than fair.

Something caught my eye out of the window. An expensive looking car had driven up to the site, but had approached the exit of the car park rather than the entrance.

One man got out from the passenger side. He walked round to the boot of the car and pulled out a short piece of scaffolding pipe.

At the same time there was a shot. A gun shot. The four of us in the guard hut looked up. There was a second shot.

'Where the hell did that come from?'

Olaia and I strained to look out of the window. There was simply nothing to see. I ran outside. Nothing.

I stood in the car park for a minute, perhaps more. But everything was still.

I realised the car with the scaffolding bar had gone too.

When I went back into the guard room Olaia was also gone.

Chapter Sixteen

I may not open mail, but when an official comes to the door and makes me sign for something, it turns out I do take an interest.

I received an official document that told me I owed about 22,000 Euros; 15,000 quid.

I turned it over in my hand several times. I couldn't make head or tail of it. I had decided to go home for my siesta period that day and see what I could do about my mother; but when I got there, there was an official on the doorstep. He didn't look as though he had been waiting long, so if I'd been a little later I doubt I would have received the court documents that day at all.

I was stunned.

I walked into the house reading it and I noticed that everything had been cleared up. All the papers had gone. All the furniture had been rearranged and dusted.

'Gabby?' I called.

No answer.

I think I'd have known if I owed 22,000 Euros.

Some time later I wandered upstairs.

Gabrielle was standing in a doorway. Just standing there. She was wearing grey combats with big pockets. She was stripped to the waist. She had broad shoulders for a woman. Full breasts. A perfect, even tan. She was beginning to look pregnant. Faster than I'd have thought. She looked good on it.

I thought there must be something wrong. It was like seeing an apparition, so I stood on the stairs just staring at her. She must have been asleep on our bed and I'd woken her. Neither of us said a word for a very long time.

'Did you clear up?' I said at last.

'Yeah.'

'Where are all the papers?' I asked.

'What papers?'

'The papers and letters and stuff that were on the floor downstairs,' I said.

'I have no idea. I presumed you took them.'

Silence again.

'You mean to say that all the documents, everything, had gone.'

'That's what I just said,' she replied.

'So you walked into the house and they were just gone. There was space on the floor where they should have been.'

'Yes. Stop repeating yourself.'

We were still just standing there; Gabby in the doorway, and me on the third from top step.

The phone rang.

I was loathe to go for it. It was as though we were in a stand off and if I answered the phone I would be the first to blink.

I answered the phone.

It was Olaia.

'I've made you an appointment with the gestor,' she said.

She read me out the address and I copied it down.

'Why?' I asked.

'Because you were not going to do it evidently, and I am trying to organise things,' she said. 'The appointment is at 10 o'clock tomorrow. I've also found out from the police that they may be charging you with some offences. They are not finished with you.'

I decided that the last phrase sounded more dramatic than intended. A Basque would not know a more subtle phrase like, 'you're not totally in the clear yet'.

Gabrielle walked past me to the kitchen and put on the kettle.

'Do you want a drink?' she asked.

She'd put on one of my white shirts. It was unbuttoned. In theory she looked fantastic, but when you think someone isn't straight, they suddenly don't look so sexy.

I slipped my arms around her from behind and kissed her neck. She was spooning out coffee; she turned her head towards me and kissed the air affectionately.

'I am getting so tired with this pregnancy,' she said. 'I keep shutting my eyes for a moment and waking up two hours later.'

I had forgotten for the umpteenth time that I didn't have my car. I had borrowed a vehicle from work but I needed to return it and collect my own. The following morning I had to take the Metro into Bilbao. My car was no longer where I'd parked it the day I'd been arrested.

At first I thought it was stolen but when I finally caught up with the gestor he suggested it had been towed away and he gave me a number to ring.

The gestor was called Felipe Guimera and I wasn't sure I liked him. He was tall and thin and played up what he thought was his Englishness.

'I'm from Surrey,' he said, with a thick Spanish accent. 'The birthplace of the gin and tonic. Do you like the office?'

I did.

It was situated in a broad street with a dramatic hill at one end. This is not an uncommon sight in Bilbao given that it is a city that exactly fills a valley, but impressive nonetheless.

The street itself was grand. The 19th Century building boom brought the city some fine terraces that have very tall, very broad, flat facades, but with boxes stuck on them: bolt-on rectangles with long windows and black framing that hang out into the air.

Felipe Guimera's firm was in one such building, made even more attractive by a blue painted effect that covered its front wall that looked as if it were meticulously tiled. It must have been at least a hundred years old and had either lasted well or been lovingly restored, because I could still see the brush strokes. His office was six floors up with a desk that backed onto one of the windowed bays. By swivelling in his chair, he could enjoy the city and the countryside in one sweep.

The day I got there he was looking out of the window.

'There's a siege going on,' he said.

He beckoned for me to look. He pointed to a side street I wouldn't have seen the way that I'd walked.

A large amount of the street was cordoned off and police were out in force wearing black bullet-proof jackets and guns.

'So what's happened?' I asked.

'They think there's an ETA hostage being held in there. They are negotiating.'

'How exciting,' I said.

'Not really. It happens a lot. They negotiate until sundown and then go storming in with tear gas and machine guns. As often as not the hostage gets killed. I think the idea is that so long as ETA doesn't win, any consequences are fine. Who knows? it's just some stupid habit both sides have got into.'

We watched for a little longer, but then lost interest. I went to sit the other side of the desk.

'I haven't had too much time to go through your stuff,' he said. 'But I've made a good start.'

'What stuff?' I asked.

'Your letters and documents,' he replied.

I let that sink in and then after much consideration said, 'Er... what?'

'The letters provided by...' he consulted a piece of paper. 'Olaia.'

'Go on,' I said.

'You appear to have a number of problems,' he explained. 'Firstly, there's the stalker.'

'The letter writer,' I said. 'The police weren't very interested.

'Now that you are more than half way to the eight they should take an interest,' he said. 'I will have a word. Do you think it's your wife?'

'No. I think it might be someone who wants me to think my wife is mad. It's certainly someone who is trying to totally ruin my life every way they can.'

'I'll ask the police what they think,' He said.

'Don't do that,' I said.

'Why not?'

Because I couldn't be bothered. I couldn't be bothered even though it was him doing the work.

'Why do you say eight?' I asked.

He handed me a pile of letters. On the top was the first letter; the one I'd never seen.

'Ah,' I said. 'And what number are we up to?'

'Five,' he said.

'I've received five letters?' I asked.

I had evidently failed to open numbers one and three. I read them very carefully. Like the others, they were on nondescript white paper. The fonts were the same, but I felt the computer printer might have been different from one letter to another.

Letter number three said,

What will be given to you, will be taken away. Remember. You don't love me.

I said, 'Leave it with me, it's a police matter, and I might know who it is, so I need to proceed delicately. What else?'

'There's all the money you owe. May I ask why you are not paying it back?'

'What money?' I asked.

'You owe about 40,000 Euros.'

'No I don't,' I said. Even I would know something like that.

The gestor tapped his desk with the end of his pen for an interminable length of time.

'You are saying you don't owe any money?' he said.

'Yes.' I said.

'Oddly enough, this isn't too unusual. There are lots of possibilities,' he said. 'Under Spanish law, money is owed on a property, not on a person. So if a previous occupant of your house has run up debts, it is you who will have to pay them. It might be unpaid taxes, community charge, loans, credit cards, electricity bills: you name it, basically. When you take over a property you have to check that all the bills are up to date from the previous person.'

'I did,' I replied.

'Yes but sometimes people just pay the most recent bill and get a receipt to show you, but they haven't paid the previous six years.'

'I'll look into it,' I lied.

'Yeah, and I'll do the same,' he said. 'And I'll keep going through your stuff.'

I noticed he had a pile of my bank statements in front of him.

'Did you take all those bank statements out of their envelopes?' I asked.

'No,' he replied. 'This is how they came.'

'How do you know I owe money?' I asked. 'Why are you so sure?'

'The police told me. One of the three people who came to your house to repossess your stuff was a policeman. They often get a policeman to come along,' he said.

'There were three of them?' I asked. 'So you're saying that my mother really did spray a policeman with oven cleaner. The policeman really was there on legal business.'

'Yes,' he replied.

'That's a problem then,' I said.

'Do you really not read your own mail?' he asked.

'Evidently not,' I replied. 'What is the official reason they arrested me?'

'It's not quite like that. They don't have an official reason often. They know they have a crime and they detain people until they feel they understand who is who. Or in the case of ETA they do it to put pressure on people.'

'Everyone says that,' I said.

'Because it's true.'

He sat back. He was finished.

'Do you really not read your mail?' he asked again in wonderment. That got me out of his office.

On leaving the building I went to have a look at the siege. I got to the end of the street in question and suddenly there was gun fire. People were running away in all directions shouting for us all to take cover.

I was very much on the periphery, I felt I'd be safe enough simply walking off at a regular pace.

I caught sight of someone across the street. I thought it was a tourist at first because he was taking a photograph. But then I realised it was Alex Lawrence. He might have been taking photos of the siege, but I got the distinct impression he was taking photos of me. Perhaps both.

He started to walk away at a reasonable pace but as I crossed the road towards him, he sped up. I broke into a run. We both pelted down the street. Almost immediately a group of Spanish got in my way, chatting and smoking. Another group beyond that, perhaps tourists, parted to reveal a yellow post-box which hit my stomach. I ran into the road. There was traffic to dodge and several recycling bins were now in my line of vision. He was still on the pavement somewhere ahead, running hard.

I am not a fit man, so after a quarter of a mile the act of running proved deeply alarming. I tried to moderate my breathing with long even breaths through my mouth. I was slowing badly, but happily Alex was slowing too; it seemed he was no fitter than me. We must have been quite a sight; two lumbering men, him in a grey tee shirt, me in business clothes, wheezing through the streets of Bilbao.

Alex ran down towards the river and past the huge stained glass of the tea rooms. Café Feve in green and yellow. The pavement was no longer keeping steady. I could hear nothing but the pulse in my head. The crowd was thicker now but I kept him in sight. He was slowing a bit. The armpits of his clothing had turned darker. My feet were thudding erratically under my tread.

As if by tacit arrangement we both slowed to a fast walk. The gap between us stayed at fifteen yards.

Down past the art deco bandstand. Beautiful fans of glass, stretching against the sun. Statues of unknown people. Stained glass. Uneven pavements. More painful breathing. Down into the old town. Was Gabby there today? Had I left her at home that day? Why was I chasing this man? Because he wanted to run. Because he must have been stalking me.

Smaller alleys. Did he turn left into the square? Why was I having trouble thinking? How hard could it be just to follow someone? Did I never get exercise? None whatever. Especially now we had less sex. I was in charge of the gym at work, why did I never go there? Where was he now? Was he still ahead? He was a little closer if anything. A shop says it sells comestibles. Surely that is not a Spanish word. He has slipped down an alley. I don't think he knows the area that well. We had almost come round in a circle so he had no real plan.

Down left now. I was getting my second wind. We had both found our pace. I sped up a little. It didn't seem to make much difference. Perhaps I would get closer in time. Perhaps I should give up. If he really was following me I would get other chances. If this was the last I ever saw of him then it hardly mattered if I did not catch up with him. Typical me. I could always find an excuse for inaction.

We were at the market now. More huge stained glass windows. Glass cabinets of meats. The clotted crowd of a market. Women with shopping baskets. Traders with fingerless gloves. Lots of butchers. A suckling pig curled up asleep, curled up dead, at peace on a steel tray. Ruddy pink. Rabbits hanging in a row with heads in plastic bags. A counter of different types of animal organ. Greying flesh in piles.

He took the stairs. Was there at least a rail for me to hold? What do disabled people do in this country? I was a disgrace I was so unfit. I was by a stall strewn with hanging dried peppers. Velvet crimsons. Long dried branches of bay leafs. Then a stall with nets of shellfish. A boarded up stall. The stained glass again. He was nowhere.

He was nowhere.

Chapter Seventeen

I caught up with Olaia.

'So you took it upon yourself to open my mail and take it all down to the gestor's office?'

Olaia rose up a few inches. She was deciding whether to lose her temper.

'Yes,' she replied.

'You took yourself into my house and took anything you fancied?'

'Sit down,' she said.

I sat.

'I just think...' I said.

'Shut up.'

I shut up.

'When you first came here, we thought you would be very efficient,' she began. 'And you *were* very efficient. You were well dressed. You had clear ideas. For, what, one week? But then... then I think you went mad.'

'What?' I asked.

'You spend day after day reading that book that your father wrote, and you want to talk about it while we are all trying to work.'

I was going to disagree but I wanted to hear what else she had to say.

'And then there is the standing and staring,' she said.

'What?'

'You talk to people and you stand like this.' She stood bolt upright with her hands by her sides.

'So?' I asked.

'You stand like that and you don't say anything, and then after, I don't know, a minute, you say something.'

'So?' I said again, after what I have to admit was a longish pause.

'So people think you are mad,' she said. She was almost shouting. She made a swirling gesture at the side of her head.

Another long pause from me, but I felt I was quite justified not knowing what to say.

'But we were okay before you came to this factory,' she said. 'So we are okay now.'

'Okay,' I said.

'Now,' she continued. 'I know you don't like me, so I have been careful to not tell you what to do.'

'Why don't I like you?' I asked.

'You stare at me. I sit at my desk and you stare at me. It's very aggressive. I have to keep my head down all the time. But I think I need to help you. So I take a chance. Your mother is in prison and you do nothing. Your mother is attacked in your house and you do nothing. I think you have a problem.'

So did I, now she mentioned it.

'And for very long periods of time you just hum.'

'I hum?'

'Yes. It is not a tune. You hum as you stare, like you do not have any thoughts.'

'I had no idea about the humming thing,' I said.

'I mean. Most of us in life are either no good at our jobs or we can't be bothered to try. But the trick is to *act* as though you're good. Don't say you don't know; say you've decided to delegate. Don't look vacant, look thoughtful.'

'Yeah. I get it,' I said. 'Tell me, do you have a key to my house?'

'There is a key here. But when I went to your house it was not locked.'

'I'm sure we lock the house,' I said. 'But you are saying you have access to a key to our house.'

'The house belongs to this company. We are the site management. But as I said, it was open. Ask your wife,' said Olaia.

'Perhaps she popped out for a moment,' I said, although I knew there was nowhere to 'just pop to' from our house.

I didn't know what to think next; which of my problems to prioritise. I didn't want to be accused of gazing into space, but I wasn't sure what I wanted to do. The funny thing was that with all my problems, the only thing that had been worrying me recently was that I seemed to be clicking less and less with Gabrielle. The other main thing I worried about were the gunshots and stuff at work. I was clearly not being rational, but that's life.

I said, 'Tell me Olaia. I always hear so much about the saint days and fiestas. But I haven't been to a good one. Not out in the country. Have you any suggestions for some we could go to?'

I happened to know the town where Olaia came from had a siesta that very weekend, and she might have known that I knew this. She chose to take me at face value.

'Yes,' she said, 'I have a good idea, you would enjoy.'

She told me about her town's fiesta at some length. I even made notes.

Chapter Eighteen

It was about that time that Gabrielle bought herself a car. It was nothing fancy. An elderly Peugeot with a deep scratch down one side and a soft top that didn't fold away properly.

I woke up one Saturday morning and she wasn't asleep beside me. This was a common occurrence. A bit later there was a car horn sounding rhythmically outside. I went to the window to complain, or at least to twitch the curtain slightly, and there was Gabrielle smiling and waving.

'Look, it's even got a CD player,' she shouted.

She absolutely loved that car.

She drove us down to the fiesta Olaia had told us about.

'You see,' I explained. 'The Spanish have a birthday and a saint day, the day that the saint with the same name as you is celebrated. Then there is the saint for your industry or walk of life. So, for example, the patron saint of caterers is St. Lawrence because during the Spanish Inquisition he was grilled to death.'

Gabrielle laughed.

We were heading south. It was a fiercely hot day. We had the hood of the car down.

This was living.

Despite the wind buffeting us, it was too hot. I stripped to the waist. Gabby did one of her favourite tricks: taking off her bra while keeping her top on, while driving at 80 miles per hour on the wrong side of the road, while dodging farm vehicles, while fiddling with the CD player, while re-doing her lippy in the rear-view mirror.

Not the least bit scary.

We passed what looked like a rotary cultivator rigged up to pull a two wheeled trailer behind. There was a bench seat on the trailer where a farmer and his wife sat side by side taking produce off to a local market. He was wearing weathered blue denims from head to toe, while she appeared to have dressed up for the day in a polka dot dress with shoulder pads. Blatantly they had been planted there by the local tourist board.

It gave me something to say.

'Every countryman worth their salt has what you might call a smallholding,' I explained. 'They grow tomatoes, beans, apples. It's a nice little earner. With an extended family with one or two working normal jobs, the whole system can support about eight people.'

We admired the countryside for a bit.

'We haven't worked on that house of yours since we've been here,' said Gabrielle.

'No,' I said.

'We'll have a blitz on it.'

'Sure,' I replied.

We drove for another half an hour and eventually came to a sturdy town seemingly in the middle of nowhere.

'We've got here early so we can park,' I said. 'We'll need to kill a few hours with a drink or two.'

'Fine by me,' she said.

'I know the town quite well, so I'll suggest a few ideas for where to park. It'll be a great day.'

I'd never been there before in my life. I have no idea why I pretended otherwise.

We parked on a verge and walked down into the town.

Everywhere we looked, makeshift bars and eateries were being constructed. Breeze blocks were being unloaded from the backs of lorries. They were placed in piles four or five high, then planks of wood were put across them to form benches and tables. Menus were pinned up on trees.

I only got lost twice while walking us to the town square.

'The bar's up there,' I said. 'Well, it certainly used to be.'

We walked up steps cut into the hill and emerged onto a terrace overlooking the square. Olaia had recommended it and it was a good choice. I scrutinised the wine list and chose a red wine for us. We raised the glasses to each other.

I pointed to an area of vineyard that we could just see beyond the town.

'This wine was made from the grapes in those very fields,' I said.

Gabrielle tasted the wine a second time.

'It didn't travel well,' she said.

I pretended to cuff her round the head.

'So what are the festivities today?' she asked.

'My favourite is a pleasingly daft tradition where one man holds a lighted torch in his mouth and runs around trying to set light to the beards of all the men in the square,' I said. 'Not surprisingly they try and run away. It's very exciting.'

'Hair razing!' said Gabby.

'Of course, the beards are fake these days,' I said with a note of disappointment.

'I'd heard all your sports involved lifting things,' said Gabrielle. 'Stone lifting, cart lifting, ox lifting, lifting a cart laden with logs, lifting a cart laden with stones, logs and an ox…'

'Yeah that goes on,' I replied. 'All that and goat fighting on pay-per-view.'

A large group of men and women turned up, all trendy and about our age, and about twenty minutes after that, Olaia herself arrived. They all knew each other.

She leaned forward and kissed me on my cheek as if we were friends. She looked younger in 'normal' clothes.

The custom in those parts is for a man to shake a woman's hand while simultaneously kissing them on both cheeks. Olaia introduced us to the first person in the crowd and Gabrielle and I had to go through this palaver, along with questions about who we were and where we were from; we were then moved on to the next person to repeat the process. This was clearly going to take an hour or more.

But then, as if there had been some invisible signal, the ritual changed and Olaia cleared a space in the middle of the table. Everyone reached into their pockets or bags and brought out ten Euros and threw it in the middle. Olaia told us to do the same.

Conversation bubbled again and a huge tray of drinks appeared.

Olaia said, 'These are *zuritos*. We sip them. It is beer, but in a small glass; it is a social thing. We'll drink them all day, one or two in each bar. It makes ordering easy. No one gets drunk.' Olaia looked as though she were saying this to me and Gabrielle alike, thus potentially blowing my cred as a local, but Gabrielle seemed not to notice.

'What is the money for?' she asked.

'That is our fund for the day. I am nominated as treasurer and I settle the bill everywhere we go, and do all the ordering. Any profit will go to the cause.'

'Is there ever any profit?' asked Gabrielle.

'No,' she laughed. 'You see, this is my *koadrila*. It's like a gang. We all knew each other at university, and we will probably all know each other when we are eighty. It's like a marriage.' She looked at Gabby and me. 'Only more important.'

I could see that despite the festivities the Basques took their *koadrilas* very seriously. At one stage Gabrielle was asking Olaia about *'koadrilas'* and a man in his twenties who was listening got cross with her. The plural in Basque is formed by adding a 'k'. She apologised for not saying *'koadrilask'* but I got the impression she was being told off for asking about them at all.

Gabrielle came into her own. She was excited by the day and kept squeezing and kissing me. She's usually best with me on my own; in group situations she sometimes mocks me and makes jokes at my expense as if to disassociate herself from me. But that day she treated the occasion like a kind of game. She busied around chatting to various of the Basques and when she had discovered something interesting she returned to me and presented the information as though it were a gift.

She discovered, for example, that bullfighting was not a tradition among the Basques, although greasing up a pig and chasing it through town most certainly was, and there was even an example later that day. She must have already known things like this from her bar work, so there was an element of theatre to her behaviour. She was making sure to please me. She had an air of being falsely jolly.

She noticed a chalk board by the bar which people kept writing on and asked Olaia about it.

'We love to gamble,' she said.

'And?'

'Think of an event you could bet on,' said Olaia.

Gabrielle looked around. 'Okay, I bet that the event where you grease a pig and try to catch it will not start on time. It'll be over an hour late, because you Spaniards...'

'We are not Spaniards,' said Olaia, but she was clearly amused.

Olaia turned and shouted something in Basque to the bar. She went over to the blackboard and wrote Gabrielle's name on it.

'How much are you betting?' she shouted to Gabrielle in English.

'Twenty Euros.'

Olaia shouted this above the noise and in no time she had found two people willing to put ten Euros each on a bet that the pig greasing would start less than an hour late. She wrote it all on the board.

Later, sitting down with me again, Gabrielle said, 'You know, you didn't seem Spanish or Basque when I first met you: you seemed very English. But now I see you in your natural habitat you seem Spanish after all.'

Olaia then did something odd.

She sat herself opposite Gabrielle and said, 'What are your intentions with Sal?'

Gabrielle despite her pregnancy was more than a little drunk.

She said, 'Intentions? Today? I'm going to fuck him so hard that he can scrub but he'll never feel clean again.'

Olaia was expressionless; she wanted to keep it serious.

She said, 'You are lucky to have Sal.'

'We're both lucky,' replied Gabrielle, which I thought was very quick.

Later Gabrielle said to me, 'What was that about?'

I said, 'Jealousy?' I pulled a 'who knows?' kind of face, so that it didn't seem conceited. I followed it up with a joke. 'What is it the jealous say? My friend's friend is my enemy?'

'Have you noticed that you don't get jealous of someone you like?' said Gabrielle. 'You get jealous of someone you love.' Very profound when you're feeling as drunk as I did. *Zuritos* may be a sipping drink but unfortunately I'd had the benefit of the two bottles of red wine we'd ordered before that.

'Okay,' shouted Gabrielle to no one in particular, 'I've got a bet.'

A few people looked her way.

She sprang up to the bar.

'I suggest,' she started. 'I suggest that each of us put five Euros on what we think the next person to walk in will order for a drink.' Gabby stopped, wondering if that sentence made any sense through the alcohol.

A Basque who I didn't know translated what Gabby had said, and by translating, endorsed Gabrielle.

'Okay Gabrielle, you choose first,' he said. Whoever he was, he'd remembered her name straight away.

A worrying number of people in Spain drank red wine with coke so Gabrielle made that her prediction. The man who had told her off about not adding K to plurals predicted *sagardoa*, a local cider. Gabrielle put an arm around his shoulder, in that way you do when you're drunk and feeling affectionate towards whoever happens to be next to you. Olaia predicted *zurito*. She reasoned loudly, and twice, that the next people into the bar could easily be a group like themselves.

Someone was writing all this on the chalkboard and money was going into a beer glass.

Someone suggested sherry, another person suggested Rioja.

There were plenty of people still waiting to place their money when a new customer came through the door; prematurely in most people's opinion.

The woman in question was unnerved by the hush.

The crowd parted for her to get to the bar.

She looked around the room carefully. It was entirely possible she hadn't intended to buy a drink at all, but was just trying to find someone.

'Aren't you going to order?' asked the barman, who himself had put money on Coke.

'No prompting!' shouted Gabby.

'Coffee?' said the customer nervously.

Eighty eyes turned to the blackboard.

No one had chosen coffee.

There was a groan and Olaia announced in Basque, then English, 'It's a rollover!'

A man and a woman behind her started fighting over the chance to put five Euros on 'coffee.' They started slapping each other over the head in a manner that was almost good natured, while a third person held the chalk out of their reach.

At least another ten bets were laid on various drinks and there was a commotion on the terrace. One lad had been spotted trying to climb over the balcony in an attempt to jump down to the square, then run back upstairs and be the next customer. A hand reached out and grabbed the back of his shirt, leaving him dangling and protesting his innocence. A further crowd formed to watch in the square below.

As a result, two customers came in together completely unnoticed. They were a middle-aged couple, probably tourists. There was a hush, then one punter broke ranks and suggested in broken English that the tourists buy Sangria. There followed a torrent of bellowed suggestions to the bewildered pair about what they should order.

'I will buy the drink for you,' shouted one, followed in turn by recriminations and jostling. A sea of people moved in on the innocent tourists, waving money at them to allow them to pay for a drink, not necessarily of their choosing.

The couple chose to drink San Miguel.

All necks craned towards the blackboard. But I knew that I was the winner.

I waited for them all to work it out for themselves.

Eventually I moved forwards through the parting crowd. I held my hands up triumphantly and acknowledged my people.

Olaia brandished the jar of money. She kissed it and ceremoniously handed it over. I held it high in the air.

'Every person in the bar must have a drink on me,' I shouted.

A huge cheer went up.

Gabrielle hugged and kissed me. She was jumping up and down, laughing and holding me tight.

As far as I'm aware, in all the excitement the tourists never, in fact, got served.

That night I drove us home while Gabrielle's head slumped with sleep against the window. But I had put off mentioning Alex and even I had to face up to doing that. I was dithering as usual. Was it a strength if we could always discuss whatever worried us or was it just the sign of a weak worrier? I certainly wished I had more confidence, and more experience with relationships. I wished I had a greater number of key relationships so that this one didn't have to be so important, so I didn't get angst ridden about my every move. I could be lighter. Urbane. Charming. Strong. A rock that women loved, and men admired.

'I saw Alex in a crowd,' I said.

No response.

'I think he was following me,' I said. 'He took my photograph.'

'You have to do that, don't you?' she replied.

'Do what?'

'You wait until we've had a great time, and then spoil it at the end.'

Silence. More driving. I sneaked a look at her. She was doing her sulky truant look.

'When was this?' she asked.

'A couple of days ago,' I said.

A sigh.

A sigh that we still had problems with Alex, or a sigh that I'd raised the issue?

'What do you think we should do about him?' I asked.

'I don't think you should do anything. I think I should try and contact him.'

'Has he tried to contact you?' I asked.

'Yes,' she said.

'When?'

'At the bar,' she said.

'You didn't mention this before.'

'You didn't mention you'd seen him either,' she said.

Yes, but in my case it's because I didn't want to do the wrong thing. In your case it's because you're secretive.

'What did he say?' I asked.

'Not much. I told him to piss off or I'd call the police.'

'Do you think we should call the police?' I asked.

'He hasn't done anything wrong. In this country. I don't really know, to be honest.'

Another long pause. The road was unlit and winding so I had to concentrate on the darkness ahead.

'Actually,' she said, 'I don't want to talk about it now, if that's okay.'

She sighed again. I wanted to ask whether she was upset with me, but I couldn't.

About ten miles later she spoke again.

'Have you really not visited your mother in prison?'

'They're still not admitting exactly where she is,' I replied.

'You seem very concerned,' she said.

Chapter Nineteen

A sense of industry surfaced.

Gabby, Olaia and I all put in stints in our various ways to ring up banks, prisons, and officials to try and make headway with our various problems.

Gabrielle even made an attempt to track down Alex. She was open and good-natured about it.

She looked in her address book and rang the number of Alex's last known workplace in England. I could hear only her half of the conversation.

'Hi,' said Gabby, 'Can I have extension 4-8-8?'

A pause.

'Yeah, can I speak to Alex Lawrence please?'

She was then presumably asked her name.

'Gina Tremain,' she said. 'Thank you.'

A long pause. I'm not sure why.

'Yes, hi, is Alex Lawrence there, please?'

Pause.

'On holiday or ill?' she asked.

Pause.

'Well I suppose what I'm asking is, when he'll be back,' said Gabby.

A longer pause. It seemed to me she was then passed to another person.

'Yes, indeed, it's Gina. Oh hi, yeah, I thought I recognised your voice. How are you?'

There followed a lot of chatter about this and that, where the woman who evidently worked in the same department as Alex was avoiding direct reference to the fact that Gabby had once done a runner. This phone call would no doubt prove to be the main piece of office gossip that day.

'No, it's simply that I wanted to contact him in a hurry,' said Gabby. 'His mobile doesn't seem to work. As you know, we don't live together now. Oh, you didn't know that?'

Gabby mouthed 'liar' at the phone.

'When will he be back?' asked Gabby. 'It's quite urgent. Have you got a mobile number that I could use?'

Gabby raised her pen ready to write, then realised she was being told a phone number she already knew. Her pen lowered again.

There was a bit more conversation, but nothing useful. Gabby put the phone down.

'She says he's been away for a while. She implied he was chronically ill or something. Perhaps a nervous breakdown type thing.'

'But he still has his job there,' I asked.

'If he goes back, yeah.'

'So perhaps he's just taken a few weeks off to harass us and if we don't respond he'll go home.'

'You never know your luck,' she said.

'And we're still no clearer where my mother is?' I asked.

'No.'

'That is appalling,' I said.

About half an hour later, Gabrielle wandered off for a bath. While she was in there, I went back to the telephone and pressed redial.

The phone seemed to take for ever to sort itself out and ring at the other end in England.

I heard Gabby open the bathroom door and pad across the landing.

I still wasn't connected.

There was a creak on the stairs.

I tensed my hand ready to put the receiver down quickly.

The stairs creaked again and then there were footsteps back along the landing and the sound of the bathroom door shutting. She had probably been looking for a towel and found one drying on the banisters.

'Metropolitan Police, Dulwich, what extension please?'

I put the phone down.

The same day as that conversation, I had another appointment with the gestor. He was very pleased with himself.

'I have made progress,' he beamed.

'Great!' I replied.

'But it raises more questions than it answers.'

'Oh,' I said.

'Firstly it seems that no previous resident at your address has run up debts and left them for you, so that's good.'

'Great,' I said.

I already knew that.

'However,' he said taking a breath. 'It appears that two major loans have been taken out, secured on your property,' he said.

'Who by?' I asked.

'By you,' he said. 'And you haven't been paying the loan repayments. Thus the problem.'

'How big are these loans?'

'A total of just under 40,000 Euros, about 28,000 pounds,' he said.

'I know how much a Euro is worth,' I said.

He shrugged.

'How do you know this?' I asked.

'I've tracked down the official who authorised the repossession of your stuff. Next they will want to sell your property in the country.'

I was incredulous.

'Why don't you just pay the loan repayments?' he said.

'Because I haven't taken out any loans,' I replied.

'You are saying you haven't raised money with these banks at all,' he said.

'Definitely not.'

'What about your wife?' he asked.

'What about her?'

'Has she taken out any loans?'

I wanted to say no definitely not, but I actually said, 'I'll check on every possibility before we proceed. Have we got any details about these supposed loans?'

'Not yet. I was told this by a policeman. I'll try and work backwards. It shouldn't take more than a day to find out who thinks they are owed the money. Then perhaps we can ask to look at the paperwork that he or she signed to raise the loan.'

'I do have a court document somewhere which might say,' I said. 'It's amazing though. I can't believe they would just lend a large sum of money out without double checking the person had the right to borrow it.'

'Really?' he replied. 'The last time I can remember borrowing money from a bank, I did it over the phone. One phone call.'

'Yes but they then send the forms to your house and you have to sign something and return it,' I protested. 'So he or she would have to receive the documents at the house upon which the loan was secured.'

'I'd have thought so,' replied the gestor.

I spent the rest of my morning retrieving my car from the compound. They didn't take credit cards and when I returned with cash, it turned out that I also needed proof of residency. They had not made any of this clear in the first place, so one way and another I lost all of my morning and was not in a good mood.

I finally got to work in the afternoon, and Olaia greeted me with the news that my mother had been located and could be picked up that evening.

'Thank you,' I said.

'And that man was looking for you,' she said.

'What man?'

'The man you talked to before.'

'When was this?' I asked.

'He said he'd come another time today. He was here at three o'clock.'

Thirty minutes ago.

'He said he'd come back?' I asked.

'Yes.'

I really didn't feel like working, so on a whim I took myself off to look around the grounds. There was a chance he was killing time just having a wander.

It took me less than five minutes to find him.

He was sitting in a car in the visitor's car park.

I approached with caution, half expecting him to drive off.

He saw me and immediately got out of the car.

'Why are you following me?' I asked.

'I'm not,' he said.

'Okay. What do you want with me today?'

'I want to talk.'

'Let's go and have coffee,' I said.

We walked to the canteen. It made no sense to make small talk so we said nothing.

'You must think I'm mad,' he said when we'd settled at a table. 'Perhaps I am.'

'Whatever,' I replied.

In fact I didn't think he looked mad; I thought he looked energised. The first time I had met him, he had looked withdrawn and reserved; pushed back into a corner by life. But now he seemed more in his stride. He was certainly more chatty.

'You have to see it from my point of view,' he said. 'I had a perfectly good relationship and it finished without warning.'

'Sure,' I said.

'So it's going to make me a little funny, but that doesn't make me insane.'

'I'm not saying you're insane. I'm not saying anything.'

'After my initial shock, I found I wanted answers,' he said. 'I wanted to know what had happened. Had there been another bloke? Had she been wanting to leave for some time? Was I an arsehole to live with? Was she an arsehole?'

'Er, fair enough,' I said.

'I have been ill,' he said. 'I do know that. It's made me ill'

'So,' I said. 'What do you feel I can do for you?'

'It turns out, that it's more what I can do for you,' he said.

'How so?'

'When I tried to track her down, I had to do a lot of research. I had to talk to people, ring around. You can imagine.'

'Sure,' I said.

'The trail eventually led to you, but it also led backwards.'

'What do you mean?'

'I looked into her past,' he said.

I had been game about the conversation so far, but now I wasn't sure I wanted to continue.

'You looked into her past,' I repeated.

'You see, she's done this before,' he said.

'She's done what before?'

'Hitched up with someone, drained them of every last penny they owned and moved on.'

'You are saying, .that she…' I said. 'What are you saying exactly?'

'There was at least one person before me.'

'Okay,' I said. 'People have previous relationships. What are you claiming about the finances?'

'She fleeced me. She cleaned me out. I went to see this previous guy and he said the same. She spent every last penny he had, ran up huge bills and one day she simply fled. William Barfield. Bill Barfield. He lives in Salisbury.'

'You sound as though the name should mean something to me,' I said.

'I'm just suggesting you make a note of the name mentally and then you can do your own research. You obviously don't want to take my word for it.'

I made a deliberate point of not writing down anything. It would be disloyal to Gabby.

'Look,' I said. 'I don't know exactly what you are hoping to achieve, but this is pointless. I can assure you that I am not being fleeced as you put it. My relationship with Gabrielle is entirely my business. I am sorry things didn't work out for you, but that is the nature of relationships. Get over it.'

He put his hand out across the table and held my wrist.

'You are in danger,' he said.

'I am not in danger,' I said.

'I have reason to believe that she is dangerous. I mean, I don't know what the actual word for it is, the syndrome or whatever, but she's dangerous.'

'I think I've heard enough,' I said.

I rose to go.

'You don't have to believe me,' he said.

'I'm going now. This doesn't add up. I mean, why did you run the other day, if you are so innocent? Why were you taking my photo? If Gabby owes you money, take it up with her.'

'You need to listen to me. The woman is dangerous. She has an extraordinary problem with jealousy that makes her virtually psychotic. No, not virtually psychotic; she *is* psychotic. I am not mad.'

'Frankly,' I said, 'This is the point where you have lost what little credibility you had.'

The man had been stalking me, and now that he had my attention he was just burbling away. Even if Alex was correct in every detail, it was a fact of life that if he tried to communicate in this manner, I was unlikely to believe him.

I walked out of the canteen and back to my office. I found a scrap of paper and a pen. I was going to write down the name William Barfield and Salisbury, because I can't always rely on my memory. My pen hovered for a while and then I decided against it. I put the pen back in my draw.

Chapter Twenty

I picked up my mother from prison.

That's not the sort of thing you can say every day.

She was admirable. She didn't moan about how long she'd been banged up, even though it was far longer than I'd put up with. Nor did she moan that I hadn't visited. She did moan about the food, however, which was unfair.

'They've taken my passport away,' she said. 'And they are going to charge me with assault. I'm not allowed to leave the country. I'm going to have to stay with you for several months.'

'Unless they lock you up again,' I volunteered brightly.

I was stuck with her for months. *I was stuck with her for months*. My foot weakened on the accelerator.

When we did get home it was to an evening when Gabby was out working.

I decided to go through her stuff.

She had a couple of drawers that we considered hers, plus a wardrobe, a suitcase under the bed, and a couple of handbags, one of which looked new but I didn't recognise it. I started with the drawers.

I was careful not to disturb anything, although I needn't have worried, because people don't tend to remember exactly how each drawer of clothing looks every morning before they go to work. I mainly lifted the clothes up a bit to see if there was anything below.

'What exactly are you doing?'

'What?' I jumped a mile.

It was my mother.

'I'm tidying,' I said.

'It's a funny place to start,' she said. 'The whole house is a tip.'

'True,' I said. 'So you're welcome to tidy downstairs.'

'I don't think I can do that,' she replied.

Because you're so bloody lazy.

'Do you fancy making me a cup of tea?' I asked.

I got on with the search. There wasn't much to look at, but I kept going because I hadn't even found things like her birth certificate, so I felt I hadn't found 'the good stuff' yet.

In the suitcase under the bed I found a lot of photographs. They were still in Boots envelopes but inside they were sorted out and weeded. There were no duds or irrelevancies. I took them out and looked at each one carefully. It was mostly people I didn't know. Beaches, parties, a couple of children, a couple of photos of what looked like a gymnastics competition. One or two of Gabby with blonde hair, another showing her with the dark hair and light eyebrows combo she now sported. Did she dye her eyebrows because they were too Neanderthal, or were her eyebrows naturally blonde and she dyed her hair black? I'd never seen roots, and I'd never known her to dye it. I wasn't sure either way.

I didn't really know what I was looking for. A fresh supply of stalker's letters perhaps, still warm where she'd been writing them. A pile of documents showing she'd taken out loans against the house? Proof that I could never have landed such a gorgeous woman without there being a serious catch.

A thought popped into my head that was unconnected to my search.

I raced downstairs to find the summons that I had been given by the official. It was somewhere in the kitchen. It would have the name of the finance company who were aggrieved. I would be able to ring them up and ask what they remembered.

Gabby walked in.

'Hiya,' she said. 'I've finished early.'

Her photographs were still on top of the bed, along with her case.

'I'll get changed,' she said. 'I thought it would be nice if we went out. The three of us.'

'That would be a fantastic idea. That *is* a fantastic idea,' I said.

She walked towards the stairs.

'Sweetheart,' I called.

She turned and smiled, 'Yeah?'

'I was looking for that letter that arrived. The one I had to sign for.'

From where I was standing I could see the letter I wanted, but Gabby wasn't to know that.

Gabby looked at me blankly.

'From the court saying we owed money,' I said. 'It's quite important I find it now, because I need to phone someone in the next ten minutes before they leave the office.'

Gabby walked towards me a little way.

'We have really got to sit down and talk about finances and all the problems,' she said. 'We need more of a strategy. I think we keep hoping it'll all blow over.'

She turned to go up the stairs.

'I need it now. I need help now,' I whined.

'What does it look like?'

'A4 brown envelope, with a "signed for" sticker in Spanish on the front. You look downstairs, and I'll look upstairs.'

I raced past her up the stairs.

I hadn't made a huge mess with the photos but I wanted them to look roughly right when she next opened the case. It was a thirty seconds that lasted for ever.

'Is this is it?' she asked from the doorway of the bedroom.

I was pretty sure she hadn't seen me but there was only about a second in it.

I looked quizzically at what she was holding.

'No, I checked that,' I said.

I walked over and took the envelope from her and looked inside.

'Oh, yes, it is the right one,' I said. 'I am so stupid. I did check that as well.'

Gabby said, 'Why are you such a liar?'

'What do you mean?'

'When you lie your face looks all…' Gabby pulled a face. 'Why would you lie about looking in an envelope?'

'I wasn't lying,' I said.

Gabby raised her eyebrows. Her lips dragged to one side. She walked past me to her wardrobe.

'I'll wear these,' she said holding up a pair of emerald green velvet trousers. They looked ghastly in theory, but there was a chance she would carry them off: she has a world-beating arse and legs.

'I bought them yesterday,' she said. 'What do you think?'

'Fantastic.'

I went downstairs reading the letter.

The aggrieved party was a bank called BDM, The Bank of Deron and Madrid. I'd never heard of them, but that meant nothing.

I didn't phone them. They would be shut at that time of day. I paced around reading the letter.

There was no escaping it. I was a mess. I'd had a stream of problems and I wasn't giving myself time to even fathom them out, let alone act. What had I done about the stalker's letters? What had I done about the letter I was holding? What had I done about the action the police seemed hell bent on taking? Nothing, nothing and nothing. What would it take to stir me into action? Well, I suppose I had at least gone to the gestor. He seemed quite able and knowledgeable.

'Did you make that phone call?' asked Gabby after she'd changed. She was only making conversation. She was admiring herself in a mirror.

'They weren't still there I guess. I couldn't get through,' I said. 'Where shall we go for supper?'

'Mandoya?' she said.

'Shall we go somewhere cheaper?' I asked.

'Yeah sure,' she said. 'Where?'

I made a number of suggestions but Gabby didn't like any of them. We'd either been to a place too often, or she hadn't previously liked the food there.

The three of us went to Mandoya and each had a fantastic lobster. It was perfect, genuinely perfect, but that wasn't quite the point.

One problem we had at that stage was that we had my mother around a lot so we couldn't discuss problems at our leisure. We frequently had to wait until we were in our bedroom. We felt like caged animals in our own house. Even in the safety of our room, my mad mother might be pacing and listening outside the door.

Late that night when we were in bed together and tired I whispered, 'Why do you think it is eight letters?'

'I don't know,' she replied.

'Scary.'

'Mmm.' she said. She didn't sound scared. 'Of all the elements, which do you think are truly a problem?'

'And which, if any, are interconnected?' I said.

'Mmm.'

'The people trying to repossess our stuff is the biggest single problem in the short term,' I said. 'And the police.'

'Those two are definitely interconnected,' said Gabby.

'We'll start there,' I said. 'I think there's a chance they won't want to prosecute a dotty old woman. We might be able to get my mother off.'

'Mmm,' she said, sounding sleepy now. 'I also have to decide whether I want to go to England to have this baby.'

We hadn't discussed the baby much. I liked the idea of having a baby but had been a little shocked at how soon we were going down that path. I suspect men often feel a bit negative when their partner gets pregnant but don't mention it, and it's certainly nothing sinister. I think, in a funny way, men often see the bigger picture earlier on than women do. You never hear a man say 'If I'd known what I know now I would never have had children.' This is partly because they do less childcare, of course; but given that a coach and horses will be run through their finances, free time, freedom and previous means of enjoyment, there is remarkably little complaining or surprise.

So I think this was all true in my case, but a bigger factor was the sheer weight of problems we'd had thrown at us.

'We may only be here for a couple of years,' I said. 'So we can take a decision later about raising him or her in a Spanish school or in England.'

'It would be great to stay here,' said Gabby.

'Yeah,' I said. 'Although, I'm not sure how many bad experiences we can take before we decide we're best off at home.'

'At home?' she said. 'England, you mean. I'm in favour of staying. Although I'm wondering if I ought to get back to England for a few months to do the basic how-to-give-birth classes. What do you think?'

'Whatever you think is best,' I said.

'Possibly to give birth too. I've been putting off making a decision. I'm getting like you,' she said.

Chapter Twenty-one

Somehow I managed to get some work done despite all the stress and traumas. Ultimately though, it was one of those jobs that could take up endless hours, or none at all: if I didn't work, people still built and repaired wind turbines, and the superconductor still got laid. One of my current jobs was the ridiculous task of logging on the computer the size and shape of every office and workshop. No one had ever done it before, and it could be used to work out whether we were spending too much on heating and whether our site was good value compared to other sites that may become available. The process was such a waste of time, and made doubly difficult by my inability to work the computer programme that had been provided.

So I spent a lot of that period wrestling with that problem while keeping an eye out for the antics of the security staff. But I also took a lot of time off. Because we were in a foreign country, it hadn't occurred to me that I was also allowed holidays, so I started taking days off to give me time to deal with my problems.

Of course, this had the negative effect of giving me more time with my mother who, for the purposes of irritating me, was employing a dual-pronged strategy of moaning about the Spanish penal system while concurrently ensuring her hearing aid didn't work.

When my mother had originally been fitted with a hearing aid she had been told that the batteries would last seven days. But Jancie, as we were endlessly reminded, was a person who only had five or six hours sleep, so her hearing aids were used up to nineteen hours a day. As a result, the batteries ran out after about five days and Jancie spent the rest of the week shaking them, and offering surreal answers to everyday questions.

My initial response to this was to try and explain the situation to her.

'Your batteries have run out!' I yelled.

No reply from her.

'It's time to change your batteries.'

Still no reply.

I suspected, because it's the sort of thing one easily suspects, that my mother heard only what she wanted to hear. I said instead, 'Your hearing aid is whistling, can I give it a shake?'

At this, my mother surrendered her hearing aid. I then shot hell for leather up the stairs, and into my mother's bedroom.

Jancie called through the house, 'Sal, are you there? Where have you gone?'

I was feverishly rifling through the old woman's possessions looking for her store of replacement batteries and fumbling to replace the old one with a new one.

'I think I've fixed it,' I gasped once I was downstairs.

My mother put it in and announced firmly that it was no better, but then gave herself away by asking, 'What exactly did you do to it?'

'I gave it a shake. I think there's a loose connection.'

She nodded. She had known all along it wasn't the battery.

It was a sign of how much she was driving me insane that I was actually glad to get into town and talk to one of the banks that alleged I owed them money. The gestor had now given me the details of both of them and I made appointments with each. My first was with the Madrid Bank I'd never heard of. When I found its branch in Bilbao it turned out I had passed it countless times but never noticed it.

The woman with whom I had the appointment didn't understand my problem.

'I want to see the original forms that were filled in.'

'Forms that you filled in?' she asked.

'No, I didn't fill them in. That's the point.'

'If you didn't fill them in, then you can't see them. They are confidential,' she said.

It took a lot of explaining, but eventually she understood and she even found me the person who had processed the loan.

He was a pleasant enough man with an office of his own on the first floor. I feared at first the whole procedure was going to be a slow paper trail but he instantly produced the relevant file. For the umpteenth time I had discovered the Spanish were far more efficient than I assumed, but no matter how many times I discovered it, I retained my original perception of them as inefficient and lazy.

He showed me a form (that had been completed in Spanish) applying for a loan. It was not my handwriting and at the bottom there was a minimal effort to ape my signature.

The form would have required a person to be able to read a small amount of Spanish, but the answers that were required were largely factual so wouldn't require much mugging up; things like my name and address, years at the current address, employer, earnings and so on. A lot of these answers could be bluffed.

'Did someone come in here to fill in the forms?' I asked.

He took the file back and looked at it.

'No, the forms have been sent in to us. They are rubber stamped as having been received.'

I had a think, and this gave the man a chance to start a cigarette.

'If this is fraud, you are going to have to act fast,' he said. 'We are hoping to repossess your property soon. You'll need some proof of your story and you'll need to get the police to believe you.'

'So you personally have never met the person who signed these forms,' I asked.

'No, but the final offer document would have been sent to your house for signing,' he said. 'Definitely.'

'Can I have a photocopy of this for the dates and for the handwriting and stuff?'

'Sure,' he said.

At home I went off to look at the calendar. The date on the loan agreement was June 3rd. I wanted to know what we were doing that day. If we had been out, it was possible that someone had broken in and gone through our mail. But it was so unlikely. He or she was taking a chance that we wouldn't open the mail first and wonder what the loan forms were all about. Or was I so predictable in my inability to open my own mail? I suppose I was, but it was still a risky strategy nonetheless.

The calendar showed nothing for June 3rd.

I looked again at the loan documents. There was a bank account from which the loan repayments were supposed to come. It wasn't an account I recognised: probably fictitious. Would checks not have shown this up? Perhaps there was a different attitude in Spain, based on the fact that they were always in a position to foreclose on your house. But two banks had been fooled, not one: surely that in itself showed the system didn't work.

The phone rang.

It was Olaia.

'I have uncovered something very important,' she said. 'Well, at least I think it's important.'

She sounded tense, not quite herself.

'Uh huh?' I replied.

'Do you know where the Chillida Installations are?'

'Roughly.'

'You should go down there at six tomorrow morning.'

'Why?' I asked.

'Trust me. Six tomorrow morning.'

'How do you know this? I mean, what do you know?' I asked.

'I can't tell you that. Remember what I told you about phones the other day? Will you go there?' she asked.

'Yes,' I replied.

'On your own.'

'Okay!' I said.

I was going to ask another question but the phone went dead.

I was a little dazed but then thought of some good supplementary questions and decided to ring Olaia back.

I rang work, but she didn't pick up the phone. I rang a colleague in the same building. He wandered off to look round the door of my office.

'Apparently she hasn't been in today,' he said.

Chapter Twenty-two

Gabrielle had done a late shift at her bar and must have come home at about 4.30 or thereabouts. She was fast asleep beside me when I woke. I crept out of bed. My mother also appeared to be asleep, but as I tiptoed down the corridor she called out from her bedroom.

'Where are you going?'

'Out,' I said.

I could have said that I was going to the toilet but somehow she knew that wasn't the case, otherwise she wouldn't have asked. But how had the deaf old bat even heard me in the first place?

I drove to San Sebastian, parked my car on the edge of town and walked to the cliffs.

The Basques' single biggest contribution to Western culture is probably in the field of modern sculpture. The Chillida Installations are giant metal pieces set into the rocks on the coastline, and the locals were justifiably proud of them.

The sea was rough that day; it lashed the coastline and I wondered whether the art would look best on a calm day with the sun rising through it, or whether such bold pieces would look best defying a storm.

I couldn't help feeling I had chosen the wrong route. I was forced to climb down a semi-path that took me to a precarious position on the rocks at the foot of the cliff. I continued gingerly. I had worn the wrong shoes and clothes; I had presumed I would go straight to work afterwards. I inched my way round a corner and the first of the three installations came into view; giant metal pliers set into the rock. Soon I saw the second pair; the same as the first but set at a right angle. As brutal and as elegant as the sea.

I loved them. They looked a bit like Euro signs, or those old-fashioned tin openers with the blade. But these were bigger. They were proud to be solid and functional.

The third installation was now in sight. This one was shaped a little differently: it had an extra vertical line hanging down.

The light was not yet what it could be and the third installation was still some distance away. I concentrated on picking my way along the rocks, so I was quite a bit closer before I looked up at the sculpture again.

My stomach didn't contract, nor did I salivate. I was standing upright and the vomit simply poured out of my mouth, down my chin and onto my clothes.

It was the most frightened I had ever been in my life.

I had to sit for a while and then, when I was able to, I felt it was my duty to walk forward towards it.

The nature of the rocks forced me to climb a little higher in order to get closer. I could now see a single rib bone, greyed and bare, as if an animal had been eating it, stripping it of its flesh. The rib was horizontal from the body; it had been forced out from behind but still attached at one end.

The body itself had been impaled onto the metalwork of the sculpture, so that the steel emerged through the middle of her abdomen. It was a woman. She had a white vest-type top raised up to her rib cage; it was brown with stale blood. The remains of a shirt was on her shoulders, flapping furiously in the wind.

Her head was slumped forward to the left at an angle over her chest, an angle that is impossible for a person who is alive. Perhaps her neck had been snapped. Her right eyelid was swollen and sealed shut with blood. Her torso was held upright because the lower edge of her ribcage had jammed against the metal. As well as the rib, there was grey small intestine smeared and stretched on the steel in front.

It wasn't until I was a lot closer that I realised it was Olaia.

Chapter Twenty-three

The metal that Olaia was impaled upon was so thick that there was absolutely no chance she was alive. There was no point in getting any closer. My instinct was to run, to create thinking time as much as anything.

I made my way back along the rocks and prayed the whole episode wasn't a sting. I had images that whoever had done the murder probably knew I was going to meet her there; they might also tip off the police to frame me. I could easily be arrested.

Presumably Olaia hadn't come down much before six. That wouldn't have given the murderer much time to kill her, impale her, and run for it. The murderer could easily still be there watching.

I looked along the cliff tops, along the coastline. I couldn't see anyone.

I could ring up the police and report the crime. That would be the action of an innocent man. But, presumably, the body would still be warm, which implicated me. I definitely needed to get away.

As I picked my way along the rocks, I racked my brains as to what she could possibly have had to say to me. Was it so incriminating that someone felt they had no option but to kill her before she talked to me? Who the hell could it be? And why did she want to meet out near San Sebastian? It was a long way from work or where either of us lived.

I remembered my vomit. I had thrown up on a rock. I think the rock was above the tide level so it wouldn't get washed away. Could they do a DNA test on vomit? It was some of last night's food and a lot of stomach acid. I thought I should go back. I could get handfuls of sea water and try and wash the rocks. But what if the police came and saw me doing that? Not the actions of an innocent man. My God, why do I dither so much? I've always dithered. All my life I've been ineffectual and dithered.

I turned the keys in the ignition. I drove off at a slowish pace. On some level I didn't want to go far in case I had a new thought and needed to return. I looked out for police cars. I kept thinking about the pile of vomit, about Olaia. Poor Olaia. Poor, poor Olaia.

There was so much I didn't understand.

If or when the police asked me what I was doing there I had no alibi. Olaia herself was the only proof that I had been rang up and told to go. There was no plausible reason why I would be there by coincidence.

I started driving faster away from San Sebastian.

Was there any chance at all that my vomit would get washed away by the sea? Probably not. But there would be a fair amount of sea spray in the wind. The rocks I had been walking on were probably above the high tide mark, but they weren't exactly dry.

I realised I had vomit on my clothing as I drove. Even if it wasn't possible to match DNA from vomit, it seemed likely they could match the vomit on my clothes with the vomit on the rocks. In that case I needed to drive home, get changed and put my clothes in the wash. I then had to try and get into work on time so that it wasn't noticed that I was missing or late that morning.

It was 7.35 by the time I got home. Gabby and my mother were both up and in the kitchen.

I ran upstairs and feverishly took my clothes off. Gabby followed sleepily up the stairs.

'Where've you been?' she asked.

'I wanted to get into work early because I'm so behind, but the car had trouble and when I fixed the bloody thing I got oil on me.'

Gabby appeared to be only half listening. Distracted perhaps by my bared hairy arse and my legs that were tangled up in an underpants and trouser combo.

'Are you all right?' she asked.

'Yeah. A bit hassled,' I said. 'You all right?'

'I couldn't sleep. I woke up after only about two hours. Perhaps I'm turning Spanish,' she said.

I folded my clothes into themselves to trap in any stains and wandered off to find something else to wear.

When I came back, Gabby was picking up my clothes. Since when did she ever do anything like that?

'I'll handle it,' I said. 'I want to get them in the wash straight away. It really helps with oily stains.'

It sounded wrong and Gabrielle sniggered.

'Whatever you say,' she said. 'I'm going to have a shower.'

I got myself into my new clothes. I reckoned I just had enough time to get to work and affect a look of studied nonchalance.

'Oh by the way,' said Gabby, wandering back. 'I have some good news. I rang up Alex's work for the umpteenth time and the woman said that he has made contact.'

'Yeah?'

'Yeah. She says he's going back to work. He'll be back in two days time.'

Chapter Twenty-four

I got to work and made sure to engage the security guards in some light conversation.

Once in my office I got a couple of files and wandered off to discuss them with a few colleagues. Some of them weren't at work yet, so I left post-it notes on their desks about this or that, each with the date and time on them.

I kept getting flashbacks about Olaia. A life gone. A beautiful, full life. I'd really liked her by the end. She had been very kind to me. Strong, bolshie, kind Olaia.

I could think about hardly anything else.

I couldn't settle at my desk, so I took myself for a walk around the grounds. I spotted a car drive up to the exit of the car park. I hovered out of sight and watched. It was quite an expensive sports car driven by a man in a suit.

He got out and took a scaffolding pole from the back seat. He then walked to the other side of the barrier and rolled the scaffolding pole along the road. The metal detectors under the road evidently sensed it, thinking it was a car trying to *leave* the car park. The barrier went up, the man got back in the car and drove through.

After he'd found a parking space, I walked over to him. I reached him as he was getting an overnight case out of his boot.

'Can I ask you what you're doing?' I asked.

'Parking,' he replied.

'Do you have business here?'

The man raised an eyebrow, which could have meant anything.

Then I realised what had been happening all along.

I said, 'You are going to the airport, aren't you?'

The man looked neutral.

'How much is long stay parking at the airport?' I asked.

The man broke out in a smile.

'Twenty Euros a day,' he said.

'So if I clamped your car and charged twenty Euros a day for you to have it back?' I asked.

'That's a bargain. Because if you clamp it, it can't be stolen. That is better than the other car park. And your car park is closer to the airport than the official long stay,' he said. 'Do you need me? Because I've got a plane to catch.'

'That's fine, mate,' I said. 'If I do clamp it, then you'll need to go to the guard hut to get it unlocked.'

'Thanks,' he said.

He wandered off on his walk down the road to the airport.

I walked back to my office doing my sums as I went. I reckoned that clamping would put a lot of people off parking, but if I set the price right I would retain perhaps a quarter of the airport commuters and make enough money to make the car park self-financing. I would check with the British powers that be, and get it organised. I predicted that the British would like it, but the Spanish wouldn't.

I got back to my office and decided to ring Gabby. I needed to force myself to puzzle through all the elements one by one.

'Hiya,' I said, when she answered.

'Hi.'

'Tell me. That loan that was taken out was signed on June 3rd.'

'Okay,' she said.

'It means that the forms were sent to our house and whoever signed them must have been in a position to pick them up from our place without us realising.'

'Right,' she said. 'What are you thinking?'

'Well I'm wondering what we were doing on the 3rd of June, or the second.'

'Right,' she said. 'I'll just get the calendar.'

'I've tried that. There's nothing written down.'

'I'll look anyway,' she said. 'It might jog my memory.'

She returned to the phone.

'It was before I worked at the bar,' she said. 'So I was in most of the time.'

'Okay.'

'So the postman when he did come, which wasn't that often, either used to put the stuff through the door or when I was decorating he used to knock on the window,' said Gabby.

'Why?'

'Well the front doorway was boarded up for a week or so because I had taken the door off its hinges. I had to repair it and fill it and stuff, before I could paint it.'

'So he used to knock on the window and give you the post himself,' I said.

'Yes.'

'What happened if you weren't in?' I asked.

'I put a box outside the front for him to put the post in,' she said.

'Ah,' I said. 'So someone could have easily stolen our mail.'

'Sort of,' she said. 'The person would have had to have kept an eye on our daily routine for that to be possible. And you reckoned they did two loans. That means they took the chance that they would be able to intercept the mail each time.'

'I don't know for sure if the second loan involved forms being sent by post,' I said. 'It might have been done by someone going down to the bank in person. How often did the postman use the box outside?'

'A few times. Now I think about it, I only had one tap on the window at that time,' she said. 'But we live abroad, how

143

often would we get mail? The postman used the box a couple of times, I think.'

'I suppose from the stalker's point of view, the worst that would happen is we'd get some mail about a loan that we didn't recognise and we binned it. It still doesn't feel right though,' I said.

'How so?'

I could hardly say that a scenario that fitted the facts better was that she had arranged the loan herself.

'Oh I don't know,' I said.

That afternoon, a policeman visited me at work.

'Site management?'

'Yep,' I replied.

'Salvador Gongola?'

'Yep.'

'I need to ask you a few questions,' he said. 'My name is Juan Pairnez.'

He was one of those people in the habit of touching any furniture he passed, either with the tips of his fingers, or stroking it the way people do when wondering what to buy in a furniture shop.

He was well dressed. Not so much an expensive suit as a suit that was made to last.

I decided to ask for identification, 'just for safety's sake', and he reached into his jacket. The 'badge' he pulled out was a worn plastic wallet which he flicked open with great panache. I was half expecting to see a big shiny metal crest as heavy as a doorstop. Possibly with an American eagle on and LAPD.

In reality it was just a bit of beaten up plastic with 'POLICIA' written in silver. It was a disappointing moment.

'We have reason to believe that an employee of yours has been murdered.'

'Okay,' I said.

'A Senora Olaia Mujika.'

'Olaia?' I said. I went for 'puzzled' rather than a 'say it isn't so, Inspector!' style.

'When did you last see her?'

'Well, she's not been in today, so yesterday,' I said. 'Oh, hang on, no, the day before yesterday.'

'Were you expecting her today?' asked the inspector.

'Yes, but she has various duties. Sometimes she is at the Pamplona site. Do you want me to ring and check?' I asked.

'No. She is dead.'

'God. I mean how?'

'It was a very brutal killing and very public so we are thinking it could be to do with the Separatist Movement. It is possible she was an informer that ETA has executed.'

'Really?' I said, genuinely surprised.

This policeman was obviously from the 'you give some gossip out to get some back' school. Or garrulous.

'Certainly she had reported to a colleague that some people here are using firearms,' he said.

'But I heard she was in ETA herself.'

'That was the official line apparently, and the line most police were led to believe. We couldn't possibly trust anyone to know she was an informant, not even the rank and file police.'

'Most reassuring,' I said.

'But having said all that, it most likely has nothing to do with ETA at all,' he said.

'No?'

'All we ever hear is ETA, ETA, ETA, but have you ever, even once, come across something they have done?' He asked.

'It's in the newspapers all the time,' I said.

'Oh it's in the *newspapers*,' he said. 'But, for all the talk, have you personally come across anything they've done, apart from the odd bit of graffiti? Let's look instead at the guards and their guns, and clues like that.'

I was stuck as to what to say. Did I admit that I knew about the guns but had done nothing? If Olaia was concerned about the guards, why hadn't she helped me more? Or was she trying to get their trust, trust that would have been lost if she'd been seen to help me.

'You see, she had a theory,' said the inspector, warming to his theme. 'You are laying superconductors, right?'

'The first in Europe.'

'She said that to keep them cool they are sheathed in a cooling gas, yes?' he said.

'Yes,' I replied. I couldn't see where this was going.

'Her theory was that a terrorist outfit could change the gas for something explosive. The gas could be pumped in and would go down the line for kilometres and then it could be ignited or it would explode when it got to a certain temperature.'

'So, in fact, you are saying it *is* ETA?' I said. 'In either event I don't think that would work with the superconductors.' I was freezing to my core just contemplating it.

'It is the line we *have* to look at first,' he replied. 'It was her theory, after all. And now she's dead.'

I was furiously trying to think how far the superconductor extended. Could it be used to blow up an entire section of a city? And what about the one in Frisbee, USA? Terrorists love getting themselves on the map with strikes like that. Something big that goes down in history: invading the public consciousness and forcing reactions.

He asked me for my phone number and I gave it to him. He then wrote down his name and a phone number on my pad which I thought was a good sign.

'You have to appreciate that if this does prove to be ETA we have to be seen to stamp on it very hard,' he said.

'But they *want* you to overreact,' I said. 'It confirms their sense of being hard done by.'

He looked at me as though I were very thick.

'We can't just *forget* what they do to us,' he said.

After he left, I spent more time than usual gazing into space.

I tried to think things through. If Olaia was correct and ETA had their eyes on the superconductor then they may have wanted both me and Olaia out of the way. We were in charge of security, after all. I had no idea whether it would be possible to cause widespread explosions using our cabling. It would depend on just what they pumped down there instead of coolant. The least they could achieve would be to destroy the superconductor itself, which might be a satisfactory outcome for them. At most they might be able to blow up an entire city.

Perhaps the whole strategy had been one of making my life a misery in the hope I'd go back to England. But then how to explain away Alex?

Then something else occurred to me.

The murder was too complicated.

If Olaia was going to tell me important information and someone panicked when they realised this, then the murder would have been hurried and ill-prepared. But it would be very difficult to impale a body on those sculptures. It was not a random act. The murderer must have felt they had lots of time in hand.

Either they didn't know I was going to be there, or Olaia had been down at the coast much earlier than me.

Why? She had clearly said six a.m. to me.

A horrible possibility struck me.

When she had rung me, she sounded strained. Could it be that when she was speaking, the murderer was there with her? He or she had told her what to say, then took her down to the Chillida Installations to murder her. By doing that they had removed my alibi for being down there, and possibly were trying to frame me for her murder.

147

Chapter Twenty-five

I told Gabrielle everything. She stood in the kitchen holding a mug of coffee, listening intently. She was very calm about it.

'The trouble is,' said Gabrielle. 'They might check the phone records.'

'What do you mean?'

'Well, you say Olaia rang you,' she said. 'So it might look like you told her to meet you at the Chillida Installations.'

'Why would I do that?'

'To murder her,' she said.

'Why would I want to murder her?'

'Who knows?' she said. 'The fact remains you didn't tell the police you'd talked to her that day. That's going to look terrible. They are bound to check Olaia's phone records and your number will come up.'

'I'll have to say that someone rang from her number but it wasn't her,' I said.

It would sound really unlikely.

Gabrielle was beginning to look angry.

'How could you be so stupid?'

'Why am I stupid?' I asked.

'You should have told me about the phone call. We could have worked at it together.'

'You weren't here. You were working. Besides, she told me not to tell anyone,' I said.

'Christ you're stupid!' she said.

It came completely out of nowhere.

It was as if some sort of mental incendiary device had gone off. Her face twisted with rage, her skin glistened with hate.

'That doesn't mean you can't tell me!' she shouted. She started coming out with stuff that wasn't even relevant. 'When I met you, nothing fazed you. No matter what happened you would sit us down, you would reason it out. Now you are just this little mole of a person. You are pathetic. You bury your head in the sand. You are lazy. You are weird. You are secretive. You are pathetic. Pathetic.'

'Yeah, I get that you think I'm pathetic.'

'Pathetic.'

'Shut up.'

'I mean, it's not as though you are Brad Pitt, or rich, or amazingly interesting. The whole point about you was that you were solid. You were even. You were normal. But really, what have we got now?'

She hit me hard in the face. I lost my footing and tilted back to right myself. She then unleashed a flurry of punches; sideways swipes at my chest.

After the initial shock I got my footing back.

I hit her in return. I don't know where it came from. My fist shot up like a bullet. Of all places, it hit her high in the neck. Her jaw jerked back and up. She lost her balance, possibly from the surprise. She fell backwards on her heel and in the same movement the back of her skull caught the edge of the work surface. It made a dull crack. Coffee shot over her face.

She was on the ground.

I was shouting at her.

'Is this what you want? Is this what you want? You want a man who reacts?' I don't know where it all came from. I started screaming obscenities at her over and over again.

She wasn't moving.

I don't recall when I went from shouting at Gabrielle to concern at the fact that she wasn't moving.

I spoke her name, softly now.

I should have known what to do in these situations but my head was blank. Check her heart? No. It wouldn't be a heart attack.

It came to me. I had to check her breathing. I listened with my head close to hers. Is that the best I could do? Listening? Is this all we are supposed to do in an emergency?

She was breathing. I could see her chest rise and fall.

Now what?

I stood.

Her eyes opened. She looked relaxed. As if she'd woken from a gentle sleep.

She sat up on her elbows.

There was blood on the floor. A red rectangle about two inches across. The edge of the rectangle was well defined; the blood seemed to have already clotted. In the middle of the rectangle, the blood was so thin it was almost transparent.

Gabrielle said nothing. She ran from the room.

I spent the evening talking to my mother. Or rather watching the television and telling her what was going on. I had no idea where she'd been when Gabrielle and I had had our argument; in her room perhaps.

I went to bed at exactly the normal time and put out the light.

About an hour later I heard Gabrielle walk up the stairs. She went into the bathroom and was in there a long time. She slipped into bed.

There was no sound in the room.

'I am very sorry,' I said.

My voice was dampened by the silence.

Normally at night I'd have leant across and kissed her. But I felt I no longer had the right to even be near her. She was the only one who could make a move. But it was absurd for *her* to have to offer comfort to *me*. An impasse, then.

Chapter Twenty-six

The next morning the three of us had coffee in the kitchen. The weather was beautiful. I was due to take my mother into town that day to see an official about a possible court case. There wasn't a country in the world which was lenient about someone assaulting its police force, so we were a bit gloomy.

The three of us talked about nothing in particular.

'We need more bleach,' said Gabby. 'And also milk.'

'No problem,' I said. 'Anything else?'

She shrugged.

I couldn't see any sign of a wound on the back of her head.

My mother and I were summoned to attend the prosecutor's about the assault on the policeman. We were seen promptly. The prosecutor was elderly and exuded competence. Two armed policemen entered the room and stood either side of his desk, presumably to show gravitas, unless they thought that my dotty old mother posed a threat to them and had concealed some oven cleaner about her person. She had been frisked on the way in.

'We can't drop the charges against you,' he began. 'It is not an option. We must always be seen to protect the police and make an example of people who attack them. Especially with the war against ETA. So prison is the solution here.'

I couldn't quite believe we had been told to attend this man's office just to hear that but, worryingly, he had the look of someone getting into his stride.

'Six months to a year,' he said.

Six months to a year of visiting my mother. Six months to a year of my mother moaning about the prison food and the fact that she had to wash the soap before using it.

'We may be willing to listen to representations on the grounds that she is old,' he was saying. 'It will be my position that we will require a prison sentence to be passed, but once passed we will then accept the idea that we may be asked for clemency. She may then be deported, but I doubt it.'

He appeared to be saying that ultimately she wouldn't have to go to prison, but that we would have to present the correct defence to make this happen.

'We have to listen to representations, and then we will meet again, just like this, at a later date. Then the court date will be after that,' he said.

This was good news and it was reasonable that the authorities were looking for a line to take that was fair to both us and them.

I thought we'd got a good result but the sting came in the tail.

'Could you leave the room now, please,' said the prosecutor.

We stood up to go, but at the door I was collared by an official.

'Could you wait a moment?' he said.

Within in a minute I was in another office on my own with an Inspector: the furniture stroker.

'I don't think you have been honest with me,' he said.

'In what way?' I asked.

'It turns out we had a tip off.'

'It turns out, what?' I asked.

'It was phoned into another department so it took time to reach me.'

152

'A tip off about what?' I said. 'I'm a bit lost.'

'We had a tip off that you were down at the Chillida Installations at the time Olaia's death.'

Bum.

'The Chillida Installations?' I asked. 'What have they got to do with anything?'

'Oh come on!' he said.

'What?'

'You must know perfectly well where Olaia died. You would have read it in the newspapers; it would have been a topic of discussion at work. You must know perfectly well where her body was found.'

I stuck to my guns. 'You are saying her body was found at the Chillida Installations down near San Sebastian?' I exhaled thoughtfully, sadly. 'You have to understand that I have had a lot of problems of my own. I have not been reading the newspapers.'

'That is where the body was found,' he said.

'Oh, God,' I said.

I had a think. I always believe that the best lies are the ones closest to the truth. But if I admitted to being down there, what would my excuse be? I couldn't now admit to having talked to her on the phone because it looked as if I had a lot to hide that had to be forced out of me. Or did that make no sense at all? Come on brain, work!

'The reason I am slow to reply is that I think someone is trying to frame me,' I said.

'Why do you say that?'

'I was asked to go down to the Chillida Installations that morning,' I said.

'Why?'

'Look,' I said, 'we have been receiving hate mail. All sorts of things have been going wrong. I was told that if I went down there first thing this morning I would be able understand what had happened,' I said.

'Who told you to do that?'

'It was an anonymous phone call. You have to understand we have been very thrown by all of this. I am not sure I am acting rationally anymore. So I went down there.'

'Can anyone confirm this?' he asked.

'What do you mean?'

'Can anyone confirm that you received this call and that you were told to go down there?'

'No,' I replied. 'But there will be phone records.'

'Who was the person who rang you?'

'I don't know,' I replied. 'It was a woman. She sounded in her twenties or thirties. After all, it was in Spanish. When you are not a natural Spanish speaker it is harder to differentiate between what different speakers sound like.'

'I can imagine,' he said, almost sarcastically. It was hard to tell given that he was speaking Spanish.

I looked as if I was thinking for a while, then perked up.

'I did report the letters to the police. The inspector concerned might remember it. I might be able to find the name of the police inspector I talked to.' In reality I hadn't written the man's name down because he had been such a waste of space.

'There's a gestor who can confirm what's been happening,' I said.

'A gestor,' laughed the policeman. 'Well, that's all right then.'

It was not looking good.

'So you are saying that you went down to the Chillida Installations,' he said. 'Then what did you do?'

'I went down there. I had one of those kind of situations where I kept chopping and changing my attitude.' I realised I wasn't making much sense, but at least my speech was plausibly chaotic. 'As I was driving along I kept changing my mind as to whether I was doing the right thing. I mean it could have been a trap. Well, it probably was a trap as it turned out. So, anyway, I parked the car and I walked towards the Installations a bit. I could just about see them. I couldn't see anything of interest. I think I imagined there would be someone there to meet me or something. So I sort of turned up and nothing happened and I just went home again.'

'And that was it?' he said.

'That was it.'

He looked at me for a long time but I felt he'd bought the story.

'It's the sort of story that doesn't sound very likely. But don't worry too much,' he said. 'This is a strange land. We are used to false tip-offs and layers beneath layers and all sorts of trouble. The thrust of the investigation is that we are assuming it is to do with ETA. I personally don't believe that's the case, but so long as that is the line you won't find us breathing too deeply down your neck.'

I smiled. He didn't return the smile.

'It was a violent death, Mr Gongola,' he said.

'Yes.'

'The metal she was impaled upon is very thick. The evidence is that the murderer hacked at her back before impaling her. We think she was murdered a few metres further along the coast and they cut and cracked through her spine. They put a hole in her torso so that she could fit over the steel. It was either a show killing or the work of a very weird person.'

'Heavens,' I said, picturing it.

'Have you got your passport with you?' he asked.

'No.'

'You'll need to hand in your passport and not leave the country while we investigate. I will need the passport within 24 hours.'

As we left the building, my mother asked me what had happened.

'You're going to prison,' I said.

'Oh.'

'But we might be able to prevent it.'

'Oh. Thank heaven's I've got you, Sal.'

'Yeah,' I said.

We got home to find Gabrielle packing her belongings.

'Have you been going through my stuff?' she asked.

'No. Why?' I said.

'My suitcase under the bed,' she said.

'What about it?'

'Someone's been going through it.'

'No,' I said.

'There's a number of photographs missing.'

'Really, what photographs?' I asked.

'This and that. Photos from my past.'

'How many?' I asked.

'It's hard to tell. But there's quite a few missing. They are mostly of me at the time I was with Alex. In fact, I think that every single photo of Alex has gone.'

'Er, you appear to be packing,' I said.

'I'm going back to England.'

I sat down, my energy drained from me.

'I'll just go there for a while. Clear my head. Get some baby and birth classes under my belt,' she said. 'I'll have a think.'

Don't go.

'I had promised myself a few things,' she continued. 'I promised myself that I would never stick around in an abusive relationship. The first sign of trouble I would go. I also think we've run out of steam.'

As she spoke she kept herself busy with the packing. Her eyes stayed within the case.

'Abusive?' I said.

'You're just so limp,' she said.

'Abusive but limp,' I said.

She was making no sense. She didn't care that she didn't make sense; she wanted out.

I stood up. I couldn't think what to do or say.

She turned and faced me. I approached her and we held each other. We cried and rocked together forwards and backwards.

Chapter Twenty-seven

After my initial shock, I felt cheated. I thought we had far more mileage in us. I thought we were nowhere near the stage where anyone throws in the towel. Sometimes I reasoned that I'd misread what had been happening. Had we drifted and lost what we had some time ago? After my mother had arrived I had certainly spent less time alone with Gabby, but surely it was obvious that that was a temporary problem. My mad mother wasn't going to stay forever. And there was bound to be the odd phase where things slid, where one has to put a relationship on the back burner and feel confident that everything was fundamentally strong enough.

Would it have been different if we hadn't been under so much pressure? Would it have been different if we'd jumped off the cliff together that time?

She stayed at a friend's flat and texted me the phone number. I waited a day and rang her.

Her friend picked up the phone.

'Is Gabby there, please?'

She replied, 'Who is it?'

'Sal.'

She said, 'I'll see if she's in.'

See if she's in? She would know whether or not her flatmate is in; she actually meant that she would find out whether Gabrielle would take the call.

'Yep?' said Gabrielle.

What should I say? Launch straight in with an in depth discussion of domestic violence? A few light anecdotes about life at the office? The weather? The state of the roads?

'I was wondering how you were,' I said.

'Fine,' she replied.

Pause.

'Have you signed up for any baby classes?' I asked.

'No, not yet.'

'Oh, well. Early days,' I said.

'Yeah.'

'You didn't love me, did you,' she said.

'What?'

'You didn't once say you loved me,' she said.

'Yes, I did.'

'When? Give me one example. When?'

'I told you I loved you,' I said. I was astonished at this line of attack. It was blatantly obvious I had been infatuated with the woman. But at least by airing a grievance she was engaging with me. To simply remain monosyllabic and sealed up would have been marginally worse. At least I had something to go on.

'I love you,' I said. 'I've always loved you. Always. Almost from the first day. I'm really, really sorry I never made that clear enough.'

'You never told me I was beautiful. Or clever.'

'Clever?'

'You know what I mean,' she said. 'You never told me the hows and the whys; why you loved me. If you did.'

That was totally unfair. I was angry with her for deliberately taking a line she knew wasn't true. It was a sign she would be happy to create false obstacles hereon in. I was angry, but I was determined to be big, and loving and apologetic. Think big, Sal; even though you hate her for this.

'I love you,' I said. 'I love your energy. I love how wonderful you've been to me. I love that you light up a room just by walking into it. I love that you're kind. I love that you're sexy. I love you when you paint the house. I love you when you're pulling pints for the waifs and strays in Bilbao. I love you. I don't care if I have to say that every day of your life, for the rest of your life.'

Silence.

'Are you there?' I said.

'Yeah. I'm looking into the option of going back into the Force.'

Silence.

Never criticise, always support.

'You should do what's best for you, Gabrielle.'

'Well, of course, I should do what's best for me. I've got a bloody baby.'

Another letter came.

It was posted in Spain. The date of the postmark was the last day that Alex was thought to be still in Spain. The last day that Gabrielle was known to be in Spain. Several million other people were also in Spain at that time too, of course, but it nonetheless felt relevant.

The letter had a number six on the envelope. I tapped it against my hand several times. I decided not to read it. I'd had enough. More than enough long since.

I found some matches and I set fire to one corner of it. When I was sure it wouldn't go out I took it for a walk outside to the metal bin.

About ten minutes later I went back out to see if there was anything left of it. I should have read it. There were a few leafs of charcoal. Impossibly fragile. A word or two had survived in molten purple lettering against the grey. I could just make out what looked like 'baby'.

It is difficult to clearly explain why I had burnt it. Perhaps it was to prove to myself that I had nothing to fear from these letters. Perhaps I'd had so much stress that I simply didn't want any more to think about.

Mother improved a lot in that period. She stopped pacing outside my bedroom door, she changed her own hearing aid batteries; she was even genial company.

We would exchange stories about my father.

He was a strange man. He was obsessive about cricket, which was very unusual for a Spaniard. But he couldn't bring himself to fork out for satellite channels so he would spend his afternoons watching the score on Ceefax or Teletext. The big boxy letters would change in their slow rhythm and no one was allowed to talk, although we couldn't understand why not.

'He could be witty,' said Jancie. 'I remember the first day we got a television he stood in front of it and said, "You know, if you shut your eyes it's almost as good as the wireless," he was very quick like that.'

Given that we were both stuck for a couple of months waiting for decisions from the authorities, there was a general air of us getting to know each other. It was not unpleasant.

I tried to pinpoint why my mother irritated me so much. It was something to do with my childhood but, after all these years, it was hard to remember exactly what. Had I felt ignored? Was it that my parents argued too much? I had no idea.

Work was the usual mixture of the bizarre and the banal. People were in shock about Olaia's death but, as an outsider, no one particularly wanted to talk to me about it.

I had the task of clearing out her desk. It was eerie and depressing. I had a bin sack for rubbish and a box for possessions to hand over to her family.

She obviously liked pens. There were about eighty Biros of various shapes and sizes. There were loose keys from long forgotten padlocks. A woman's magazine that was a few months old. It was open at one of those quizzes where you answer lots of questions about yourself and get evaluated at the end.

One of the questions was, 'When making love, how many orgasms do you have on average?' Olaia had ticked the 3 to 5 box. 'Have you ever had anal sex?' She ticked the box that said, 'My boyfriend pesters me for it, and I have to fend him off.'

Should I throw the magazine away or put it in the box? It was personal; a trace of herself left behind. But it was rubbish and not something her family should read.

There was a present wrapped up in green paper with a purple ribbon. It was a box about four inches square and deep. There was no label and could have been a gift to Olaia or a gift she was going to give to someone else. I shook it. I don't know what I was hoping to hear. I put it in the possessions box.

There were two dictionaries for Spanish/Basque and English/Spanish. I wondered which language she felt shaky in. There was no Basque spell check on her computer so it could have been to do with that. Or did she work furiously hard to be good at languages? She had always made it look effortless and natural and yet some of the pages of these dictionaries were almost worn through.

There was not much else of interest and the desk was soon empty. I put the box of her possessions by the door, but when I then worked at my desk I discovered it was in my line of vision, so I moved it to behind her chair.

Runty little Juan Crusie was going to fill in for Olaia for a month or two. The idea was that he would come in most mornings and use Olaia's desk. He started on the second morning after her death.

I was still struggling with the computer program that logged the various room sizes on our site, but now I didn't have Olaia to help me with it.

The third time that I asked Juan to help me, he completely lost his temper, shot across the room and seized the mouse from me while unleashing a stream of Basque that it is reasonable to assume was best left untranslated. I felt like my mother with her hearing aid.

Another thing I did about that time was to set up standing orders with the two banks that claimed I owed them money. Obviously, when I proved it was all a mistake I could have the payments back, so I wasn't too worried. But in the meantime I had the peace of mind that they weren't going to be knocking on the door and taking our stuff away while my addled mother tried to assault them.

Not that we had that much stuff left. We had gone out and chosen a new TV and video. Mother and son in an electronics shop, fussing about our wide-screen options.

I also made sure to ring Gabrielle regularly. She never rang me, but then she had a new life to sort out and no doubt had her hands full. I was determined to keep up the effort regardless of the response I received. After all, I had a baby to think about. I think also at that time I had a general feeling that my problems were beginning to go away. The police hadn't contacted me about Olaia for a long time, although they did still have my passport, which was a pest.

All in all, then, the chronic sense of 'another day, another life threatening disaster' that had blighted the summer, had ebbed away. Life was stabilising. Above all, there were no more letters. It had got as far letter six and stopped. And, yes, I did now check my mail.

My phone calls with Gabby didn't get any easier. She was unwilling or unable to come up with the little stories from her daily life that would have given us conversation and something for me to ask about in subsequent calls, and she obviously wasn't up for the lovers' staples of discussing sex or reminiscing about past escapades.

She did at one stage divulge that she was applying for a clerical job with SO19, the firearms squad, with whom she had some connections. But having mentioned it once she was cagey thereafter and I was left to wonder whether this was because she had not been successful.

'Have you got a reliable due date yet?' I asked.

'November 5th,' she replied. A whole two months earlier than I'd been led to believe.

'We could call him Guy if it's a boy and Catherine if it's a girl,' I said. 'What have they based the date on?'

'The scan. They measure the circumference of the baby's head and the length of the femur. It is the single most accurate predictor apparently.'

'So why is it earlier than we thought?' I allowed myself that much.

'I think it's just a statistical thing,' she replied. 'It could be born at eight months but the scan has predicted that it's likely to be a month early, if you follow that.'

I didn't. Largely because it didn't make sense.

.

Chapter Twenty-eight

It transpired that in the course of later police investigations, Alex Lawrence made a number of statements to the police.

The first is relevant here even though it wasn't written until some months after.

The following is the first statement made by Mr Alexander Lawrence of 49 Harringdon Road, London E8, UK, taken in the presence of DI A S Hopswain and DC N E Liddle and on behalf of the Cuerpo Superior of Bilbao, Spain.

Gabrielle Gongola, known to me as Gina Gabrielle Tremain, came to visit me, Alex Lawrence, in September of last year at my London flat.

She seemed agitated and informed me that she wanted to tell me about recent events in her life, the reason being, in her words, 'in case anything happened' to her.

She had recently married a Salvador Gongola and moved with him to Northern Spain. She said that his behaviour had become increasingly erratic and that he had recently hit her, thus her reason for coming back to England. At that time, however, she was hoping for a reconciliation with him. She told me of one specific incident where she had been assaulted by her husband but it was my impression that she had had other, previous, problems, and that she was loathe to share them with me either out of loyalty to her husband or out of pride; not wanting me, a previous partner of hers, to know the worst.

She then asked whether it would be possible to have a reconciliation with me. I felt that this was not possible and when I explained this she became hysterical.

Although she and I were estranged from a seven year relationship, she was carrying my baby and this gave me a direct interest in her welfare, along with my natural concern for her. I am also aware from my police work that women frequently leave it too late before reporting incidents of domestic violence. I felt, therefore, that I should assume there had been more incidents than she had divulged.

I was surprised that she chose to visit me in London because I had, on a prior occasion, visited her in Spain and she had stated that she did not wish to see me further. She had previously contacted me about the baby and I had an opportunity to visit Bilbao in June of last year. I visited her at her house and she was decorating. She seemed distraught at that time and accused me of stealing her mail that day and of writing letters to them. I did not see the letters in question but she described them to me. The letters were threatening letters to her husband that looked as if they had been sent by herself, Gina Tremain. She denied this was the case. In some way she thought these letters had been written by me in an attempt to make her husband think she was mad. I found the whole story confusing and told her so. I mention this in my statement because she stated that she was going to make similar claims to the local police, and also to explain why I was wary of direct involvement with her, but nonetheless went on to help indirectly. I had felt that she was behaving erratically, that I didn't know what she might accuse me of next, but I wanted to help her in some way, which preferably didn't involve direct contact.

I contacted the police authorities in Bilbao to say that she felt threatened. I was led to understand subsequently that her husband Salvador had been arrested on a separate charge where a police officer was assaulted at his home residence. When, at a later date, Gina Tremain was subsequently held hostage it was then easier for the police to take the issue seriously and take relevant action. I feel this vindicated my previous discussions with the police, which are on file.

Chapter Twenty-nine

I had a visit at work from one of the many police departments.

I furiously tried to remember what I'd previously said about the morning I found Olaia's body.

The policeman was young, and seemed friendly enough. He took out a notebook and some documentation.

'We wondered if you have a policy on people being arrested on this site,' he began.

'Excuse me?' I said.

'Do you prefer that people are asked to leave the site before we arrest them?'

There were so many branches of the police that I wondered exactly which branch I was dealing with here. The Policia Con Buenos Modales – the Police With Manners?

'We want to question and detain a number of your workers,' he said.

'On what charge?'

'Carrying unlicensed weapons,' said the Inspector.

I almost said 'Be my guest' but then self interest intervened and I was concerned about how I could replace them.

'Can you at least wait until the end of their shift?' I said.

'That depends when their shift ends,' he said genially.

'Can you tell me more details about the crime, please?' I asked.

'It appears that some of your staff have been stocking your artificial lakes with fish.'

'Fish?'

'Carp and the like,' he said.

This was complete news to me, but hardly a crime.

'Okay,' I said. 'And?'

'And at various times of the year birds of prey or sea birds come past this region and try to eat the fish. You will have to excuse me but I don't know anything about fish, or indeed about birds of prey,' he said.

'Okay,' I said again.

'So your staff have taken to shooting the birds from the windows of the second floor.'

I almost blurted out, 'So that's what the buggers have been doing!' Instead I said, 'Well clearly this is a serious matter. You have my full support. How did you know they were doing this?'

He shrugged, 'Bizkaia is a small place.'

He might have been tipped off by the same person, presumably an employee, who had been sending me the leaflets about birds. That was one mystery solved at least.

I was doubly pleased with this development because it gave me something to talk about in my weekly call to Gabrielle. There had been a marked lack of arrests, murders and threatening letters of late so my conversation had been getting a decidedly dull. Gabrielle and I had gone from being exciting lovers to a weekly chore.

By chance, that week she had plenty she wanted to talk to me about too.

'I went to see Alex,' she said.

'Oh,' I replied. 'And how was he?'

'Fine,' she said, as though I'd asked a reasonable question. 'I wanted to see him.'

'Okay.'

169

'Because I feel that I have been the cause of so much upset, so much trouble. I wanted to put a stop to it.'

'I wouldn't say you've been the cause of all the trouble,' I said. I was lying.

'You and I could have got on very well. We *did* get on very well. But relationships are hard enough without someone from my past popping up to drive us crazy.'

'So what did you say to him?' I said.

'I told him to leave us alone. I think he has been sending those letters to us.'

'Well, obviously, that has always been a possibility,' I said.

'If he has been hoping to make me look mad, insane with jealousy, I think he might have murdered Olaia.'

'Why?' I asked.

'He was trying to show that I was jealous that you got on with her and that I murdered her.'

I was doubtful about this.

'The police think it's something to do with ETA,' I said.

'Well, anyway,' she said. 'I went to see him. I said to him that he was ruining my life and asked him to walk away.'

'Was that wise?' I asked.

'I have absolutely no idea, Sal. What else could I do? I feel I have brought all this on us. But by going to him it made him feel he was having an effect. It allowed him to feel power. It could have been a very silly idea. Perhaps I should have just pretended that everything that had ever happened has had no effect whatever. How long would he have kept going then?'

'Until he'd killed one of us?' I hazarded.

'He wouldn't kill,' she said.

'You just said he might have killed Olaia. It was a sickeningly grisly murder, Gabrielle.'

'Yeah,' she said. 'Look, I think one element to all of this is that I've felt guilty about what's been happening. I think that is one reason why I ran away. I think perhaps when I have this baby, I'll then come back and we'll start again. Is that okay? A fresh start.'

'Of course it's okay. It's great news. I'll try and get rid of my mother by then.'

'Have you got your passport back yet?' she asked.

'No, why?'

'I was hoping you'd be able to come over for the birth,' she said.

'I'll see if I can retrieve it,' I said.

Chapter Thirty

By an irritating coincidence, my mother and I were summoned to the prosecutor's office on the very day that Gabrielle gave birth.

'You will be happy to know that we have finalised a solution to your problem,' he said. It was the man who had summoned us before. This time he had no armed guards to flank him. It said something that I had seen so much of these officials that I now knew most of their names. There had even been the odd instance of one or two of them saying hello when passing me in the street.

'We have agreed that we will press charges,' he said.

That didn't sound like good news.

'But,' he said, 'we have then agreed clemency. So I am today confirming that we will do this, on account of your age. You will need to attend the trial and you will need to plead guilty, but I give you my personal guarantee that this is the end of it.'

'As simple as that?' I said.

'As simple as that,' he said.

He then handed me my passport. I couldn't help feeling that they'd got themselves confused. My passport had been taken away because I was a suspect in Olaia's murder but they must have felt it was to do with the assault case. I didn't question it.

'We will keep your mother's passport until the court hearing,' he said.

My mother and I went to a bar to celebrate.

A promise of freedom and the news that she was a grandmother!

We had no idea to what degree we were going to be allowed to interact with the baby. Gabrielle had so effectively walled me out of the whole process. I didn't even know how she was supporting herself. But we would celebrate nonetheless.

I spent several hours getting completely rat-arsed with my own mother. It was a joy.

When we got back home, however, I knew I needed to face up to her.

'We need to talk,' I said.

She was standing in the hallway at the time. She seemed smaller than I remembered. A little old lady.

'I think we have to admit that, on the whole, we drive each other mad,' I said.

'No, we don't,' she replied.

'No. We have some great times, but we can't possibly drive each other mad for ever. It will taint what we have.'

'You don't drive me mad,' she said. 'I mean, what things are we talking about?'

'Things like your hearing aid,' I said.

The hearing aid? It was a pathetically slight example of what wound me up.

'We can sort out the hearing aid,' she said.

'Well, it's not just the hearing aid.' I couldn't stand there and list every last thing that was irritating about her. It would have been unreasonable and unpleasant. But I couldn't not have a reason for wanting her to move out.

'We've got a new baby coming into the house,' I said. 'It will be a trying time, and I feel I need my life to be a little more simple.'

'What can I do? I can help,' she said.

Yeah. By leaving.

'No,' I said, 'I can arrange a small flat for you nearby. We can sell up your place in England, if you ever get your passport back. You are welcome to live nearby.'

She had long since resigned herself to never being liked by her own son. I could see that and felt sorry for her. But I felt this was my big last chance with Gabrielle. We were a little wiser; we knew the pitfalls, the stakes and the joys. I didn't want to feel I hadn't tried everything.

The next day I went to an estate agent and did two things. I put my broken down *baserri* on the market, and asked how much it would cost to rent a cheap place for my mother.

I took a plane to England to go and see Gabrielle and the baby. She was staying with a friend called Ellen, whom I had never met, at an address in Stevenage.

I used my mother's place as a base and took the train up from London, then walked from the station. It was a mile or more, and had got dark by the time I found the house. There were no lights on at the windows, and no answer when I knocked on the door. I couldn't hang around outside; I would look like a stalker. How does the joke go? Women can be groupies but men are always stalkers. A man can't just hang around outside a house.

I walked back to the main road where I'd seen a pub, and had a pint. I thought I'd do the crossword but I didn't have a pen so I sat, feeling self-conscious and alone, pretending to study the crossword clues.

I had a second pint then walked back to Ellen's. The lights were on this time. I knocked on the door.

A woman answered; I recognised her from Gabby's photos. 'Ellen?'

'Oh, hi,' she said, 'It's you.'

Perhaps she had likewise seen a photograph of me.

'Is Gabrielle in?' I asked.

'What did you want her for exactly?'

'I want to say hi.' I was perplexed. 'I want to see the baby. I've come all the way from Spain.'

It was a thoroughly weird conversation.

'Yes, of course,' she said and made way for me.

Gabrielle was sitting in the lounge. She stood up when I walked in the room.

'Sal,' she said.

I kissed her cheek.

'Shall I make some tea?' said Ellen.

'So how's it going?' asked Gabrielle.

'Where's the baby, then?' I said.

'Upstairs. She's asleep.'

Ellen had come back in the room.

Gabrielle threw an arm up over her own head and took a step back so that she was behind her friend.

'I am coming back to Spain, you know,' she said.

'Yes,' I said.

The atmosphere was indescribably odd.

I leant forward by the merest fraction.

Gabrielle flinched.

Ellen said, 'You'd better go.'

'I've come to see my baby,' I said. 'I've come to see Gabrielle.'

I had absolutely no explanation for their behaviour. Perhaps Gabrielle had just got over-flustered about seeing me after such a long break. She was known to get herself worked up. Possibly her friend had fed off that nervousness and thought I must be some sort of threat.

I did get to see our baby, though. She was beautiful; impossibly tiny and content. She kept unleashing a broad toothless smile. She was dwarfed by her cot. She was called Amy.

Gabrielle was completely besotted. She held Amy and rocked her and looked as though she would never ever let her go. She had been through a birth that I'd heard little about;

she must be going through the chronic tiredness of a new mum, but there was no sign of it. There was also no sign that I was going to be fed. I had last eaten an alleged sandwich at King's Cross so I suggested we went out for a meal.

Big mistake.

'We can't possibly go out, you idiot,' spat Gabrielle.

'I meant a takeaway,' I said.

'You have no idea what it is like having a baby. Life is completely different now.'

She was simply pulling rank.

She agreed to a takeaway, but even that was a struggle.

The three of us ended up eating a Chinese on the floor of Ellen's lounge in front of the TV.

The other mistake I made that night was to raise the subject of the bank loans. I was largely making conversation.

'I still haven't been to that second bank,' I said.

'Why am I not surprised?' said Gabrielle.

'I wondered if you had any photos of Alex I could borrow?' I said.

'Why?'

'Well there is a chance that the bank will have met the person face to face,' I said.

'What person?' she asked.

'The person who took out the loan. They might be able to identify the person as Alex from a photo.'

'You're so stupid,' she said.

'Why?'

'Because I had my photographs stolen,' she said.

'You had every single picture of Alex stolen?' I found that very hard to swallow.

'I didn't have that many in the first place.'

I looked at Ellen. She was apparently engrossed in *Blind Date* but her ears were definitely wagging. I was hoping she'd volunteer that she had a few photos somewhere. I stopped short of actually asking her though. In fact, I stopped short of raising anything difficult after that.

When I was in England I also went to visit Alex Lawrence. It wasn't hard to find him; I remembered half of his address, and the other half was in the phone book. It wasn't hard to make an excuse to Gabrielle; I simply said I was going to visit a few people while I was in England. She was glad to get rid of me.

When Alex saw me he went a shade of grey that made me wonder if his heart had stopped.

I deliberately hadn't rung him first. I had half an idea that I could walk into his flat and find all sorts of stalker memorabilia; perhaps a spare room with its walls covered in photos of victims, newspaper cuttings of his exploits, and a daily diary open at the day when he first decided to go on a killing spree.

'It's you,' he said.

'Can we talk?' I asked.

He reluctantly moved to one side.

He had a tasteful place; the ground floor of a Victorian terraced house. I caught a glimpse of the front room. A Picasso print, but not one of his more difficult pieces; a number of books; a wide-screen TV that looked overly large for a small room. The flat in general was very clean and tidy but not obsessively so.

'Can I offer you a drink?' he said. He was directing me down the corridor to the kitchen. 'A beer?'

'Yeah,' I said. 'Thank you.'

'What can I do for you?' he asked.

'I want to hear all about your time with Gabrielle. Or Gina as you call her.'

'In what way?'

'I want to know who was violent,' I said. It was an ungainly sentence. 'I want to hear your view of her mental state and your view of your own mental state.'

'Gosh,' he said.

'Let me first say that I know for a fact you were not married,' I said.

I took a chance saying that. I had no proof either way.

'Yeah,' he said. 'We weren't married. One problem is that we were both a bit deranged. When Gina left me, I became a little insane. I see that now. It means that I don't have too much credibility. I see that too.'

Alex was careful with his words. Every so often he was stopping, as if to check whether he agreed with the words he heard himself saying.

He talked about their life together. There was no mention of money or car parts on the sitting room floor; it was a bittersweet collection of memories. Holidays spent together, dreams they'd had; first dates and last straws.

I wasn't entirely sure how much I could get from all of this. He was a self-confessed liar and therefore it was hard to know what to believe. Certainly I felt I was being confronted with yet another Alex. Not the steely Alex I'd last met who had detailed Gabby's alleged sins; not the stalker or the man who'd run away; not the hesitant man on my doorstep all those months ago, but a man who was maturely considering the past and what to make of it. He brought that side out in me too.

I caught myself saying, 'So, all in all, what do you make of her?'

'I think she's ill,' he said. 'Borderline personality disorder, or a bipolar who hides it well. I don't know. She'd fly into these amazing rages that would come out of nowhere, or she would spend two solid weeks shopping, or we'd have to ditch everything and go on holiday that very instant. Was that someone who's tremendous fun or dysfunctional? The whole point about the borderline personality is that, in many ways, they are well adjusted; they seem almost normal.'

'Have you any specific proof that she was violent?' I asked.

'I think she could kill someone. I genuinely think that.'

'Then why did you want her back?' I asked.

'I was in love. It doesn't happen a lot. I became a total wreck when she left. I would have cheerfully lied and cheated and scammed to get her back. But I'm getting on with my life. I've moved on psychologically,' he said. 'I feel that, at long last, I am myself again.'

'You mentioned a previous person who you claim she bled dry,' I said. 'Did you make that up?'

'No, I didn't make that up. But when I came across his story, that was when the scales fell from my eyes and I saw her more for what she is. I see that as the beginning of my recovery.'

I said, 'The trouble is, you cheerfully throw out generalities like "she could kill" but you're not offering proof; nothing a neutral observer would swallow.'

He gave me a pitying look.

'With one previous boyfriend, she pretended she had cancer and needed chemotherapy,' he said. 'She kept hair in an envelope and would show it to people saying it had fallen out of her head. She's a horror. She preys on weak people; it's like she can smell them. I know you wouldn't think it to look at her. I think it's some sort of attention seeking disorder. I mean, hell, you would have to be really sick and really want to seek attention to pull a stunt like that.'

'That's the umpteenth disorder you've cited,' I said.

'I'm not a psychiatrist, I have no idea,' he said. 'I did a lot of reading at one stage, and found one disorder that fits the bill. It's an identity problem. It's people who feel insecure with their own identity, so they endlessly try to assume roles. They throw themselves into their career, or being a mother or whatever; they buy all the kit and become obsessive about doing it right. It was the disorder Zelig was based on, but in real life they get unaccountable rages, they often drink heavily or take drugs...'

My instinct was that he was just making up some syndrome to fit the facts. I changed tack.

'You see yourself as a weak person?' I said.

'I was hopelessly infatuated with her. It made me very weak.'

'When you say Gabrielle did this chemo thing,' I asked, 'was that with the Bill person you mentioned?'

'No, that was someone else.'

Alex stood and left the room purposefully. It was a curiously exciting moment.

He returned with what looked like a ledger but in fact turned out to be one of those files with plastic sleeves inside.

The stalker's diary.

Or a rather sane meticulous set of typed notes.

He skimmed through various sections. As well as the typed pages, there were handwritten notes and some photographs.

'Why do you take people's photographs?' I asked.

'In case they go missing,' he said.

'If you don't mind me saying so, that is really weird.' But the sheer fact that I was happy saying that to him showed I was quietly convinced he was rational, not someone who was just about to attack me, boil up my carcass and dispose of me down the drains.

'Yeah, it's weird,' he agreed. 'So people drive you mad. I think we can all agree on that. Here we go. I'll jot down his name and number for you. For your own sake, ring him.'

'No, don't do that,' I said.

'You should talk to him. I'll jot down his number.'

'Don't,' I persisted.

He had a pad and pen ready, but caught my look. He evidently wanted to keep me on side so put them down.

'I have another question,' I said.

'Shoot,' he replied.

'What do you do for a living?' I asked.

'I'm a civil engineer,' he said.

I considered this for a while.

'Have you been off work recently?'

'Yes,' he replied. 'As I said, I really haven't been well.'

'If you were in the police, isn't there some law that if I ask you whether you are a policeman, you have to admit to it?'

'Ask Gabrielle,' he laughed. 'She's the one with the code book and the pixilated number plates.'

'But I'm asking you,' I said. 'Are you in the police? Directly or indirectly?'

'No,' he said.

For some reason that I can't now remember, Alex left the room. I wondered whether he deliberately left me alone with the file.

I got the pad and pen and jotted down the name, address and phone number of the man who Alex claimed I should contact. I ripped the paper off the pad and hastily stuck it in my back pocket.

Why would an innocent man keep a file like this? From what I could see it was largely trivial details; people's jobs, where they lived when they dated Gabby, where they lived now. But he had evidently talked to them all because he had quotes and transcriptions of conversations.

I leafed through a little way, listening out for creaks in the hallway. One person was talking about a baby and how they had had to call an ambulance a few times. The suspicion was that Gabrielle was smothering the child when left alone, then raising the alarm when it passed out. Did Gabrielle have a previous baby? The file wasn't clear, or rather I had at most a minute to gaze at it.

Alex came back into the room. The file was back on his side of the table.

I was puzzled why Alex hadn't mentioned the suspected baby smothering. Perhaps there was no proof. Possibly he was only offering me ideas he could substantiate. If that was true then I was admitting to myself that the hair in an envelope incident could indeed be proven.

I mentally shook myself. The book, the barrage of concepts from borderline personality disorder to baby smothering; these could easily be the workings of Alex's deranged mind.

He could have gone mad with jealousy and his loss of Gabby and come to hate her, come to have insane fantasies about her. What was the statistic? The majority of murders in Britain involved a woman who had been killed by a man she'd jilted. And they say men don't fall in love.

He started talking to me again about their past. He was very sunny. He told me about a dog they once had whose party trick in the pub was to open up packets of crisps and eat them. He told me about how a visit to the Dordogne where they'd gone deep underground to some lakes and rivers. Gabrielle had refused to wear a cagoule Alex had offered. 'They're just so menial,' she'd said. When they got down there she discovered it rained incessantly as water ran through the layers of the earth. She got drenched.

'Ooh, she was raw,' chuckled Alex.

I could recognise Gabrielle in all of his stories. He would certainly know her well enough to be able to guess what sort of problems I would encounter when living with her. If he had written the letters, he would probably be able to make them resonate. He would certainly have a shrewd idea about the problems I was likely to face with her.

Alex was in his stride now and opened a couple more beers. He treated us like friends, drawn together by the common bond of having been victims of this woman.

'I found I had to make it so that she always felt things were her ideas,' said Alex.

'Like what?' I asked.

'Well, we were staying on a Greek island and I walked her forwards and backwards in front of shop where they hired out Vespas. Eventually she suggested we hired them to buzz around the mountains and down to the beaches and stuff. If I had suggested it, she'd have said it was a bad idea.'

'So she hired Vespas?' I asked.

He nodded. He was obviously in love with her still.

'Tell me,' I said. 'I was once walking along a cliff edge with Gabrielle and she simply jumped in the water. We were a hell of a way up.'

'Okay,' he replied.

'What should I have done?'

'What?' he asked.

'I felt a kind of dull loser for not jumping just like she did,' I said. 'I would love to be the sort of carefree person who just threw caution to the wind and dived right on in with her, but I'm not.'

Alex could barely conceal his pleasure.

'You are asking me for relationship advice with Gabrielle?' he said.

'I suppose,' I said.

'Be solid. She is unhinged, but very likeable. She is looking for a rock. Try not to be too dull or predictable. But you don't have to jump in the water.'

I had been intrigued at my own motives for visiting Alex and my ambivalence towards him. In many ways I shouldn't have gone to see him, I should have ignored him. I feared that I had been sucker punched into believing ill of her. She was a Godsend to my life, and the nature of relationships is such that there will always be misunderstandings, mismatches, petty jealousies, grievances, disappointments and freaky ex-lovers. It's no good listening to the voices as well.

I think deep down I didn't believe Alex. His accusations about Gabrielle were too random. Okay, I think I seventy per cent didn't believe him, let's put it that way. I evidently thought he might have some insight into how to deal with her day to day. I think I also felt at that time that he was a spent force. That he was going to stay in England and not cause us any more trouble.

As I was leaving I pulled out my main reason for visiting. A camera. I took two photos of him. He was incredulous.

I fled before he could complain.

Chapter Thirty-one

Gabrielle came back to Bilbao with me. She, too, had a character transformation. She was relaxed, sunny and chatty. There was a definite sense we were into a new, positive era.

She started wearing mummsy clothes, which was disconcerting. Especially the pastel dungarees. They were undoubtedly a crime against fashion but not in themselves enough to get her committed.

We redecorated the spare room together to make it into a child's room. We'd found some fun wallpaper of various animals trying out for all the wrong jobs; an elephant ballet dancer, a giraffe in a submarine with its head up the periscope, a kangaroo as a coal miner which kept bumping its head on the roof of the tunnels.

Amy herself was a dream. She was very healthy looking, which is another way of saying she was fat. But we were assured there was every chance that the number of folds in her neck would drop into single figures when she grew. We had to get cotton wool every night and dunk it in warm water; lift each fold in turn and clear out the bits of crud, food and small toys that claimed to be a choking hazard. We then had to dry the folds with talcum and repeat the process where her legs met her arse, and so on.

She was very communicative for a newborn. To show pleasure she employed a broad toothless grin. To show displeasure she swiped me once, hard, with her hand. And to say, 'You're ignoring me. I've put everything I have into this relationship and you barely even acknowledge that I'm in the room anymore' she'd throw her bottle at me. She was a girl, after all.

She had slightly bent feet, which looked dramatic but again we were reassured it wasn't a problem. Her position in the womb had evidently tucked her feet inwards, so six times a day we had to gently mould her feet with our hands, coaxing them outwards. The improvement was steady and reassuring.

Well, I say 'we' did it but, in fact, Gabby was possessive about Amy. When I tried to do stuff she got literally fidgety. She sort of hovered over me and her hands kept coming out to take over, then retreated again. But, undoubtedly, Gabrielle was trying very hard. She was all smiles, all day. In fact, that's what I remember most about that period: Gabrielle smiling the broadest of grins. It was a new beginning.

Gabby literally sang as she walked around the house. We drank together, we danced on the wooden floors. We leant side by side on the balcony as the sun set, swapping tales from our day.

With motherhood, there was no sign of diminished irresponsibility.

'I know it's not PC,' she said, 'but I was determined to bottle feed. I really missed alcohol. I mean, I want to be able to have a good drink. I can see I had a bit of a drink problem…'

'I have never ever thought you had a drink problem,' I said, truthfully. It was obviously something she was self-conscious about, though.

'I thought I'd have a few rules, that's all,' she said. 'Not have my first drink before I'm awake in the mornings. If we're going out for a few drinks then line my stomach first, with a few gin and tonics. That sort of thing.'

It was a new Gabrielle. As witty and energetic as when I met her, but now also more reflective about life; I fell in love all over again.

She still had her odd moments.

We were both on the balcony one evening and she was rocking Amy in her arms.

She said, apropos nothing whatever, 'It's barely worth bringing them up is it?'

'What?'

'Well, life's so bloody hard isn't it?' she said. 'Relationships, careers, finances, learning to be happy. I mean, we've brought a child into the world just so that it can go through all that.'

'Might as well just smother the poor mite while the going's good,' I said. I was joking.

'Exactly,' she said grimly.

The thing is, that this is the sort of frivolous conversation almost anyone can have. But after what we'd been through, I was sensitised to every last bit of evidence that she was barking mad.

But, broadly speaking, there was nothing odd about Gabrielle at that time.

Even my mother was well behaved. The three of us agreed on a plan for her to return to Britain and ultimately sell her house and move to near us.

As a prelude to that, we looked at various flats. They were demonstrably cheaper than the one that Jancie would sell, and that in itself was an incentive for her to do it.

After four weeks Jancie set off back to England, or to be precise, Gabrielle gave her a lift to the airport while I was at work.

I'd say we had a total of six good weeks.

One night we were congratulating ourselves on Amy's sleeping pattern. She would have her last feed at 9.00 p.m. and then that really was it until nearly 6.00 in the morning. We could put her in her cot and our life was our own.

We knew we were very, very lucky. We had heard plenty of tales of four year olds who hadn't slept for four years and we fully accepted that in the future there may be six month colic and the terrible twos, but in the short term we were pitifully grateful. It was going well.

I can remember that we mentioned all of this that night.

And I remember going to bed.

It was quiet that night. No mopeds or skateboarders, no mice in the attic.

There might have been some slamming of car doors and the like as the local populace went home for their well deserved two hour sleep, because I can remember vaguely waking up and Gabrielle returning to bed having had a pee, or similar.

But when you have a young child you always sleep solidly unless the child herself wakes you, because you're constantly exhausted. Insomnia is an impossible luxury for the young parent.

The first thing I remember in the morning was Gabrielle popping her head round our bedroom door. I had been asleep.

'Where's Amy?' she asked. She smiled as she said it.

'No idea,' I said. 'Not in her cot?'

I turned over in bed. It was too light in the room.

Gabrielle disappeared, then reappeared within a moment.

'I can't find Amy,' she said.

I leapt out of bed and ran to the nursery. I don't know what I was expecting to see. The cot was empty.

Chapter Thirty-two

Gabrielle, who was previously animated, became still. I looked around the room to see if anything else was missing. A blanket, perhaps. I couldn't be sure.

'Her carry cot. Moses basket thing,' I said. 'Shouldn't that be in here?'

'I think so,' she replied. 'I'm not sure. We might have left it downstairs.'

'We'll search the house,' I said.

We knew the child couldn't walk or crawl, we knew we hadn't moved her, but nonetheless we searched the house.

I tried to recall the previous night.

We had eaten. What about Amy? Had we left her in the car? Had we come back from somewhere and forgotten her? I instantly discounted all of those. Gabrielle had put her to bed. We had been chatting in the kitchen and Gabrielle had been holding Amy.

She said, 'I'm tired, I hope Amy's tired too, because I'm putting her down.'

'Not in the veterinary sense I presume,' I joked. I don't remember saying goodnight to Amy. I might have kissed her before they left the room. I'm sure I would have done that, but I don't recall.

I had checked every room upstairs, I had even checked under the beds. It occurred to me that one of us could perhaps sleep walk. Perhaps the baby cried in the night and one of us got up and then didn't remember it. She might be on the sofa downstairs or in any number of places.

I had now checked the lounge and the kitchen.

Nothing.

Gabrielle was pacing up and down.

'We should phone,' she said.

'What?'

'We're wasting time. We need to phone the police.'

I had this ridiculous notion that we would somehow be disturbing the police and it wasn't our place to do so.

'I'll look in the car,' I said.

'I'll ring the police, then,' she said. 'But my Spanish isn't that good.'

'Yeah. You're right. I'll do it,' I said. 'Who shall I ring?'

'Oh, for God's sake!' she screamed.

'I'm serious,' I protested. 'There's the local police which is 092, there's the national police which is 091, there's the civil guard which is for rural areas and I think we're in a rural area, they're 062.'

'Shut up, shut up, shut up, you arsehole,' she shouted. 'You are such an arsehole! Give me the fucking phone! What number did you say first?'

'Er, let's go with Civil Guard. I don't think they know us. 062.'

'062 then. You are such a prat, you know that don't you?'

She handed back the phone.

'Okay, so I don't actually speak good enough Spanish,' she said.

Within minutes the lights of a police car were flashing through our front windows.

The two men who arrived were very much on the ball. I had indeed rung the wrong number but nonetheless the correct squad was on the job instantly. One of them was a dead ringer for Charles Aznavour which was disconcerting; but they both had walkie-talkies that crackled incessantly, and

I found that reassuring out of all proportion. These men were going to get things done.

'Let me first reassure you that we are very used to dealing with kidnapping,' said the Aznavour look alike. 'We have approximately one every two weeks. We usually get the child back. ETA do not want to turn public opinion against themselves.'

'So you think this is ETA?' said Gabrielle.

ETA hadn't occurred to either of us.

'Have you had a ransom demand yet?' asked the policeman.

'No,' I said.

I sat down. Yet more nightmare.

'Can I look around?' he asked.

'If you can find the baby somewhere in the house I will personally kiss you,' I said.

He laughed.

'No,' he said, 'I am looking for how they got in. Did you lock the doors last night?'

'Yes, of course.' Even as I said it, I realised I couldn't remember what we'd done or not done.

'Were there any broken windows?' he asked.

'No. I don't think so,' said Gabrielle. She was pacing around clenching her jaw; the muscles formed pulsing bars in her cheeks. She was chewing the skin on the sides of her fingernails.

'Oh God, this is just so awful,' she kept saying.

The policeman was making an attempt to rally our concentration. He was saying something but I was having trouble hearing.

'It's very important that you recall,' he was saying.

'Recall what?'

'This morning, was the front door unlocked? Or the back door?'

I tried to recapture my memories. When would I have looked at the door or tried it? I phoned the police from within the house. I had talked about looking in the car for the baby, but I hadn't actually gone out and done it. In fact, thinking about it, we hadn't even looked at the front door until the police had arrived. Gabrielle had let the police in. I had been in the kitchen.

'Gabrielle?' I called. She was in a total daze. 'Gabrielle?'

'Yes?'

'When you opened the door for the police, was it bolted from the inside?'

She looked at me as though I were speaking some other language.

'The front door?' she said. 'Yes.'

'So you had to unbolt it to let the police in?' I asked.

'Yes.'

I stood up and walked to the back door.

The backdoor was a stable door in style. It had a separate top and bottom that could be bolted together to turn it into one unit. The bolt was secure to make that the case, but the door as a whole was simply shut on a Yale lock. It could be pulled shut behind someone who was leaving. It certainly hadn't been deadlocked or bolted.

So someone could have left by the back door and it would have looked exactly like that, but they would have needed a key if they'd come *in* that way.

I ran back into the front room.

'Should we dust for fingerprints before I touch the back door?' I asked.

I didn't wait for an answer, I went out the front door and round to the back garden.

The sun was up fully now.

There was nothing to see. Just another beautiful day.

Chapter Thirty-three

The police called in a large number of their colleagues. They were all over the house like ants at a picnic, but they should have been out looking for the baby.

I jumped into my car and drove off round the neighbourhood. I had no idea what I thought I was going to find.

I was looking for abandoned cars, or cars that looked parked in a hurry. I was looking for bits of dropped baby clothing or recent footprints; perhaps a dropped dummy. Amy's dummy was still in the cot but I imagined that the kidnappers might have planned the operation and decided to bring one along. Stupid thoughts, but that was what I was thinking. Would the kidnappers have nappies? I imagined some burly Hispanic changing the baby's nappy. Surely there was a chance the baby would have cried when woken up by them? Did I hear anything in the night that I hadn't remembered yet? I might have been woken by a baby crying and then when I was properly awake it might have gone quiet again when Amy was off the premises. It didn't ring any bells though.

I drove down to the town and along to the river. I parked my car with two wheels on the pavement and ran out to look at the cars waiting for the transporter bridge. I had had a character transformation. No longer the meek Sal. I was pressing my face against car windows to see if there was any chance of a baby being stowed away. I was insisting they wound down their windows. I was getting people to open the boots of their cars.

I went to talk to the woman who takes the money.

'Have you seen some people come through here in a car, with a baby?' I asked. 'It is desperately important.'

People took me surprisingly seriously. Perhaps it was obvious from my face that something truly awful had occurred.

It was hopeless of course.

The kidnappers would have gone by motorway and not used the transporter bridge at all. They would have got away hours ago.

I drove back to the house.

I stood in the front room asking the policeman a hundred questions and not waiting for the answers. Not hearing the answers. When does a ransom note usually arrive? How much would it be? How do we raise the money? Is it normal for a baby to be kidnapped rather than an adult? Do they murder the child even if the ransom is paid? Surely there is no point. The baby can't remember anything; she couldn't identify the kidnappers. Do they cut off an ear or a finger and send it in?

I caught sight of myself in a mirror. I had on an unbuttoned shirt and a pair of dirty jeans. A pair of black leather shoes which would normally go with my suit. Bare ankles where there were no socks. Matted hair and stubble. I imagined how I must have looked down by the quay.

Gabrielle came down the stairs.

'I've found a letter,' she said.

She was improbably neutral. In shock perhaps. She walked towards me holding it. I didn't take it.

Letter number seven. Addressed to me. Printed on a word processor like the others.

'Do we dust it for fingerprints?' I asked.

No answer from any of the policemen.

'Do we dust it for fingerprints?' I asked again.

Why were none of these people responding?

I screamed at the top of my voice, 'Do we dust it for fingerprints?'

Then I realised the problem. Gabby had been speaking to me in English and I had replied in English. I had been shouting in English. When I was down at the transporter bridge, had I been shouting in English then? The mad Englishman in the black shoes shouting at the traffic.

'Do we dust it for fingerprints?' I asked, in Spanish now.

'Hold it by the edges and open it with a knife,' he said.

I ran off to the kitchen and struggled to find a knife slim enough to work into the edge of the envelope.

It said,

Dear Sal

The next letter will be the last letter you receive from me or probably from anyone. I told you that what you will be given will be taken away. Under no circumstances ring the police. Wait for further instructions.

I held the letter and the policeman asked what it said. I translated.

'What does it mean, number seven?' he asked.

I explained.

'Where did you find this letter?'

'To one side of Amy's chest of drawers,' said Gabrielle. 'I think perhaps it might have been on top and blown off or something.'

We all trooped upstairs and looked at where it was found. Heaven knows why.

'And it was just to the left of the drawers?' said the policeman.

'Yes,' said Gabrielle.

'Why didn't we see it earlier?' I asked.

'I don't know,' she replied. 'It was sort of round the corner. It's not well lit there, and it was flat with the floor.'

It seemed so unlikely.

'And you say there were other letters,' asked the policeman. 'Were all the letters in English?'

'Yeah.'

'We'd better start with those.'

'Do you reckon the ink can be analysed?' I asked.

'Possibly,' said the policeman. 'But it would only be useful if we had someone in mind and we could analyse the ink in their computer printer and the printers they have access to. Even then, we have internet cafés and the like so it would be possible to write these letters and print them off somewhere quite neutral.'

'You'll need photos of the baby,' I said.

'We've got them,' he replied.

'We did all that when you were out,' said Gabrielle. 'Where were you exactly?'

'I was out looking for Amy,' I said.

'Where?'

'Anywhere.'

The Spanish were talking into their radios. Charles Aznavour looked really quite furtive. He was talking very rapidly into his walkie-talkie and kept looking my way as he did so as if discussing me.

He stopped his conversation and said to us both, 'Can I see your passports please?'

Gabrielle went off and returned with our passports. He leafed through them like an airport official. He moved to the table and noted the passport numbers in his notebook.

'I'll need to keep these,' he said.

He didn't explain why, and he didn't explain why he'd written the numbers down if he was going to take the passports anyway.

'What are you doing?' I said. 'What are you doing to find Amy?'

Gabrielle offered to make coffee for everyone.

This seemed to help the atmosphere.

I tried to imagine what the next few days and weeks had in store. What was I to do? Sit by the phone hour after hour? Stand in the streets of Bilbao handing out pictures of Amy? If you've seen this baby ring this number.

The two main policemen went and almost immediately they were replaced by the detective who was the furniture stroker.

'I need to talk to you,' he said. 'I'm pleased you're here.'

'Where else would I be?' I replied.

Then I realised he didn't know what had just happened to us. I explained about Amy.

'This is a bad time,' he said. 'But nonetheless I must ask you again about the death of Olaia Mujika.'

'Olaia, why?' I asked.

'We have various reports, including forensics and the records of phone conversations,' he said.

I knew to sit down.

'Firstly,' he said, 'we have found some clothing near the spot where the body was found. It was a torn piece of shirt which fell down between some rocks, it seems. It had what looks like blood on it. '

'Okay,' I said.

'So I would like to ask you to make yourself available for a DNA test.'

Whoever was trying to ruin my life was making an astonishingly thorough job of it. Had they planted an item down there with my blood on it? There was the day Gabby had hit me. What had I done with my clothing? Binned it perhaps. I remember thinking I would bin it, but did it end up in the washing pile? Or was the policeman lying and, in fact, they had found and analysed the vomit?

'But, more importantly, there are the phone records,' said the inspector.

'What phone records?' I asked. I knew exactly what was coming next.

'The night before she died, she made a phone call to your house.'

'No, she didn't,' I said. 'Well, she didn't phone me, at least.' I was furiously trying to remember what Olaia had actually said to me. She herself had once told me that the Spanish are prone to tapping phones. When the inspector said 'phone records' did he actually mean phone taps? If we really were ETA suspects because of my mother's Irish passport and her penchant for spraying the police with oven cleaner, then there was every chance our phone calls had indeed been recorded.

'I received a call,' I said, 'which I told you about. Do you think it was from Olaia's house? The killer could have phoned from there. Olaia could have been dead on the floor when he was speaking to me.'

'She,' said the inspector. 'You said a woman called you.'

'Sorry, yes,' I said. 'My Spanish gets in a muddle. Look, I'm not having a good day.'

He was unimpressed.

'Look,' I said, 'It is possible it was Olaia who spoke to me that night. I mean, if she had a gun to her head or something then she was likely to sound odd. I might not recognise her. She might have read most of what she said from a note the killer had written.'

'Where was your wife that night?' he asked.

'You don't think she has something to do with it, do you?' I replied.

'No,' he said. He looked incredulous. 'She would be your alibi.'

Chapter Thirty-four

'I must be a hell of a lay,' said Gabrielle.
'What?'

'If Alex is behind all this then he is spending an extraordinary amount of time and effort trying to screw up our lives,' she said. 'I mean, I knew he was an arsehole, a shitty little arsehole at that, but I didn't think he'd do this.'

We spent a lot of time sitting by the phone, just like I imagined. Sometimes we talked incessantly, sometimes there was nothing to say. Sometimes we would make the same point fifteen times.

'If there is no ransom note, what is the point?' I said this to anyone who would listen, and when they wouldn't listen I said it to myself.

Sometimes a police car would pull up to the house, but somehow we knew it was never good news. It was going to be a policeman saying they had heard nothing yet. No news, at all. Good news comes by phone. I dreaded that sooner or later, in a few days perhaps, there would be an instance of a car pulling up and the policeman would get out and there being terrible news. They would do that face to face.

Not yet though. Someone was making us suffer. They might want a ransom, they might just want to be cruel, but one thing was sure: they would want us to wait.

One of the police cars brought some forensic officers. They wandered round wearing white rubber gloves, carrying tweezers and sandwich bags. They put tape across Amy's doorway and spent an hour dusting the room for prints.

They left, doing a variety of shrugs.

'Did you find anything?' I asked.

'Perhaps,' replied one of them, meaning he hadn't found anything.

Time dragged on.

Gabrielle had bursts of activity. She would sit motionless on the sofa for a while and then spring up. But she couldn't think what to do.

'I'm going to search the house again,' she said.

It was something to do. It would fill the hours.

She found nothing.

We went to bed that first night at a time that made as much sense as any. It was obvious that there was no chance of sleeping. It was a ceiling to stare at, to make a change from the walls we were staring at downstairs.

The phone rang.

My eyes opened wide to the brightness in the room. Every light was still on. I must have been asleep after all.

Gabrielle wasn't in bed. I scrambled to my feet. Gabrielle flew ahead of me. She obviously hadn't slept and had been doing something in another room. She was downstairs in three leaps and I was less than a second behind her.

She picked up the phone so quickly, she fumbled it and it dropped on the floor.

'Yeah?' said Gabrielle.

There was talking on the other end.

'Yeah,' she said again.

More talking.

'Okay. Um. I see. Yes. Fair enough.'

More talking.

'Look I think you should talk to Sal. He speaks better Spanish.'

More talk on the other end. She didn't hand the phone over.

'Okay. Thank you,' she said. She put the phone down.

'And?' I asked.

'The police have had a tip off. They might know where Amy is,' she said.

'Might?'

'They were going to say where we should go, or rather where the police were going, but then they decided it was difficult to explain, and also they thought it might be a trap.'

'A trap?' I asked.

'Well, let's say if we had to go to waste ground or something, then there could be a sniper waiting to shoot us.'

'Is that likely?' I asked.

'Is it likely that someone was going to snatch our baby in the first place?'

'No,' I conceded. 'So what's happening?'

'The police are coming to pick us up.'

Chapter Thirty-five

I put some clean clothes on. It had been threatening to rain for some time, but hadn't done so yet, so we found some plastic waterproofs just in case. I had images of a dead baby; a tiny mutilated corpse in a sunless flat that smelled of fags and leaking gas. I imagined the opposite, the baby alive and healthy, her eyes following a leaf as it fell in her basket, wrapping a tiny hand around it and trying to find her own mouth; as interested in the leaf as in the distraught parent whose face had suddenly appeared, who was picking her up and was covering her with tears.

It was the Charles Aznavour-alike who arrived. I finally caught his real name. Unamuno. Another Basque surname to savour. I had a feeling I would be still be thinking of him as Aznavour.

We bundled into his car.

He drove us through the darkness. Endless unlit country roads.

Inexplicably, we didn't talk at first. Some kind of shock, the time of the morning or the occasion.

'So, what was this tip off?' I asked finally.

He stopped the car and turned on the internal light to study a map.

'We had a phone call from a woman an hour ago,' he said.

'A woman?' I asked.

'It was a mobile phone. She told us that the missing baby was on a piece of waste land.'

'What exactly did she say?' I asked.

'I don't know,' he said. 'I was in bed.'

Policemen sometimes go to bed when our baby is missing?

'Was there a ransom demand?' I asked.

'Not as far as I know,' he replied.

Gabrielle had been silent up till then, but now leant forward.

'Thank you,' she said. 'You are entitled to a night's sleep, like anyone. Thank you for coming out. We have been so much trouble. Thank you.'

She managed all that in Spanish.

I immediately had visions of Gabrielle waiting until I was asleep and wandering out the house to make a phone call. It wouldn't be hard to buy a pay-as-you-go mobile and register it under a false name. I hated myself for thinking this through.

'You have been no trouble,' said the policeman. He put the map down and drove on.

He needn't have bothered with the map. We turned a bend and saw about eight police cars scattered on the verges with their lights on full beam.

They were even erecting arc lights.

Gabrielle seemed almost excited. She was bobbing around in her seat, darting her head one way then another to take in the details.

'This is amazing,' she said. 'This is absolutely amazing.'

The police mostly looked as if they'd only just got there. Some of them were still getting out of their cars, while a few were hanging around in a group waiting for the off.

'We're looking for somewhere down by the railway tracks,' said Aznavour. 'The directions were pretty vague, probably on purpose.'

I got out of the car and had a look around. We were near a bridge where the road we were on crossed the railway. The arc lights were being placed to overlook the tracks. I suspected that was largely so that we could climb down safely.

One of the policemen was taking a thin steel suitcase out of his car. He opened it flat, then folded out three legs to form a tripod. It was some sort of incident board. He started writing stuff on it with a felt marker. He was calling out to the various men, then writing their names on it.

'Where are we looking?' Gabby asked me.

'I have no idea.'

'Down on the tracks that way,' said a policeman behind us, who obviously understood English.

We peered into the gloom. If anything the arc lights hampered us: beyond where they shone it was impossibly dark. It had stopped raining at least.

The police organised themselves; they had decided on who was going to go where and had written it on the board.

We hadn't brought torches, so it was hard to tell how much use we could be. The police were climbing down the grass now. We followed them.

'You can't go down there,' said Aznavour.

'Why not?' I replied.

'It could be dangerous. We must remember it could be ETA. They will ask us to go to a place and there will be a bomb. No baby, just a bomb. We are not allowed to put your lives in danger.'

We were a yard or two down the bank. A couple of police climbed down past us. Aznavour, however, was all but blocking our way.

'It's our baby,' I said.

'That's why it is such a good trap. They are not interested in a ransom, so why are they doing this?'

'I don't think it's ETA,' I protested. 'I think it's more personal than that. I'm sure it's safe.'

'And I'm not,' he said.

Gabrielle and I started down the bank regardless.

'Get back up there and wait in the car,' he barked.

We dithered and climbed back up. He watched us for a while and, when he was satisfied we were going to behave ourselves, he set off down to the tracks.

We stood side by side on the bridge. There was no one else with us; the marker board was still there but unattended. Perhaps it was so that they could check all the officers had come safely back out of a situation. Gabrielle was wide eyed and silent; watchful like an animal.

We could see the men below walking along the tracks, sweeping their torches before them. We could see there was nothing for them to find; if there was anything out there it was further down the line, but they had to be methodical and artificially slow.

'If the tip off is really meant to allow us to find Amy, then she must be somewhere obvious down there, not hidden away,' I said.

Gabrielle didn't appear to hear me.

A long time later, she exhaled. The night was so still it made me jump.

I could barely make out the policemen now. A train came through, seemingly out of nowhere. A long goods train. I hoped the men below had heard it.

'Perhaps we ought to go down,' I said.

'They'll find Amy,' said Gabrielle.

'How do you know?'

'I just feel it. If this is Alex... even if this isn't Alex... this is someone screwing with us mentally,' she said.

'Olaia was murdered, why not Amy?' I asked.

'For all we know, Olaia isn't related to this at all. We just assumed the two were related because *we* were involved in each.'

'When Olaia rang me she said I should go down there in order to understand everything. I think it's all related,' I said.

We were silent again. The countryside was silent.

A long time later we could hear farm animals waking up. They had been disturbed by a car somewhere, miles away probably. More animals then woke up, disturbed by the first lot; cockerels and goats, geese and sheep, all out there somewhere in the dark. The far off car kept going at what sounded like an even pace for five minutes or more. The animals kept up their din for ten minutes beyond that.

It once more became quiet. Possibly the quietest bit of countryside in the entire of Spain.

Then the rain came. A few purposeful spots, followed by a major downpour. It released an explosion of scents from the countryside. The rain was of a strength that would normally send people hurtling for cover, but we just stood there blinking furiously to keep our eyes clear. I unzipped my top to find some dry clothing to wipe my face with.

There was a man running along the tracks. He was barely visible. He had no torch. I thought he was shouting, but I couldn't make out what he was saying.

I shouted back to encourage him that we might be able to hear if he kept shouting.

'If it was bad news, do you think he'd look so animated?' I asked.

'I have no idea,' Gabrielle replied.

'I think he might be beckoning,' I said. 'We should go down anyway.'

We ran back to the end of the bridge. The earth on the bank had been so dry for so long that the rain wasn't soaking in at all; it was pouring down the slope, taking the dust and leaves with it.

Gabby and I held hands to support each other as we ran down. We gained so much momentum that it felt as though our bodies were going to outpace our legs. I was the first to stumble at the bottom; my foot caught the edge of a sleeper or something like that. Gabrielle showed surprising strength; she held my arm rigidly, and supported my weight to prevent me falling completely.

We were walking fast now. Oddly, we had lost sight of the man. We were lower and unable to see round a bank.

When we did find him we were remarkably close.

'We have found your baby,' he said.

'Dead or alive?' I asked. 'Is she harmed?'

He went to answer but then I realised we could see for ourselves. A couple of officers were clearly visible some distance away, carrying a Moses basket between them. I didn't wait to hear the answer to my question, I was afraid what that answer might be. I walked forward.

I heard Gabrielle now ask the man the same question. Is Amy alive? I didn't hear the answer but then she started running forwards, and I ran too.

Amy was living, she was breathing.

She was fine.

Chapter Thirty-six

When Amy was back with us, she felt strangely foreign. She'd been away and had experiences we didn't know about.

We unwrapped her carefully. More delicately than we had done for a long time. It was dark so I held her closely while we looked at every inch of her skin. We turned her over. No marks. Nothing to see whatsoever. I went to wrap her up again.

'Hang on, no,' said Gabrielle. 'Let me look at her back again.'

We turned the tiny baby onto her front and pulled up her clothing.

There were some marks on her skin. Black lines. Two of them, like scars.

The police hadn't understood what we were doing.

'Please shine a light,' I said.

A few seconds later a yellow torch beam was on Amy's back. It wasn't a scar. Whatever it was, it was black and flat to the skin.

'It's writing,' said Gabrielle.

I took the torch from the policeman.

We peered forward trying to make it out.

It was tiny black lettering. It formed two lines, one about two inches long and one about an inch long; parallel to her spine and just to the right of it.

It said,

You didn't follow instructions
Last warning.

Rain was blotching her skin now. The ink wasn't permanent and was already running. It occurred to me that the letters were so tiny so that it would be impossible to analyse or recognise the handwriting; among other things, the skin would move as you wrote. The ink that was chosen meant that the message wasn't destined to last long. It was such a blot on our beautiful baby that I was glad it was disappearing. I'd have rubbed it away myself if it hadn't been for the fact that it might be seen as removing evidence.

Amy was gurgling, oblivious to the fuss. We wrapped her up again and took it in turns to hug her. We hugged each other.

The police visited us the next day; the Aznavour look-alike and the sidekick who said nothing. They wanted Amy to go to a local hospital to have a full check over and X-rays, which we did later that day. They also wanted a list of anyone who we thought had a grudge against us. We could only offer Alex.

'Yet you say he is in England,' he said.

'He claims he's in England,' I replied. 'I thought perhaps you could run a check on the airports and ports.'

'People can drive into Spain from France without us knowing,' he said. He clearly wasn't going to follow it up. 'There are a number of fingerprints. Who else lives here?'

'My mother was here for a long time,' I said. 'I don't know how long fingerprints last. We don't dust much.'

'We have your mother's fingerprints,' he said. 'From when she assaulted the policeman.' He almost smiled.

It turned out the Inspector hadn't just come to tell us this. He had news.

'We have interviewed the woman who phoned us,' he said.

'Who?' I asked.

208

'The woman who rang us to tell us where the baby was.'

'And?'

'And she had a letter,' said the inspector.

'What?'

'She was sitting at home and there was a tap on the window, just one, and she ignored it,' said the inspector. 'Her house opens directly onto the street and she thought it was a passer-by who just happened to tap the window. But later she was going to bed and as she walked through the hallway she saw a letter on the floor. It was marked "urgent" in big letters.'

'When was this?' I asked.

'One in the morning?' he replied.

'The tap on the window was at one in the morning or the letter was found at one in the morning?'

'The tap was earlier,' he replied. 'But it might be a coincidence.'

'What did the letter say?' asked Gabrielle.

'It said that she must phone the police instantly. That there was a missing baby and that it could be found on the railway tracks we all went to.'

'So the letter could have been written by a man?' I said.

'Of course,' said the Inspector.

'What if she hadn't rung?' I asked. 'What if she had ignored the letter.'

'She did ring, but of course it took time for the message to get through to the right people.'

'But what if she hadn't?' I asked. 'The baby would have been stuck there. Anything could have happened to Amy.'

'Perhaps there were other letters?' suggested Gabrielle. 'He could have put several through lots of letterboxes and one is bound to work. Or perhaps the person was watching the baby that night to see if it was collected. Perhaps the abductors were there when we were there.'

'I don't think so,' I said. 'I have a feeling that this person is just playing a kind of Russian Roulette with our lives. He throws the dice and we may or may not suffer. I bet there are no other letters.'

'There's another possibility,' volunteered the inspector. 'The woman could be lying. If she is ETA she could know the importance of ringing us up. The letter gives her some cover.'

'It's not ETA,' I said. 'This is someone who is out to get one or all of us killed.'

The inspector shrugged and was soon gone.

We took Amy along to the hospital as requested and there was no evidence that she was the least bit injured.

As we were travelling back though, we had a long chat and decided that we no longer wanted to live in Biscay. Whoever was trying to ruin our lives or drive us away had succeeded. I made inquiries at work about returning to England, but in the meantime I spent an entire day of my life changing all the locks in the house and adding extra bolts. I made sure the shutters locked from the inside and that, in turn, the windows locked behind those. I even screwed a big bolt onto the outhouse door at the back. To keep the mice in, I guess.

In Amy's room, I was twice as thorough. I fitted two sets of internal locks to the shutters, and locks to the outside of her bedroom door. It felt very unsettling, and in either event we had Amy asleep in our own bedroom at night. We threw away the Moses basket she had been abducted in and got a stylish canvass travel cot instead.

We realised however that the fatal flaw with the plan was that when we put her down to sleep at eight o'clock it was in our room, and that was less secure than the nursery. So we decided instead that we'd put her down to sleep in her own room and then when we ourselves went to bed, we would transfer her to our bedroom for the night. This also meant we could have sex without her in the room with us.

This routine showed how freaky our lives had become. We would lock our own daughter into her room every night for a few hours and take the key back downstairs with us. It was a daily reminder that we needed to move back to England.

My employers were sympathetic when they heard the story but asked me to hang on for a couple of weeks while they sorted out a replacement. After all, they had already lost Olaia from our department. In either event, I still didn't have my passport, so I couldn't go immediately.

I would be glad to move on from the site. The guards who had been arrested had been released and were somehow blaming me for their temporary incarceration. They had only been in jail for a week; not much longer than I had been locked up, and I had done nothing wrong. I felt like asking them their secret. Not that that was possible because they refused to talk to me, or rather, they pretended they couldn't understand me when I spoke.

So there was no joy to be had at work.

I realised with a bump that I hadn't spoken to my mother since she'd stayed with us. Not so strange given that we'd been pre-occupied with baby abduction and the like, and also when you've put up with someone in your house for a long time you don't rush to seek out their company by phone. But the fact remains I hadn't heard from her; and more pertinently she hadn't rung me, which was unusual. I tried phoning her from work but there was no answer at her end. I'd try later.

I got home that evening to find Gabrielle had spent the day sorting out our stuff prior to packing.

She had that look on her face that she was waiting to get livid with me.

'What is this?' she asked.

She was holding a piece of paper I didn't recognise.

'I want to know what it is,' she said.

I looked at it. It was the piece of paper from Alex's flat where I'd jotted down the name of one of Gabrielle's previous boyfriends. The one to whom she'd allegedly pretended she had cancer.

'It's in your handwriting,' she shouted.

'I know it is.'

'Explain yourself, you arsehole,' she shouted. 'Go on. I am dying to hear how you are going to explain this.'

Why would I have the name and number of her previous boyfriend? What could I say?

'That man,' I began. 'Alex. He wouldn't leave me in peace unless I promised to write down the name of this person, whoever he is.'

'When?' she said.

'What?'

'When did he make you write that down?' she asked.

'Ages ago, I don't know,' I said.

'What?' she said. 'That time you said he came to you at work?'

'Yeah,' I said. 'I didn't *say* that. He *did* come to work.'

'And he made you write it down?'

'Yes,' I replied. I just knew there was a killer sting in the tail.

'So,' she began. 'You did this several months ago.'

'Okay.'

'Which doesn't explain why it was folded in the back pocket of a pair of trousers that must have been washed about twenty times since then.' Ah, that'll be the sting then.

I couldn't work out whether I should admit to seeing Alex in London.

Eventually I said, 'I found it again recently and happened to put it in my pocket.'

'Why would you keep it at all?'

'Well, who is he?' I asked.

She shrugged.

'Someone I used to date.' Then she started shouting. 'I mean, what do you want from me?'

I felt like saying, well, frankly you are pretty mad, what I want is a few answers occasionally.

I said, 'Look, I don't know what I want. I am confused. We are having a terrible time. This has been the most ghastly nightmare month after month. I get confused. I don't know what to do.'

'You don't know what to do? You don't know what to do?' This was screamed loud enough to shake the windows in the town below. 'You just have to trust me! I bring up your child. I work. I am here every day as your friend. I don't put a foot wrong. I have never ever made a fuss about the chaos that is all around us. No fuss, not for a minute.'

'Except when you hit me and when you left me,' I said.

She went ballistic.

'That was the tiniest part. The smallest fraction of our lives together. It is nothing. I put in the spade work day after day, hour after hour and... I don't believe you sometimes. I gave up everything in England for you. Everything. On a chance that we could be happy. You didn't risk anything. You were coming here anyway. I took a huge chance. I have done everything possible. I have even decorated this rat hole. AND YOU THINK I'M SOME SORT OF DEVIL. YOU NEVER GIVE ME THE BENEFIT OF THE DOUBT!'

There was a knock on the door.

Neighbours from, I don't know, France probably.

I opened the door. It was the furniture stroking detective.

'Am I disturbing you?' he asked.

'No!' we both chimed.

'I need to take you down to the station for that blood test,' he said.

'What?' I said.

'We need to rule you out for the murder of Olaia Mujika.'

'Fine,' I said. I was getting to the stage where I was submitting to whatever fate had in store. I vaguely wondered whether I should get a solicitor to come with me, or perhaps the gestor. After all a murder charge shouldn't be taken lightly.

'So you are looking to match someone's blood to the blood found on what exactly?' said Gabrielle.

'On the victim's body we found some blood that was not Olaia's,' said the detective. 'There is also blood on the piece of clothing found nearby. The shirt.'

Gabrielle looked intrigued by this; she went to ask a question and then appeared to stop herself.

The policeman continued, 'If you go down to any area of shoreline at random, you are likely to find a little bit of clothing of some sort. A shoe washed up, you know the stuff; the shirt probably means nothing. The blood on the body is more interesting obviously.'

Gabrielle looked at me and said, 'It's not as though you did the murder. Just get down there, give the blood and they can rule you out.'

Chapter Thirty-seven

At the police station the inspector was all for leaving me in a room alone.

'The doctor will be here in a minute,' he said.

'Last time I was left alone it turned out the door was locked,' I said.

'Shall I prop it open?' He was quite serious.

'No. In fact I want to talk to you.'

He pursed his lips.

'I'm a bit short of time,' he said.

'It's quite important,' I said. 'I think I might be able to help you. I think I know who might have kidnapped our daughter.'

'That is not my case,' he said.

'But it is the same person who murdered Olaia.'

'How do you know that?' he asked.

'I just want you to promise that if he comes into your radar, you'll take his prints but also consider a blood sample.'

'Sure,' he said. 'I am looking to solve the case, you know. I'll follow any reasonable lead.'

I had always had a feeling that he didn't think I was guilty. It was possible, of course, that he always showed the same dishevelled nonchalance even when he was just about to lock someone up and throw away the key, but I doubted it.

'Why do you think I might have done it?' I asked.

'Because you were there,' he said.

'Yes, but why? Why would I want to do it?'

He sighed long and hard.

'Some people think you work for ETA,' he said.

That old chestnut.

'I don't really follow,' I said.

'If Olaia was right and ETA want to try and explode the superconductor, then really it was only you and she who were in charge of the security. If she is gone then you are in charge on your own. You are her boss. If you said that day you should meet at the Chillida Installations then she might have to say yes.'

'But she rang me,' I protested.

'You said you didn't think it was her, Mr Gongola.'

'Yes, but you now tell me it was her phone. She was under stress and she might have been reading out what she had to say. I can accept it is possible it was her and I didn't realise it.' This conversation was not going the way I hoped. I appealed to him directly. 'Do you think it was me?'

He looked neutral.

'Let's say I am also looking into other lines of inquiry,' he said.

I went for an even softer approach. I lowered my voice.
'Look,' I said, 'We have been victimised. I need to feel that if I was really stuck and somehow I had been framed, I would need to feel that you would at least give me enough benefit of the doubt to completely check out the possibility of Alex Lawrence.'

'You have my assurance,' he said. 'If your Mr Lawrence appears I will thoroughly investigate him. But listen very carefully. I cannot possibly act in any meaningful way, taking blood for example, just because you say so. I would need a very good reason.'

'I understand that,' I said.

'Do you have any proof against him? Anything that links him to the crime?'

I thought for a while.

'Nothing whatever,' I said.

216

'I have given you my phone number, yes?' he asked.

'Give it to me again,' I said. 'I'm not very efficient.'

'I'd heard,' he said. 'Why do you think this man killed Olaia?'

'Because he wants Gabrielle to look like a psychopath who gets so jealous she would murder a woman who was friendly with me,' I said.

'And would she?' asked the policeman.

'No.' I replied.

'Do you think I should take your wife's blood?' He was half joking.

I think.

'Certainly I will take her prints to rule her out of the prints in your house,' he said.

'Whatever you think is best,' I said.

After my visit to the police I was quite optimistic. It looked distinctly as if all the cards weren't necessarily stacked against me. There was some credence to my idea that at least one police officer might well be inclined to believe me.

I hadn't been into work for an eternity so I drove off there and spent four or five hours doing some paper work. I rang Gabrielle to tell her I'd be late.

When I did finally get home, Amy was already upstairs and Gabrielle was a little drunk. She was in a very good mood.

'Let's get really, really plastered,' she said. 'I mean really, really, really plastered.'

'Top idea,' I replied.

We really, really set about it. A bottle of wine each, then enough Vodka to drown the entire Ukraine. We ended up sitting on the floor, possibly because we couldn't stand well enough to get to the sofa. We sang along to an old Pogues album, loudly and badly. Then a Happy Mondays CD or possibly Black Grape. Then the entire of Hunky Dory. We didn't know many of the words.

'She's so something, something, something.'

'With her something, something and hat.'

I then got it into my head that it was very important for me to ring my mother. I was barely sober enough to press the buttons on the phone.

There was no answer.

'We haven't thought what to do about her,' I said.

'In what way?' asked Gabby.

'Well, we're moving back to England but she's moving out here.'

'Perfect!' she said.

I laughed.

'No,' she said. 'We'll sort something out. She can live near us somewhere.'

'That's very generous of you,' I said.

'How so?'

'Well you don't like her.'

'Yes, I do,' she said. 'I like your mother. It's you who doesn't like your mother.'

'But you avoided her,' I protested.

'No,' she said. 'I went off to work so that I could buy that car and square a few credit card bills. I hadn't worked for a few months, what with the house to decorate and everything. I needed the money.'

'So you don't mind my mother? Well that's a turn up.'

It was that stage of drunkenness where we were talking fine, but any change at all would result in us being too drunk to be able to keep conversation going.

I stood to go for a pee and realised the room wasn't staying quite where I kept putting it. I had to make myself speak clearly and slowly to be heard.

'I think it's time for bed,' I said, at the second attempt.

We walked up the stairs together. I had two pint glasses of water in my hands that were slopping about with each step. Gabrielle had the keys to Amy's room. Her gilded cage. There was lots of comedy fumbling around where the key aimed towards the keyhole, but veered off at the last minute.

218

I decided to help.

I put the beer glasses of water down. It took a lot of ingenuity to get them to hold steady on a plain, flat wooden floor.

We both decided to hold the key between us and guide it into the lock. When even that strategy didn't work, we got the giggles. I then decided to fall backwards, crashing my back against the sharp edge of the doorframe. I spent a long time looking at the grain of the floorboards at close quarters, then realised that somehow Gabby had got the door open.

I walked into the room about two metres behind her.

Gabrielle was completely stock still. I was still too drunk to notice the change in the atmosphere.

There was no Amy.

Chapter Thirty-eight

We had shot ourselves in the foot by being so drunk we could barely stand.

The door had been locked. We had been in the house all along. Of course, I hadn't actually seen Amy that evening because I had been at work until late and I had taken Gabby's word for it that Amy was asleep upstairs. But at that stage of the proceedings I believed Gabrielle was innocent. Mind you, at that time I also believed Alex was in England. Either way, rightly or wrongly, it was definitely the case that I trusted Gabrielle.

We swayed in front of the cot for who knows how long. There wasn't proper lighting in the room because Amy usually slept in the dark, but the door to the landing was open which shed some light.

My heart was in my boots. After all that we'd been through, I didn't feel I could face any more; I just wanted to curl up and die.

The light came on. Gabrielle must have walked round behind me.

I tried to say, 'We need to ring the police,' but I'm not sure what the words sounded like.

I steadied myself on the dressing table.

Gabrielle was talking heatedly and pacing about, but I didn't catch whatever she was saying.

I was focussed on the envelope in front of me on the dressing table. It had the number eight printed on the top left.

I reasoned that we hadn't been told about fingerprints being found on other letters so I needn't be too careful with this one. I tore it open.

Gabrielle was behind me, looking over my shoulder.

Dear Sal

Letter eight. Fear the worst. One of you must go to the same place as before and one of you must go to the Chillida Installations. Now.

Do not call the police or the child will die.

'What shall we do?' I asked.

'Do as it says,' replied Gabrielle.

'Shall we call the police?'

'What have they done so far?' she asked. 'Nothing we wouldn't do. But last time, when Amy was written on, I think that was a final warning to not disobey the instructions. If Amy is there, we should get her and then just pack up and leave this godforsaken country. I think that's it, Sal. We've got to go.'

'Sure.'

Getting drunk was the biggest mistake, but not calling the police was a close second. In the cold light of day I realised that if a kidnapper says don't call the police it means that their biggest fear is that we call them, so we should have done it. But we were drunk and Gabrielle was quite correct; the police had been no help in the past.

'So who is going where?' I asked.

'We could toss for it,' said Gabrielle.

'But why two different places?'

'No idea.'

'They are expecting me to go to the Chillida Installations and you to go to the railway,' I said.

'Why?'

'Because they know for certain that I know where the Chillida wotsits are, and we are presuming that Amy is at the railway tracks and that is usually seen as a mother's place. If that makes sense,' I said.

'Right. So are we going to do that or do the opposite?' she asked.

'How did they take Amy?' I wondered. 'You are sure that this room was locked and that you had the key?'

'Of course.'

Gabrielle went to the window. It was locked. She unlocked it and tried the shutter beyond. That was also locked and unforced.

She rubbed her face with her hands over and over again.

'Look,' she said. 'I don't know. Let's sort out this problem. We'll get Amy and we'll leave the country.'

'We haven't got passports,' I said.

'Then we'll drive up through France and reason with some authority other than the Spanish. I don't know, but we can't stay here. After all, if you're stuck without a passport, you get deported to your country of birth. Presumably.'

'Okay,' I said. 'So shall I go to the Chillida Installations?'

I was feeling marginally less drunk, perhaps with the adrenaline of the situation. I certainly wasn't sober enough to drive, but it would have to be. It was very late at night so there wouldn't be any police about.

'No,' said Gabrielle firmly. 'We'll do the opposite of the obvious. I'll go to the Chillidas. You go to the railway. Besides, I'm less drunk. Yours would be the shortest drive.'

'We'll both take phones,' I said. 'If in doubt we'll arrange to come back and rethink.'

It wasn't raining, but it was dark. I had a pretty good idea where the railway tracks had been, but I wasn't too certain. I was hoping that at each part of the journey I would recognise what to do next.

I'd brought a torch with me, but I've always been convinced that batteries in torches last a matter of seconds before fading, so I was a bit apprehensive of how I was going to see.

We hadn't been told exactly where Amy had been found, and I had been so relieved that she was alive that I hadn't thought to ask.

I took a few wrong turnings and it's more than likely my navigation was hampered by the fact that I was so very drunk my field of vision had reduced to a central patch in a sea of grey. It had occurred to me I was being followed at one stage. But one car driving behind in the dark does look very much like another. After a few miles it had gone.

I was just getting to the stage where I thought I'd got the route wrong, when I turned a corner and simply knew I was at the right bridge.

I parked the car on the verge, got my torch and climbed down the bank. I vaguely remember thinking that I should have checked to see if anyone was watching me, although I don't know what I would have done.

I got my phone out and rang Gabrielle as I walked along. I felt I would have to walk several hundred yards before looking seriously, because the baby wasn't found close to the bridge. I would have time to check on Gabby. 'I'm just the other side of Bilbao now,' she said. 'I'm on the road to San Sebastian. It'll take another half hour to get there, I would have thought.'

'Okay,' I said. 'Well, ring me if there's any trouble. I'm on the tracks so I'll start looking properly now.'

'Great,' she said. 'Ring me the moment you find her, and I'll come straight back.'

That was where we left it.

I somehow assumed that Amy would be found just by the tracks but I guessed that if I saw any workman's huts I would have to look in those.

There was a bit of moonlight, so when I felt I could easily see, I saved my batteries and kept the torch off. However, I kept worrying that I'd missed out on something in the undergrowth, so the torch went on and off repeatedly. The other worry was that I could only check one side at a time by myself. The railway was twin tracked and therefore quite wide. It was inefficient to keep crossing forwards and backwards, and quite dangerous; so I thought I'd search for half a mile on the left hand side then cross over and walk back.

I saw a thicket on the other side that looked exactly the sort of place I should check, so I made an exception to my system almost before I'd begun.

I stepped clearly over a rail but found myself swaying on one leg where I couldn't see where to put my next foot.

I didn't see or hear the train coming.

I was between the two tracks of the route that goes in towards Bilbao. Something had gone badly wrong with my metabolism. Perhaps the initial adrenaline had worn off and left my body in some sort of shock as it struggled with the alcohol.

I was aware of a huge rushing. My eyes were dazzled with light so strong I couldn't see. There was a continuous warning sound from the train itself. Possibly the driver had seen me, or possibly they sound the horn as they come round every corner. I knew I had to move forward. I had to force my body to make it to the next rail and beyond. The gravel shot up towards my face. I had fallen over. My hands were on the steel of the rail. I looked at them, confused. I knew they shouldn't be there. I needed to pull hard on the rail to get my body over and safe. But I knew that if my hands were there a fraction too long, they would be sliced off by the wheels of the train.

Chapter Thirty-nine

I dithered for a fatal second. I looked to the side to see how close the train was. It was above me. It looked as high as a tower block. I pulled my fingers back off the line.

My feet.

Were they near the line behind me? When I stumbled, were my feet stuck on the rails?

I drew my legs up.

The train was over me now. Wheel after wheel shot either side of my body. It was deafening. I worried that trains might have something hanging down from them, between the wheels. I couldn't think what, but it might catch me at sixty miles an hour; tear my torso apart or throw me back onto the track. I tried to lie more flat. I tried to turn my body more in line with the rails, so that I didn't have to be so curled up and raised up. My left cheek was pushed hard against the sooted gravel.

Then it was over. The train had passed.

I had no desire to stand in a hurry.

I assumed that there were never two trains in quick succession. I lifted my head to look. My left eye was matted with oil and dirt. I didn't want to open it and when I tried to brush it with my sleeve it simply smeared and worked into my eyelids.

I was going to have to do everything with one eye.

I managed to get myself up and off the tracks. I had lost my torch somewhere. I tried to judge a safe distance from the rails where I could peer around looking for it.

And then I heard her.

There's no mistaking a baby crying.

Rather pointlessly I shouted, 'I'm coming, Amy.'

I scrabbled around. I was on my hands and knees now, trying to keep steady, but close enough to the unlit ground to look for the lost torch with my one good eye.

It was suddenly close to me, just the other side of the rail. I put my hand over and picked it up, then broke into a minor canter.

But Amy had stopped crying. She had sounded twenty or thirty yards ahead, somewhere in the darkness, but now there was nothing.

After about ten seconds of running I stopped and listened again.

There was the wind and nothing else.

There was some sort of movement in the woodland to my left. Probably an animal.

I walked on and there was a worker's hut. Black from years of train smut. If I was leaving a baby I would leave it in there.

It had a door that looked used and unlocked.

This was the first time I felt truly afraid. I was suddenly completely sure that the door could be booby trapped. I walked along the edge of the hut, hoping to find a window to look in. It appeared to be windowless. There was dense undergrowth on the other side. I was aware for the first time of a pain. I shone the torch on my left palm. There was greasy gash where I'd fallen on the rails.

I heard Amy again. I was pretty sure she was in there.

I went back to the door and pulled gently at it. I tensed every muscle, held my head away and kept my eyes closed. I have no idea how I thought that was going to protect me if several hundred pounds of explosive went off.

The door opened and there was Amy.

It was that simple.

I lifted Amy out of the darkness and walked carefully back. It was too good to be true. I knew there was a catch but I couldn't put a finger on it, so I wanted to get clear of the area. I had visions of a sniper in the woods or being set upon as I got up to the road, or my car exploding when I turned the ignition.

I got about two hundred yards into a more open terrain and I settled Amy down.

I peeled up her clothing to look at her back. There was nothing there.

I checked her stomach. No writing.

I took off most of her upper clothing to look at her arms and shoulders. There was no message written anywhere.

I took out my phone. Gabrielle's was the last number I'd called, so I pressed 'left' then 'yes' on the key pad. The display lit up saying 'Connecting to Gab.' I held it to my ear and there was no sound for a good thirty seconds, then a message.

'The number you have dialled cannot be reached. The phone may be switched off.'

I got back to my car. I looked in through the windows thinking I might see something suspect. There was nothing.

I put Amy on the passenger seat, strapped her in, and drove back home.

I'd assumed that Gabrielle was simply stuck somewhere there was no phone signal. At that point in time, I had no reason to believe otherwise.

Chapter Forty

The house was how we'd left it.

I had got to the stage of drunkenness where I really needed to sleep, but I set about making coffee, and while the kettle boiled I forced down some water.

I put Amy in the travel basket on the kitchen table, and had a good look at my cut hand. The blood and oily dirt were clotted and it was obvious that the area needed cleaning up. I ran it under the tap but it didn't dissolve. I tried washing-up liquid, but again it made little difference. It hurt like hell. I managed to find some white spirit under the sink. I poured it on some kitchen roll and tried to smear at the edges of the wound. It was astonishingly painful.

'Do you want to hear Daddy cry?' I said to Amy.

I more or less got it clean and eventually cut up an old sheet to dress it.

I had a go at cleaning up my face as well, where the tar had stuck around my eye. This was a lot more successful.

I sat at the table, then had a series of drunken thoughts.

As a result, I walked around the house checking it was empty and that every last window and shutter was completely bolted and locked. After all, whoever had taken Amy had managed to get in, and it seemed to me they must have a reason for wanting us out of the house. It occurred to me that there might be something actually in the house that they wanted though I couldn't think what that could possibly be.

I crept up through the house with Amy in one arm and an empty bottle in the other, in case I met an intruder. I undid every window in turn and checked the shutter beyond. These were seriously solid shutters and they were firmly bolted. I then relocked each window and moved on to the next room.

I was puzzled that Gabrielle hadn't been more alarmed or surprised that Amy had been taken from a locked room, but we had been so inebriated that it was hard to tell what her reaction should have been. Probably I, too, had stood there looking bemused rather than surprised.

I had finished my tour of the windows and doors but kept getting thoughts about hiding places around the house where an intruder could be, so I'd set off from time to time with Amy and my bottle to check in a cupboard or chest I had overlooked before.

Nothing.

I sat back in the brightly lit kitchen and tried ringing Gabrielle again. Again it seemed her phone was turned off or she couldn't get a signal.

I considered packing up our belongings but I wasn't really in a fit state. I then realised the phone was ringing. I had a feeling it might have been ringing for a while and I hadn't heard it. I sometimes get a sort of tinnitus when I'm drunk.

It was the land line.

As I picked it up I expected it to be Gabrielle, but it was the police.

'Senor Gongola?'

I didn't recognise the voice. He went on to explain that he was a senior policeman with one of the police forces. I am sure he gave me the exact details but it didn't register in my alcohol soaked brain.

'We need you to release Gabrielle Gongola, your wife,' he said.

'What?'

'You are holding her hostage and we need to know what terms you are requesting for her release.'

The kitchen was probably the most secluded room in the house. It was certainly the furthest from the road. But even from in there I could hear that there was something pretty major going on outside.

'I do not follow,' I said.

'Before I enter into any negotiations with you, I first need complete proof that your hostage is still alive.'

'What?' I said again, not unreasonably.

'Can I talk to her please?'

'She's not here,' I said.

'You have already rung us to say she is being held hostage. And she, herself, has given details to verify her identity and her address. Please do not cause trouble. We need to trust each other, you and I.'

'Okay,' I said, still horribly bemused.

'So could you put her on the phone, please.'

'She's not here.'

'Mr Gongola,' he said. 'We have special forces gathering around your house. We have more people on the way. You cannot leave the building. I suggest that we help each other.'

'So, let me clarify,' I said. 'You have spoken to Gabrielle.'

'Yes. You already know that, because you arranged the call she made to us.'

'When was this?' I asked.

'Do not mess with us, Senor Gongola.' He was deliberately using a calm voice so as not to antagonise me; which antagonised me because I was innocent.

It was obviously the policy never to artificially terminate the conversation, because we fell into a pattern of silences, but he never put the phone down.

He said, 'We have already established that you have explosives.'

'Have we?'

'Can you confirm whether they are strapped to you or to Gabrielle.'

Dear God, how could this nightmare get any worse?

'Why do you think I have explosives?' I asked.

'Because you have already told us that.'

'When?' I asked.

'When you phoned us before,' he said.

'So you are claiming that Gabrielle rang you and then I rang you?' I asked.

'The phone call was taped, Mr Gongola. As you know, you rang us, and then your wife spoke to us, confirming who she was and that she had been kidnapped by you, then you spoke to us again,' said the policeman. 'We have already discussed this. Please do not waste our time.'

'Did I sound the same as now?' I asked.

He laughed. The bastard actually laughed.

'Well, no,' he said. 'Now you sound drunk.'

I asked him to stay on the line. He then volunteered that it was the standard policy for him to stay on the line indefinitely. Possibly to stop me ringing out and arranging something with accomplices.

I went off round the house looking for the name and number of the detective who had half believed me before. The furniture stroker. Juan Pairnez. I had visions that with every moment I dithered, there would be armed police working their way round the back of the house, snipers would be taking good positions on the hill behind, and helicopters would be scrambled to hover above.

I was buggered.

Chapter Forty-one

The man on the phone was not interested in me talking to a policeman of my choice.

'I can't just get a policeman out of bed at random. I am the qualified negotiator. You will have to deal with me. If you want to communicate with someone, it has to be through me,' he said. He sounded shirty. Possibly that in itself was a negotiating tactic. Who knows?

It occurred to me to say, 'Look just put him on the phone within the hour or I will harm the hostage.' I seriously considered saying it, because it was possible his guidelines were that he had to concede to reasonable requests if there was a threat to life. But obviously that would confirm their view that there really was a hostage. Which there wasn't.

It felt positively ridiculous, but given that the windows were all shuttered I had to creep up to the letterbox to have a look out. I realised the letterbox pushed outwards and that my protruding finger might be vulnerable, so I went off and found a Biro.

I then realised that the lights in the house would mean that the letterbox would emit light when I opened it. A bar of light with a section of my head as a shadow in the middle; the perfect target in fact.

I turned the lights of the house out and started again.

I could see a police car to the far left and another to the far right. It looked as though they might have put a cordon across the road so that no traffic could go past. I couldn't be sure that I could see any policemen at all. It was very likely that some of the black shapes behind the cars were people, though.

The door thudded with the sound of a bullet hitting it. I shut the letterbox sharpish and scuttled away.

I tried to remember what Gabrielle had told me about sieges all those months ago on the cliff top. I remembered that every hostage situation in Europe since the 1970s had ended in arrest or death, but could I remember anything more useful and less scary? I remembered her saying that they wore night vision goggles regardless, and therefore in a blacked out house you should leave the lights on as they then saw less well than a normal person. I remembered that if a siege dragged on, they tended to storm in at the end of their shift, rather than pass the fun onto someone else. Would that be 8.00 a.m., 9.00 a.m.? Would it be true in Spain, at all? I thought perhaps so. A copper is a copper: they're an international breed. But in Spain their shift might end earlier than Britain.

What else could I remember? She said in Britain they weren't allowed to shoot unless there was reasonable evidence someone's life was in danger. I had a feeling the Spanish shot anyway. I remembered the grenades she mentioned that zigzagged around the room, and the tear gas. I would need to block up the letterbox sharpish, and perhaps the chimney.

I couldn't think what to stick in the letterbox hole. The hammers and nails and really useful stuff were in the outhouse in the back garden, along with the mice. The best I could come up with was to wedge some books into the recess and then tug a chest of drawers down the corridor and push it against the door.

Apparently, armed police did tend to use the front door and they had several methods at their disposal to break it down. They could use a battering ram. They could blow a hole in it with a shotgun that fired a special shot which spread wide but didn't penetrate far beyond the wood. Or, most popular of all, they ran up to the letterbox and pushed a kind of anchor through which was attached by a chain to a car. The car would reverse sharply and take the door with it. I hoped that by blocking the letterbox I could at least prevent the last one, because they wouldn't be able to get the anchor through in the first place.

The chimney was my next project. I got some sheets and stuffed them up. It was quite a broad chimney but I was pretty sure it was too narrow to climb down. I did think, however, that they might get up onto the roof and lob a grenade down or some tear gas.

I went back to look at Amy. She was fast asleep in the glare of the kitchen.

I put the kettle on again and staggered off for a pee.

I was pretty sure I could hear voices just outside the window of the toilet, so I peed on the upslope of the porcelain rather than make a noise. I didn't flush, which is really against my nature. I then craned my ear to the window. I was absolutely convinced they were a couple of inches the other side of the glass but I couldn't work out what they were whispering.

I had a thought or two.

I walked back to the phone.

'Hello?' I said.

'Hello?'

'If I'm going to just leave the phone off the hook, how do I know if you want to say something interesting?' I asked.

'We'll shout from outside and you can pick up the phone.'

Crazy.

I put the phone back on the work surface.

The other thing I'd decided was to alter my chimney strategy. If I was them, I'd put a grenade down the chimney anyway. They weren't to know about the sheeting I'd stuffed up it. It would get caught in the sheeting and explode, blowing a big gap in the wall or ceiling, and they would be able to climb in, or at the very least put in some tear gas after it.

I decided I'd take out the sheets and build a roaring fire in the hearth instead. No one in their right minds would climb down into a fire, and the chimney would get hot enough to put them off monkeying around up there. It wasn't a foolproof plan, but I preferred it to the blocking-it-with-sheets idea.

I thought I'd try and ring Gabrielle next; mobile to mobile. There was still no answer.

I had a curious sense that I now needed to kill time. The only thing I could do was wait until they came in. I felt that by sitting there I was submitting to my fate, but I couldn't think what else to do.

I sat down at the table next to Amy and picked up the phone.

'Hello?' I said.

'Hello,' replied the policeman.

'Look,' I said. 'How about if I come out with my hands up and no weapon and you promise not to shoot?'

Genius.

'We want to see the hostage first,' he said. 'Otherwise, how do we know the house isn't booby trapped when we go in for your wife?'

'I cannot show you the hostage because I do not have a hostage,' I said.

'You are wanted for one murder, Senor Gongola, I suggest…'

'What murder?' I asked.

'We have been issued with the papers to arrest you for the murder of Senora Olaia Mujika.'

'Why?' I asked.

'We have evidence to implicate you in the murder, subsequent to recent haematological investigations.'

It seemed that police the world over employed the same ponderous lexicon when explaining charges. I got the feeling that the arrest warrant was news to him, as though the message had got through from a colleague. Perhaps they had meant to arrest me that coming day and then the hostage situation occurred, which brought everything forward.

I knew then that they weren't going to believe me, no matter what happened. However, there was a chance they'd let me leave the house and arrest me and at least they would find there was no Gabrielle. That would clear me of one charge. Although they wanted to see the hostage first, the fact remained that if I came out with my hands up, they would probably accept that and not shoot.

But what if Gabrielle really was going to press charges claiming that I had imprisoned her, but they had somehow misunderstood what she'd said? Was she going to claim she had been held hostage by me, made the call, and then escaped before the police turned up? In that case the police had the murder charge, plus raised doubts generally about me due to Gabrielle's allegations, plus the previous implication about my mother assaulting the policeman, plus the ETA suspicions. They would definitely want to do me for something. That's how the police think. Like doing Al Capone for tax evasion. The charge itself didn't matter.

I was drunk, I was sleepy, and I simply didn't know what to do or think.

I occupied myself tending the fire. It was a nice big blaze already, so that was something.

I remembered that I had the number for the policeman who half believed me. I wandered off to ring him directly but, not surprisingly, there was no reply at the other end.

I considered burning the house down. I figured that I could hole up in one room and set fire to the other end of the house, and then in the confusion and the smoke, and the fire brigade rushing around, I could run off with Amy. They would feel a lot less confident shooting at people in the smoke, for fear of shooting one of their own.

If I did that, there was a big risk Amy and I would die.

I could give myself up and hope they didn't have strong evidence against me. It occurred to me that it was very dark outside. They had not erected floodlights, so I could open the front door and they would not have a clear view of whether or not I was holding a weapon. It struck me as odd. Surely they would want to at least direct their car beams at the door, so that they could see if I was leaving. Or was it deliberate? Were they keeping it dark so that they could creep up on the house at will? In which case their strategy was to storm.

I tried to think of other options. I could... I had no idea what else I could do.

Think, Sal, think.

Let's assume Gabrielle was innocent. She was being held by, say, Alex. He might want to murder her. I could be arrested and they wouldn't spend much time looking for Gabrielle, if any. She could be dead before they find her. There was no advantage to being arrested. In fact, only I knew that she had gone out to the Chillida Installations. She might have been followed by car. After all, Alex didn't know which of us would go to the railway tracks and which of us out to San Sebastian. So she was followed. She was kidnapped, and Alex rang the police about me, why? So that I couldn't come out and save her? So that I wouldn't be believed, at least initially, while they made a getaway. While he murdered her and had time to escape. In which case I needed to escape to have any chance of helping. Otherwise I'd either end up in a prison for several days like before, or be shot.

Okay.

As a further sign of drunkenness, I started running through the very same case I'd argued to myself a minute before. Assuming Gabrielle was barking mad and trying to engineer my death or incarceration or whatever, she would swear blind I had indeed held her hostage. She had successfully planted my bloody shirt, way back when, at Olaia's murder scene, and I was totally stuffed. In which case I needed to escape; to find evidence that helped me, or leave the country and do bar work on a Greek Island for the rest of my life. Who knows? But either way I needed to escape.

Chapter Forty-two

I figured that one of the problems was that they thought of us as foreigners. If there was a domestic hostage situation in Britain that involved a bunch of Hispanics, we wouldn't feel we understood the ins and outs of what made them tick. We'd just assume the worst of them, not trust the foreigners, and feel the need to act in a resolute manner. If the hostage takers had been English, we would feel better able to weigh them up according to things like class, attitude, and what they had to say. In short, there was no way the Spanish police were going to trust me.

There was a noise of loud-hailer outside.

'We want to talk to you.'

They had evidently dredged up an English speaker, which was surprising as I thought we were getting on fine in Spanish.

'Go to the phone,' the person said.

I picked up the phone.

'Hello?' I said.

'We are requesting that you allow us to talk to the hostage.'

'I cannot, because I do not have a hostage,' I replied.

He obviously expected me to say that, because he then said, 'In the event that you do not want to co-operate, and in the absence of negotiable demands, we must warn you that we are prepared to storm the house.'

'I wanted to talk to the policeman that I told you about,' I protested.

'As we said earlier, we understand from his office that they are now seeking your arrest on charges that are not related to kidnapping, so they will not be more favourable to you than I am.'

'Yes, but I want to talk to him anyway,' I said.

'That will not be possible until you are in custody.'

I wondered whether they would storm the house without any notice, or whether they would give me a countdown. Possibly they waited for some official or other to give the okay.

I got it into my head that the attack would be imminent, but it might have been some sort of post-pissed paranoia. Or pissed paranoia. Just how drunk was I still? Not too bad.

I finally settled for certain on my original logic that I needed to escape rather than give myself up. I might well get caught trying to flee, but there was nothing I could do about that. I had wasted time dithering.

The person who had taken Amy, and presumably my white shirt, had got in and out of our house unnoticed. I tried to concentrate on that. It might give me a clue as to how I could do it. I took Amy up to her room and looked around. The windows were bolted. There was no balcony or ledge outside that window, so I doubted that was the way in, unless they used ladders.

I went into the bathroom instead. The window in there was small and secure. I always felt that originally there would have been a second window in that room but when the outhouse was added they had built it up against one of the walls and presumably bricked it in. It looked secure in there.

I went back to Amy's room.

The attic.

There was an attic hatch in the ceiling. I moved a chair and stood on it. The hatch moved easily, but it was dark up there so I got a torch.

Even with a torch I couldn't see anything of interest. A dark windowless attic with no other exit.

It still seemed like the most likely option though.

I put the torch in my teeth and struggled up into the loft space. My cut palm complained about the pressure, but that was the least of my problems.

It was dark outside, of course, so any link with the outside world wouldn't show up as a glimmer of light. I didn't give up, though. I crept around in the shadows, balancing on rafters, looking for a gap in the wall.

Success.

At one end the bricks were loose. It was an internal wall rather than a wall that supported the house, and the cement had apparently crumbled between the bricks.

I pulled at a few top bricks. There were already dusty bits of cement by my feet where mortar had previously fallen away. It was entirely possible that these bricks had been removed in the past and piled up again.

I now had a gap about four bricks wide and three bricks deep. I shone my torch through. On the other side was the lean-to outhouse where I kept my tools and lawn mower. Despite the fact that it was on the highest side of the hill, the attic was, nonetheless, about nine foot from the ground. It was a bit of a jump, but possible. It was the nearest to some good news I'd had, well, for months really.

If Amy's kidnapper had got in this way, it was a precarious climb, but possible. Also they would have had to force the bolt on the outside of the outhouse door. Or unscrewed it, which now I thought about it, wasn't very hard. After Amy was kidnapped the second time I hadn't gone out into the garden to check whether or not the bolt had been forced or removed. I was now praying that it had been, otherwise I wouldn't be able to get out that way.

I climbed back to Amy's room and went off to the kitchen. I was looking for some Elastoplast but found some sellotape instead. I tore off some sections with my teeth and stuck them on the gas cooker; over the metal igniters. I turned on the gas rings. The gas flowed but they didn't ignite. I turned the kitchen table over and dragged it up at forty-five degrees so that the surface pushed hard onto the knobs and kept them on. In no time at all the smell of gas was thick in the air.

I picked up Amy and walked around the house, wedging open all the doors.

I had to assume my plan would work so I got a plastic bag and put a couple of cartons of ready made baby milk and a bottle in it. I then jotted down a few phone numbers and found some documents and photographs that I thought might be useful. I put them in the bag too, along with some extra strappings for my cut palm. It was already bleeding beyond the bandage but I didn't have time to do anything about it.

I found the baby sling and strapped Amy against my chest. I got my wallet and phone.

I had a sense that I was now setting off.

I found a broom and pushed it up into the attic. I then stood on the chair and climbed up after it. I got the broom again and, holding it by the handle, extended it back down through the loft hatch. I hooked it through the back of the chair below and managed to drag the chair off to the wall, so that it wouldn't look as though I'd climbed up there.

I pulled the broom up into the attic and shut the loft door.

A big mistake. Call me stupid, call me drunk, but I'd forgotten the torch.

I had to open the hatch, hook back the chair, climb down with Amy, find the torch and start all over again. The smell of gas was permeating the house well now.

I was soon back in the attic.

I figured the police were likely to storm the building at any given moment and that if they fired a shot or used a hand grenade they might blow themselves up. When they finally caught up with me they would want to prosecute for murder. But as likely, the leaking gas would become sufficiently concentrated in the air to reach the fire in the lounge. The house would explode of its own accord. Whatever the case, when the explosion went off I needed to run like hell.

For an amateur I thought it was a pretty good plan.

If I didn't kill us both, that is.

I took away brick after brick from the connecting wall to the outhouse. They came away very easily, but that in itself didn't prove that anyone had done it before; walls like this were quite common in houses of this age.

One of the bricks fell down the wrong side. It knocked against a shelf and then smashed something glass, perhaps a jar. I waited, listening hard, but there was no flurry of activity, no police storming in.

Amy had been very good up until then but was beginning to make noises. She was preparing her lungs ready for a cry, by doing a few pre-emptive squeals.

I had a dummy in my back pocket. I gave it a sterilising lick and offered it to her. She seemed happy with this, but made it clear she was reserving the right to wail in the not too distant future.

I tried to climb down into the outhouse. The wall was lined with the shelving I'd put in; it formed a ladder of sorts. It was secure and well made, though I say so myself. It was ironic that I myself might have constructed the means for the kidnapper to get in.

The problem was avoiding the precariously balanced power tools, socket sets, and the twenty-odd glass jars with unwashed paintbrushes in. Why hadn't I simply thrown them away?

Something cracked under my tread. A plastic box I kept old screws in. Perhaps I thought people couldn't hear me because I couldn't hear them. That had a kind of logic to it, surely. Although, no doubt they were creeping around quietly, while I was busy crunching about and knocking things over.

One way or another, Amy and I got down to the floor of the outhouse.

It couldn't be long before the house exploded. Should I test the door to see if it opened, or would that blow my cover? It wasn't just that I wanted to know if I could escape; I was dying to find out whether the door had been previously forced and opened.

I sat in the darkness for an eternity. I realised I'd forgotten to bring any painkillers. It was hard to tell how drunk I was in the darkness but I couldn't be that far from having to deal with a hangover.

Amy started making more than the occasional noise. I jogged her up and down rhythmically. She cried louder. I added a swaying motion to the mix. She subsided a little but was still making a noise.

I thought I could hear police moving outside the door. I strained to listen. There was definite movement. I readied myself so that if they opened the door, I could run hell for leather out and past them. I might be able to catch them off guard, but more likely they would have marksmen arrayed in a semicircle. Amy was really wailing now. I tried to jog her up and down in a way that felt relaxed, so as not to convey my stress to her. I heard definite movement of men running. They must have heard Amy. The running stopped and I could hear whispering. Amy was between cries but was going to start again.

It was a WHOOMPH! of a noise.

It took me completely by surprise. I had been so sure Amy had given me away that I had temporarily forgotten about the gas. When it dawned on me that this was it, this was *really* it, I realised I hadn't even worked out which side of the door had the hinges, and which side had the lock. It certainly opened outwards and there was no internal handle so I kicked hard on the left.

It didn't budge.

I kicked hard on the right.

The door gave a bit but didn't open. I smacked it with the sole of my foot. I used all my weight. Suddenly I was outside and running. It was completely dark at the back of the house. I scrambled up the bank.

I was soon about twenty feet clear of the house when I thought I saw someone run diagonally behind me. I had no time to look back, but I had half a hope they were running towards the kitchen door and hadn't noticed me. The explosion hadn't caused a total fire, at least by that stage, but I hoped that the shock of it at least made the police startled. Certainly it should have blinded them temporarily. They might, perhaps, waste some precious time discussing what to do, before then organising themselves to move in. This should also have the effect of making them temporarily far less observant.

I heard some shouting.

'Police! Lay down your weapons!'

Then another voice shouting the same, 'Police! Lay down your weapons!'

The voices were well behind me now. I was at the top of the bank. Were they storming the house and this is what they always said, or had they seen me?

I ran sideways high up on the side of the bank. I wanted to stay up on the hill for a hundred yards or more then get back down onto the road, but running over rough hillside without any light at all is very difficult.

There was a loud shout and then some running, and a torch beam swept up onto the hill.

My leg slipped into a rabbit hole or something similar and my weight jarred down onto the side of my ankle.

There was another shout.

'You there! Stop! Stop or we will shoot.'

I had definitely been seen.

Chapter Forty-three

I simply wasn't with it enough to decide what to do.

I was running as fast as my legs and the darkness allowed. But I didn't know what was best, so I never actually made a decision. In the absence of a decision I just kept running.

I must have been five or ten yards further on than when the policeman had shouted at me.

At least two torch beams were now focussed on my every move.

They would have to make a decision whether to shoot or not. Few people would take that decision lightly, they were likely to dither. But was I getting away at enough speed to make running a worthwhile option?

'Stop now or I will shoot,' shouted the man.

I had visions that he would have to stop and steady himself to get a proper aim. There must have been three or four of them. A few to hold torches and at least one to shoot.

A shot.

It cracked so loud that it felt as if the gun itself were within feet of me.

I was on some sort of grass ridge. I knew I had to run erratically, so I veered to the left.

My foot caught as I turned and I slipped sideways. I slid, rather than fell. I was shooting down some sort of bank. It was, literally, a life saver. I had somehow fallen somewhere safe. I soon had my balance again and felt for Amy, to check she was still safe against me.

I changed direction. I was looking for a path that Gabby and I used for short strolls. I knew that it looped back to Portugalete. Hopefully, the police wouldn't know the area well. They wouldn't know to head me off.

I ran and ran into the darkness, pain shooting up my leg in electric jolts.

I finally began to feel I was sufficiently far away. I was feeling my luck had held firm. I was feeling my luck would stop me getting shot. I was feeling I could escape. I was feeling… extreme pain, to be honest. My right ankle really had taken a nasty twist.

I strained to hear if there was anyone behind me. I thought not.

I got lost. There was nothing in the dark to give me any clues. I was pretty sure the path I was looking for was up there somewhere. It ran left to right, but should I go higher or lower to find it?

I was suddenly on ground that at least felt more flat. I was picking up pace but had to do a sort of constant skip, with my leg swinging out sideways, to avoid putting pressure on my right ankle.

Eventually some lights from Portugalete came into view beneath me. I had run a lot further than I imagined. Before I knew it, I came across the road from our house down to the town.

I did have a plan, it's just that it wasn't a very good one.

I got down amongst the houses. I refused to look over my shoulder. I managed to mostly avoid running down any actual roads, because a police car would have been able to catch up with me in a moment. There are plenty of paths down between the buildings of Portugalete which link the roads, so I was able to make my way around without too much trouble.

It must have been about 5.30 in the morning; the time when there are fewest people about but, nonetheless, there was the odd person wandering here and there which didn't help at all. It wasn't as though it was a crowd to get lost in: it just provided the police with people they could ask whether they'd seen me.

If I wanted to use the tube trains in the morning which, in itself, was risky, then I was going to need to cross the river. There were also some decent bits of dockland on that side that I could hide out in. There were some docks on the side I was already on, so I reckoned that whatever plan I went for, I needed to get down to the river.

I had a large weight pressing down on my head and my thoughts. The hangover was beginning. I found myself standing at the transporter bridge entrance, reading the opening times. It was a totally stupid move. If the police were looking for me at all they would be down there sooner rather than later, just as I had been the first time Amy was kidnapped.

I looked left towards the docks. It would be the best of the options, I reasoned. I started to walk that way when I spotted two cars tearing down the hill towards me. There were no flashing lights or sirens so, like an idiot, I waited until they were close enough for me to be sure they were police cars before running for it. With the crucial seconds that I lost, I'd also lost most of my options.

I limped back to the transporter bridge. The police ran their cars up onto the pavements. The car doors were opening. I climbed over a three foot high barrier and up some metal stairs that took me onto the roof of the ticket office.

'Police. Stop!'

I didn't.

They were moments behind me.

I climbed up a second barrier. This one was tall and meant to deter. It was almost impossible with a baby strapped to my front because I had to constantly hold myself a little away from the metalwork. It's the sort of thing you can only manage when you're really desperate. It took me onto the unit which received the lift cage when it came down. The police had slowed a little, discussing whether they wanted to follow me; one of them started talking on his radio. Even if I could climb up and across the 160 metres of bridge then I might not manage it before they got police waiting for me on the other side.

I climbed anyway.

I had to edge across a piece of girder three inches wide. On the slim chance that the police had somehow lost sight of me, Amy took the precaution of wailing loudly.

I had now found the thin emergency ladder, used to evacuate people when the lift failed. The dark was helpful in that I couldn't see the drop below as I climbed although, in fact, I could tell from the edge of the sky that the sun was beginning to rise.

There was an ominous creak as I climbed; a slow moaning in the metal as it took the strain. It wasn't reassuring. After about fifty rungs the ladder stopped at the tiniest of platforms and the next ladder began at an angle to the first.

I was a little baffled that the police weren't still directly behind me. Possibly they had stopped to discuss tactics and tell their colleagues they'd found me. I presumed they weren't far behind though.

I must have been climbing for a full five minutes and stopped to catch my breath. I looked down for the first time. I was only about half way up but already high enough to feel the swaying of the bridge. God knows what it was like on a windy day. I could now hear the metal thunk, thunk, thunk, of someone else on the ladders, but I couldn't see them.

I looked up.

Big mistake.

The dawn was starting to colour the sky in yellows and pinks. The clouds were moving swiftly. I had the sense that I was rolling, that the whole bridge was rolling. Or was that drunkenness?

I started again. It was harder now. The steel was ice cold against my hands: so cold that my fingers were pulsing with the pain of it. The only good news was that my cut palm couldn't feel much worse than it already did, so the different kind of pain made a break of sorts. In either event, it wasn't as though I had a choice; I had to keep grabbing at the next painful rung and the next after that.

Some lights came on below at the ticket office. Had they managed to get the staff to open up or was this the time they normally started? I couldn't remember what the sign had said. It made no difference. They would soon have the lifts up and running, and the police would be able to get to the top of the bridge in large numbers.

I tried to climb faster. Amy had shut up at least.

I looked up again. Two more ladders to go. A hundred or so rungs. I might conceivably make it to the top before them. I tried to look to the other side of the river without slowing my climb. I couldn't see any activity there yet. The police would have to come from Bilbao to get there by car; that was the nearest bridge across the river and the nearest police station. If they had called for help when I got to the bridge that might give me a quarter of an hour. Five minutes to sort themselves out, and ten minutes to drive down. It would probably take them longer than that, certainly not less time. Alternatively, there might not be any extra police to summon up at this time of the morning so they would have to drive all the way down the river on my side, down to Bilbao, across the bridge and back again. That was at least twenty minutes. I was beginning to think my idea to cross the bridge was inspired. If I didn't drop dead from exhaustion first.

I was now on the last ladder from the very top.

The swaying was getting worse; the cloud spinning was much faster. It was totally out of control. I was beyond exhaustion. There was a shifting and droning. I couldn't work out what it was, at first.

The lift mechanism.

The pulleys and machinery were turning. The lift cage was kept at the top at night; it was now starting its long journey down. The lights were on inside it and as it went down, it illuminated me. I heard someone's shout on the wind.

'There he is!'

I kept climbing. Perhaps another thirty rungs to go now. I reckoned I could get to the top before the lift could. Everyone knows lifts take for ever.

The clunk of the lift docking at the bottom of the steel towers rang around the silent river. The doors shunted open.

Half a ladder to go. Twenty five rungs. I could barely see with the exhaustion.

I'd perhaps managed another eight or ten rungs when I heard the doors shut below. Another rung, but I was going so desperately slowly. I felt sick with the strain.

A dramatic pause from below, then I saw the steel cables pouring down beside me; steady and immutable.

I simply had to stop for a while. I was so tired.

A counterweight drifted down in the silence. I managed another three rungs. Then one more. I could do this. It was in sight now. But if I did get to the top I would barely be able to stand. When the police got up there they would be fresh. They'd taken the bloody lift; of course they'd be fresh. The bastards.

The lift went up past me. I had five rungs to go. Five measly rungs. It takes time for lifts to dock. It takes time for the doors to open.

Three rungs.

Light cut down onto me as the lift doors opened. There was a clank of boots as the police surged out. If I went onto the main walkway they could shoot me. I ducked my head as they ran out of the lift. They were getting their bearings. They were working out where the emergency stairs came up.

Beneath the tourist walkway there was a service deck. It was about three planks wide and had very little head clearance. It gave access to the rails that the automated trolley ran along, that in turn held up the gondola beneath. It had a railing on one side only. The other side was a sixty metre drop. Presumably workers would have safety ropes attached to them when up there. I reached out for a girder and swung myself out and down to it.

I ran along the planking. I kept my head ducked at first because, otherwise, it was only a few feet beneath their feet. The police were pleasingly confused. They started running along the upper walkway and then twigged that I wasn't on it with them. They ran back to look at the ladder I'd come up. I was already about half way across the bridge when they got themselves onto the same walkway as me. They'd have done better to stay at the top, run across and head me off at the other end, so they'd made a mistake.

The mistake I made was to look down. It was a stomach churningly awful drop. There was nothing whatever to stop me plummeting. I knew that if it were on a pavement at ground level, I could walk along that width for ever and never fall off the side, but at sixty metres in the air it seemed an impossible feat. To add to my panic, there was now even a wind.

The entire bridge rumbled and swayed. I turned my head back while still running, to see what was happening. It was the gondola setting off from the bank I'd left. I had originally assumed they would drive round to the other side. I hadn't banked on them getting the bridge operational so quickly. I had perhaps another sixty yards to run but it wasn't going to be enough; it would take me far too long to climb down the other side.

I was two thirds of my way across now. There was shouting behind me. The police were gaining ground. They had fresh legs, they were fit; they didn't have a baby and a lifetime of sedentary habits impeding them.

The front edge of the trolley system was level with me now. I could jump on it and hitch a ride. It would help, it would get me to the other end in a mere twenty seconds, but it still wouldn't buy me enough time.

I knew what I had to do.

I had to jump.

Chapter Forty-four

I got my plastic bag of bottles and documents out and refolded it over and again to minimise the chance of water getting in. I put it inside my jacket, then zipped it up.

I toyed with putting Amy inside my clothes as well, but I wanted to be able to directly hold her. I wanted to clamp her nose and mouth hard against me before we hit the water. I adjusted the strappings so that I could do it with my good hand. That would leave only my bad hand to swim with.

When I realised deep down I was actually going to try this stunt, I thought I was going to throw up with fear. Obviously in the cold light of day, and sober, no rational person would have done what I was going to do.

The police were within five yards of me. I knew that I had to step off that platform.

'Lay down your weapons or we will shoot.'

They stopped a few yards away from me. They obviously thought I was armed. Perhaps they thought the baby was, in fact, explosives strapped to my chest. With the gas explosion, they might not know for sure whether Gabrielle had been in the building. I had no way of knowing whether any of their colleagues had been injured. Had the gas ignited before they got in the house, or did they themselves set it off? I might already be responsible for some deaths. Despite my previous innocence I would now be seriously guilty. They would be pleased to shoot me.

There were four of them. One had a pistol and three had rifles. The ones with rifles knelt. They nestled their rifles into their shoulders and cocked their heads to look down their sights at me. There was absolutely no way that all three of them could miss.

The policeman with the pistol shouted.

'Lay down your weapons on the count of five, or we will shoot.'

I was paralysed.

'Five.'

The water was so very far beneath yet I would see the eddies and turbulence within it.

'Four.'

I jumped.

I threw myself forward into the air. I needed to be clear of the bridge so as not to crack my head on its metalwork.

I had got my jump wrong. I was facing downwards and would belly flop against the wall of water with Amy on my chest taking the full brunt of it. She would die instantly. She would break her neck or something.

I should have given myself up to the police.

I took my hands off Amy and swirled my arms furiously. I was soon on my back. That was marginally better, but still dangerous. When I hit the water I couldn't afford to break anything serious as I needed to get us up to the surface as soon as possible.

I kept thinking, 'Surely I'm going to hit the water soon. *Surely* I'm going to hit the water soon.'

I dropped and dropped and dropped, and managed to turn so that my feet were more or less the lowest part of me, but by then my body was slanted at about forty-five degrees to the left. I was going to hit the water largely with my side.

I clasped my fingers over Amy's mouth and nose, and with my other hand I pushed her into my clothing. But still we didn't hit the water. Perhaps it was one of those moments where fear made me feel everything had gone into slow

254

motion. I could feel her struggle. I let go of her mouth for a second. She didn't seem to breathe at first, she was so outraged, then I felt her lungs draw in deeply as she prepared herself for a major cry. I covered her face again.

WALLOP, we hit the water.

We had fallen so fast that the water felt solid: it jarred my legs. Pain shot up my weak ankle. My hip was slammed and felt pulled where my legs had been torn to one side. I kept my hand on Amy's face and with my other hand I flailed the best I could but we still seemed to be going deeper. The muscles on my chest constricted with the cold. Pain braced my ribcage. I didn't know which way was up; once under the water I was sure we had somehow turned. How long could Amy possibly go without oxygen? She was wriggling and thrashing against me. My wet hand could not hope to maintain a perfect seal over her mouth for long.

I was kicking the water helplessly with my legs, but it didn't seem to have any effect. Surely I had some natural buoyancy that would assert itself, but it appeared to be ineffectual. I was convinced we were still going deeper and deeper.

My clothing seemed to be hindering me. I could flap my arm or my legs but the loose clothing seemed to negate the stroke: my arm was simply flapping about *within* loose clothing. It was hopeless. Water was echoing in my ears. Everything was now slowing. My chest was burning, crying out to be allowed to breathe. My throat felt pressurised, strangled; my stomach ached. Surely the surface of this water couldn't be far now.

I thrashed and thrashed. I thought that if I could only concentrate on the swimming it would distract me from the pain in my lungs and in my throat. I kicked the water as if I was trying to kill it, beat it to death. I wanted to cry and die and submit to my fate all in one go.

It was my free arm that hit the air first. I had put it above my head to gain a really long, powerful stroke and it was suddenly free. I splashed clear of the water but seemed to tumble backwards and underneath the water again in the same movement. I had breathed out but I was submerged again before I had a chance to breathe in.

Amy. I needed her unstrapped. I somehow needed to hold her high in the air, even if this meant I myself sank.

I was up again. My head was above the surface. I breathed through the water that had half filled my mouth. I tried to get on my back. I pushed Amy away from my chest. Was she breathing at all? She didn't seem to be moving in any way whatever.

I couldn't see the bank. The water was choppy and obscuring my view. After all, we were only a few hundred yards from the Atlantic Ocean. Which way was the current? Was I still under the bridge, or had I been swept down towards the sea? Possibly the tide had pushed me the other way, up the river towards Bilbao. I shook my head as hard as I could. I didn't have a free hand to clear my eyes of water. I could see light, but little more. I held Amy high.

She still wasn't moving or crying. How long had we been under water? Less time that I might have feared in my panic, but still too long. I could see lights from a town. They seemed some distance away. A wave enveloped us. The water was more choppy now. There were definite waves. I kicked my legs in a more solid backstroke. I had Amy on my chest. I thought I saw what looked like a beach. It inspired me to swim harder. I was now sure it was a beach. Probably Areeta. It was about a hundred yards away and I was worried about the current being too strong and taking me out to the ocean. I swam as if my life depended on it, which it did. I was unable to see if I was making headway because the shoreline was behind my head.

With every kick of my foot, pain spasmed from my ankle and up through my body.

I made myself not look again for a minute or more, so as not to be disappointed, so as to concentrate on the swimming.

When I did stop to crane my neck, it was definitely closer. I could see a couple of people on the beach. If they were police then that was the end of it. I had given it my best shot.

I swam on and then stopped to venture a foot down to find the bottom. Nothing yet. Another minute of swimming should do it, if not less.

I hit the beach with my arse.

I stood up on what seemed to be a sandbank because I was still some way out. I pulled Amy completely free from her harness and held her upside down. I shook her and patted her back. I turned her the right way up.

She was limp and cold.

Her skin was metallic blue. Her lips were black.

I put her upside down again and patted her back. I half expected water to fall out of her lungs, but it didn't happen.

I turned her the correct way up again and held her close to me, rocking her.

I was so stupid. So, so stupid. I should never have jumped off the bridge.

I held her close to my face and shook her.

Her eyes jolted open, then focussed on me in an accusing manner.

She cried.

I was sobbing with gratitude; hugging her close to me and kissing her. I pulled her away to look at her yet again.

Thank God, something had gone my way.

Chapter Forty-five

I turned and waded to the shore. The two people were still there, they could easily be police. They were the right size and shape.

They were standing and watching this man and his baby who had emerged, fully clothed, from the sea.

Then I saw the dog. It was playing in the waves. Then another dog further off. Just a couple of early morning dog walkers who now had something to talk about.

I walked left and up onto the road.

I didn't recognise where I was, and then decided it was indeed Areeta, but much further along the coast than I thought. The tube stations would be open now, but they would probably be watched by the police. I wouldn't be hard to spot. I wouldn't be hard to track down; they'd just have to follow the trail of wet.

I would need to walk up to the next Metro stop at Gobela or even Neguri.

I didn't know if there were any plain clothes officers at the Metro station; there certainly weren't any in uniform. I bought a ticket for Bilbao, and no one seemed to follow me down the steps.

On the platform I got some milk sorted out for the very hungry Amy. I had neglected to bring nappies with me and she was sodden. Part pee, part sea. I was also regretting the lack of painkillers. I hadn't slept for nearly twenty-four hours and there was no chance of me getting a rest that day.

My hand had lost its bandage. A lot of the torn skin looked dead. There were dull greys of muscle layers showing but, curiously, no blood. The sea water must have done something odd.

I got into Bilbao and there was still no sign of the police. There was an hour or more to kill before any shops opened.

I wasted minutes limping down to the old town. I wanted to see the bar where Gabrielle had worked. It was shuttered up, of course. There was every chance our relationship was over, and I wanted to mark the end of it somehow. I tried to picture her inside, throwing eggs in the air and catching them on the edge of the cleaver; amusing the crowds with her pidgin Spanish; flirting with the men and making jokes with the women.

Better to have lived and loved and lost and loathed, or whatever that saying is.

I couldn't find anywhere suitable to flop down for half an hour, so I walked along the river, past the Guggenheim and various building sites, and eventually found a park where I laid down for a while.

I just felt worse and worse. My sinuses were throbbing, I felt sick, and I was in constant fear that if I did drift off to sleep I would be woken by a policeman. Nonetheless, one way or another, the time disappeared.

It was going to be a reasonably sunny day. I figured that I could ditch my coat and buy a new shirt, a new babygrow for Amy and some nappies. At least I wouldn't look like a tramp any more. I needed a shave and a hair wash, and there was little I could do about that except perhaps book into a hotel later. Unless they'd want my passport before they let me check in.

It took me less that half an hour of shopping to sort us both out with some new clothes and nappies, and I transferred the baby's bottle and my documents into a new plastic bag. I looked almost human.

Now to take my first chance.

I went off to visit the bank that had issued the second loan in my name.

It was one of those banks where the front door is locked; you sometimes find them on the continent. I had to look up at a camera and be buzzed in by a member of staff. They already had a picture of me, therefore, by the time I was inside.

I approached a woman at a desk.

'Hi. I have a loan account with your bank and I need to talk to someone because I think there's an irregularity.'

'Okay,' she said. 'Your name, please?'

I gave her my name, but she didn't appear to do anything. She just looked distracted, as if something had occurred to her.

She picked up the phone, dialled a number and talked quietly into the receiver. She could easily have been calling the police. We sat in silence opposite each other. I attempted a smile at her, but it wasn't reciprocated. I must have looked too rough.

Eventually, there was movement.

A woman came out of a door and sat down with me. She had a file with her and she brought the details up on a computer. The first woman disappeared.

I explained myself, with Amy perched on my knee. The woman understood completely the concept that someone might have taken the money out in my name. She looked willing to help.

'The forms weren't sent out,' she said. 'They were collected by someone and then a day later there is a note in the file that the forms were received; they had been filled in.'

'Do you have a note of who dealt face to face with the person who brought the forms in?' I asked.

'Of course,' she replied.

With a blank expression, she looked in the file for a while. Then she tapped at the computer and studied a few screens.

'I'll get her,' she said.

'She's on duty?' I asked.

'Mmm. She's the assistant manager.'

She smiled at Amy, who was looking decidedly endearing, and left through a door.

It was going too well, but after all these months I was probably due a run of luck.

The door opened and the first woman I'd talked to came out. It turned out she was the assistant manager, but now she looked busy and distracted. She stood to give the impression she didn't want to hang around. She nodded as I explained the problem again, then got distracted by the state of my cut palm.

Finally I said, 'There are a couple of people who might have done this to me. It was either a man who came in, or a woman who would have claimed she was simply picking up the loan forms and bringing them back on my behalf. So I want you to look at these two photographs and tell me who you dealt with.'

I got out a photograph of Gabrielle and the photo I had taken of Alex. I laid them side by side on the desk, and turned towards the assistant manager.

'Which one of these people did you meet?'

Chapter Forty-six

There was a wail of sirens as first one police car then another screeched up onto the pavements. The staff turned as one to look out through the glass of the doors. Police jumped out. This lot had pistols rather than rifles. They were attached to their belts by coiled wire, like phone flex, so that they didn't have to suffer the ignominy of having their guns pickpocketed. Presumably this meant they were regular police, not the dedicated firearms squad. There was a good chance they didn't want to storm the building until their mates with grenades had arrived.

The police chose not to look in at us through the glass doors, possibly through fear of being shot at by me, by my invisible gun. They chose instead to stand on tiptoes to look through the other windows, which were set quite high up. As a result, we could see the occasional pair of eyes bob up into view, then go back down. Mostly we could see their police caps only. The caps turned towards each other as they conferred.

The assistant manager who had been helping me, went off to talk to them.

'No,' I called after her. 'Don't go out there.'

I didn't want it to sound like a threat. In either event she didn't hear me. She let herself out the door, and we could see the police hats turn in her direction as they took in this new development. The hats nodded as they talked to her. Then the sets of eyes bobbed up in turn to have a look at me. Then the hats turned towards each other for more conferring.

I wondered who had called the police. The bank perhaps, but more likely someone had seen me walking through the streets of Bilbao earlier.

I considered taking a hostage. I could easily overpower one of the female staff, but what could I threaten her with? One of those Biros on a little silver chain? I was so tired and felt so ill that a nice warm cell with a plastic mattress on the floor was becoming a very tempting option.

The door buzzer rang. The assistant manager wanted to be let back in.

She came through the door with the two policemen. They had their guns drawn and looked nervous. The assistant manager just looked irritated by the disruption to her day.

'Would you come with us please, Senor?' asked one of them.

'Yes,' I replied. 'But first I need to hear from the bank employee, who she dealt with. I need her to point to one of the two photographs.'

She sighed and moved towards the desk. The policemen stiffened because she was getting close to me, and they didn't understand what was happening. One of them started flexing his neck rhythmically. Never a good sign in a copper.

She looked at the photographs again.

'It was that person. I am sure of it,' she said pointing. She tapped the photo with the end of her fingernail.

The whole bank peered at the photograph.

It was Alex Lawrence.

My hangover chose that moment to take my metabolism by storm. I salivated uncontrollably. I opened my mouth and, for the first and only time in my life, I threw up on a policeman's legs.

Chapter Forty-seven

We were in the bar where Gabrielle used to work. The owner's teenage daughter had expressed an inexplicable desire to 'get into childcare' and wanted to be our part time nanny. We'd discussed terms, as in, 'Yes, please, dear God, yes!' and then she'd taken Amy off our hands for the day to 'see how she got on.' If that was all right with us. Now let me think...

With the heat off us, we had decided that the Basque Country wasn't such a bad place after all and we were busy making plans for the future.

The bar hadn't changed much. New posters of prisoners who needed to be pre-soaked had replaced the previous ones, but the same teenage Basques were in the corner plotting all-night raves and how best to overthrow the state.

We were temporarily living in a hotel near to our house, while I organised its repair, but it was so cramped we had already spent most of the time out and about, having coffee in bars and going for walks with Amy.

'Okay,' I said. 'When you were kidnapped on the way to the Chillida Installations, what exactly happened?'

'Alex followed me in a van he'd hired. He must have been waiting near our house; he had followed me for half an hour before I spotted him. He forced me to pull over and threatened me. Before I could think straight I was in the back of the bloody van.'

'What was the phone conversation with the police?' I asked.

'Well,' she began. 'He was hoping that the police would detain you long enough to allow him to get out of the country with me. I mean, it was all some major jealousy thing and he was getting less and less rational. I mean, was he planning to hold me prisoner for the rest of my life? It makes no sense. Possibly he was planning to kill me.'

'Keeping you alive made little sense,' I agreed.

'He'd spent months trying to either ruin your life or turn you against me by making you think I was mad, sending you those letters and the rest. He took the view that if he couldn't have me then no one else should.'

'You were saying about the phone call to the police...' I said.

'Yeah, so he rang the police, pretending to be you and claiming you had me hostage, then put me on the phone. I was in the van so I didn't hear what he'd said to the police: I didn't realise he'd framed you. He simply asked me to confirm my name and address and that I had been kidnapped. I didn't say who by. I didn't know what he'd said to them, you see?'

'What did Alex do for a living?'

'Something in Intelligence and, yes, I know I said civil engineering, but you really don't go around telling people that someone is in the secret services, not least because no one believes you, even though between them and GCHQ they employ tens of thousands of people. But he was going mad and he took a huge amount of unpaid leave and ran up debts, so he really needed that money he conned you out of with the loans.'

'So how did you get out of the van?' I asked.

'I just kept banging on the panels. It was the only thing I could think of to do. Eventually he stopped and I said I needed a pee.'

'And?'

'And when I got the chance I hit him incredibly hard and ran even harder. We were, mercifully, near some houses and I managed to knock someone up. In fact, it turned out I was just over the French border, so they weren't Spanish at all. They rang the French police, which really slowed up the process of getting you off the hook all the way back in Biscay.'

'Well that's something to tell our grandchildren,' I said.

Our fourth bottle of wine arrived. I was far too drunk to concentrate properly.

'Here's another question,' I said. 'Is there any chance that you are a little, er, unhinged?'

I was pushing my luck, but Gabrielle really was in a very good mood.

She giggled like a girl.

'Believe it or not, this is something I've thought about a lot and looked into,' she replied. 'There is an official diagnostic test for borderline personality disorder. There are eight major symptoms and I'd have to have five of the eight to qualify.'

'And how many have you got?'

'Me?' she asked. 'Oh, all eight.' She was pouring wine out and laughing so much it was shaking either side of the glass. 'Violent mood swings, inexplicable rage, dramatic impulses, addictive personality, a desire to take on roles according to the people around me, a chronic sense of not being loved enough. I can't remember it all, but it's something like that. It's definitely what I've got.'

She was trying to control her laughter, as though she should feel guilty about who she was, but it kept hiccupping out.

'I mean,' she continued. 'What can I do? I can't be hang dog about it for the rest of my life. I've just got to get on with it. It's not as though I've done any serious harm. I'm just very flaky. I've had the odd lapse while with you, but I've done well, I think. That's why you need to be the sane one, sweetheart.'

She looked deep into my eyes, the way drunks sometimes do, and started patting the back of my hand.

Then she bit it.

It was meant to be funny, but in fact it was alarming.

'Anyway you can't talk,' she said. 'You're the one who left your mother in jail as we swanned off to a fiesta. You're the one who took to riffling through my belongings.'

'You knew about that, huh?'

'You're at least as mad as me,' she said. 'Certainly as secretive and at least as unbalanced. Does that mean we both aren't allowed relationships? Besides, we didn't mean it to drag on so long,' she said.

'What?' I asked.

'Well, Alex and I had already fleeced you successfully. Scammed tens of thousands out of you and discredited you with the police, should you want to complain. But then Olaia got in the way.'

'What?' I asked again.

'She'd twigged what Alex and I were up to. She was reading our mail, after all. She would have spoiled everything. She was going to tell you everything that morning.'

There was a horrified silence.

'Okay,' I said. 'Let's assume you and Alex were in it together and, for the record, I think you're kidding. You raised forty grand in the first few weeks. Why didn't you just run off then? There was no point in hanging around for months after that. It wasn't cost effective.'

'Exactly right,' said Gabrielle. 'The original plan was to run the moment we'd got the money. That's what we've always done before. But, as bad luck would have it, I got pregnant. I really didn't want the sodding baby. So I had to wait until I gave birth, and then come up with a plan to leave you holding it. Thus the kidnapping.'

I was stunned.

'Why two kidnappings, not one?'

'With the first kidnapping, you weren't supposed to phone the police. But you didn't see the letter left behind when Amy was kidnapped, and so the police did get called. We couldn't then send the letter saying to go down to the Chillida Installations because the police would have escorted me. So the whole process had to be repeated.'

'I don't believe you,' I said.

'But, when push came to shove, I couldn't bear to leave Amy. It turns out I'm quite maternal. Alex didn't want a baby. So I fell out with Alex as we drove away in the van and I came back.'

There was a very, very long silence.

'Why are you telling me this now?' I asked.

Gabrielle looked at me for the longest time imaginable.

'Because I am kidding,' said Gabrielle. '*Kidding*. Jesus Christ, Sal, I am kidding. I'm kidding. Kidding! Can't you take a joke?'

'No,' I replied. 'Have I not made that clear?'

She poured yet more wine.

'Think about it,' she said. 'If I wanted to leave you with Amy, I could simply walk out, couldn't I?'

'Are you sure?' I asked.

'Sure, sweetheart. And, remember, it was me who wanted us to call the police the first time Amy was taken.'

She leant forward and kissed me.

'Happy?' she said. 'I'm sorry I teased you. So how come your blood was found near Olaia?'

'The police took the view that it was planted there,' I said. 'On Olaia's actual body they found Alex's blood. They were able to have him arrested on the strength of the bank employee's identification and once he was in custody they took a blood sample. Then there was your testimony.'

'My *fabulous* testimony,' she said.

'In his first two statements to the police, he claimed that you were trying to escape with him, but when the blood evidence came in, they started to believe your statements instead.'

Gabrielle wagged a finger at me.

'I should be very angry with you,' she said. 'I didn't put a foot wrong. Not one. I was loving, I was fun, I worked hard, I was nice to your mother, I even decorated your house. How do you pay me back? You blow it up in a gas explosion, and subject me to a year of suspicion. You were prepared to talk yourself out of the single best relationship you'll ever have by half believing Alex.'

'You're right,' I said.

'What's going to happen about that house?' she asked.

'Happily,' I said, 'I am in charge of property at work. So I just wrote that it was a gas explosion. I didn't go into details. It wasn't too badly damaged.'

'Terrific,' she grinned.

'Why eight?' I asked.

'What?'

'Why eight letters?'

'Apparently I'd written him eight letters when we were together,' said Gabrielle.

'What do you mean?'

'Eight love letters,' she said. 'Hell, he was the obsessive, not me. If he says there were eight letters, he's probably correct. No one ever blew up your superconductor cables, then?'

'No. But I'd better look into it.'

I looked out of the window, half expecting a huge explosion in the direction of our factory.

'And there were no police injured in the gas explosion,' she asked.

'No,' I replied.

'So we're going for a happy ending, you and me?'

'It looks like it,' I said.

She kissed me.

'Can we cut a deal whereby, in the years to come, I try and pretend to be as sane as possible, and you try and pretend to be solid and capable?' she asked.

'Sure,' I said. 'Or… we can do what comes naturally; being batty and abstract and lurch from one drama to another.'

'That *would* be easier,' she conceded.

'Mad woman.'

'Div.'

'I'll tell you something that puzzles me,' I said.

'Mmmm?'

'The third letter that was sent to me refers, I think, to Amy being taken away.'

'That's barely arguable,' she said. 'But go on.'

'I didn't read it until some time after it was sent. It was the gestor who showed it to me.'

'So?' she asked.

'So, whoever wrote the letter knew about your pregnancy before I did.'

Gabrielle looked at me blankly, then went to the toilet.

The entire story, my entire belief about what had occurred up to that point, still relied on believing Gabrielle's version of events.

When she came back from the toilets, she didn't mention it.

She said, matter-of-factly, 'What happened about your mother?'

Oh, my God. My mother.

Chapter Forty-eight

I got out my mobile and rang England.
   No answer.

'How many times have you tried ringing her?' asked Gabrielle.

'Umpteen,' I replied. 'But not in the last few days.'

'Shit.'

'Shit.'

'So?' she said.

'So you were the last person to see her, Gabrielle.'

'Really?' she replied.

'Yes. I was at work, and you said you'd driven my mother to the airport. And I never heard from her again.'

'Okay,' she replied. 'But I saw her onto the plane.'

'Do you think Alex could have got to her?' I asked.

'In what way?'

'It wouldn't be hard to find her address in England and, I don't know, the man was mad. He killed Olaia. And it was a very violent death, at that,' I said.

'I'll get a policeman to call on her,' said Gabrielle. 'Jot down her address.'

I wrote my mother's address and phone number on a napkin and Gabrielle disappeared into a quiet corner with a mobile phone.

'I have found a policeman in England who will make it his business to sort it out,' said Gabrielle. 'He says he has a pal in the right patch who will go along and visit your mother. When he has news he will ring you on your mobile.'

'Thanks.'

The mood of the afternoon had changed.

'You don't trust me do you?' she said. She looked quite neutral about it. 'It's understandable. So much happened that you will endlessly be able to find bits and pieces that don't quite make sense; that will raise doubts.'

I looked neutral.

'So I think you need to look at it another way,' she continued. 'We are not our pasts. Not if we choose otherwise. Examining the past should be about finding ways to improve the future, not about nursing grievances. We are individuals. If you and I want a great future together, we simply have to opt for it. I am opting to be with you here and now. You have to ask yourself what you are opting for. Here and now.'

Gabrielle smiled in a resigned fashion.

'I'm tired. I'm going back to the hotel,' she said. 'You have a think.'

I needed some air and took myself off for a walk. I held my mobile phone in my hand, willing it to ring.

I left the old town and made my way off to the funicular railway that runs up the hillside to the east of the city. I sat in the first carriage; it had a broad glass window so that tourists could admire the view. The train rose up and away from the Victorian buildings. I was soon above Bilbao and soaked in sunshine.

Still no phone call.

At the top of the hill I was surprised to discover I could see all the way off to the factory where I worked, and the sea beyond. I toyed with walking that way but opted instead to sit at the top for half an hour, then set off on a leisurely walk back towards Bilbao. I set the glinting Guggenheim as my notional target. There were some good bars in the streets near the museum.

There are fields on the hillside that stretch all the way down to the city boundary. They are full of wild flowers and cows, and the occasional dog walker. It is a joy that the countryside should be pressing so hard against a major city.

It could take hours before the policeman rang me, time I was determined to kill before making a decision about my future. I tried ringing my mother directly, but there was nothing but the ringing tone on the other end.

I wondered whether I might fancy walking all the way along the river. Upstream, not downstream towards Portugalete. Just keep walking and seeing where it took me.

It occurred to me that the whole drama had taken me from the first moment I had met Gabrielle to a point where it all ended. The entire trajectory of a relationship. If my mother was alive, she would probably come and live near. I quite liked her after all these years. It would be fine. Fun, even. There were worse lives than that.

I was now at the edge of town and decided I'd sit in a bar for a while.

I tried ringing my mother again, but to no avail.

Almost immediately afterwards my phone rang of its own volition.

'Hello?'

'Mr Gongola?'

'Speaking.'

It was a man. It sounded like a policeman.

'Your wife Gabrielle gave me your number. It's DC Andy Walker from Stoke Newington.'

'Hello,' I said. 'Thank you for taking the trouble...'

'We've visited your mother,' he said.

He didn't sound as though he was breaking bad news.

'She is fine,' he said.

'Thank heavens.'

'I think she has a hearing problem,' he said.

'Indeed,' I said.

'Even when I was there, the telephone rang and she didn't hear it. I suggested she needs a new hearing aid.'

'Or a new battery,' I said.

'What?'

'Never mind,' I said. 'Thank you very much, Inspector.'

'DC,' he said. 'My pleasure.'

He chatted some more about this and that. I couldn't think why. I got the impression he once knew Gabrielle and liked her. He eventually rang off.

So the silly old bag was walking around without hearing. There had never been a problem. That figured.

I ordered the most expensive brandy I could see on the shelf.

Sitting there, I did a little inventory of my life. I had a job that paid well. I had a new life. All the problems of the last year had now gone. I had a beautiful new daughter.

And then there was Gabrielle.

I knew in that moment what I had to do. It would solve everything.

I downed the drink within seconds of its arrival and left some money on the table.

I took the Metro down to Areeta and walked across to use the transporter bridge. I felt self-conscious using it, as though the people around me would know that I was the man who had jumped off it a few nights before.

'He was being chased by police you know. Some say he had a baby with him, some say it was explosive. But it was actually a dog.'

I laughed as I thought that and a couple of passengers looked my way for the first time, then looked away as I returned their stare.

At Portugalete I took my time walking up the hill to the hotel. I was nervous about what I knew I had to do.

At reception, I could see our key was already missing. Gabrielle was in our room.